Out of Breath

JULIE MYERSON

JONATHAN CAPE
LONDON

Published by Jonathan Cape 2008

2 4 6 8 10 9 7 5 3 1

Copyright © Julie Myerson 2008

Julie Myerson has asserted her right under the Copyright, Designs
and Patents Act 1988 to be identified as the author of this work

First published in Great Britain in 2008 by
Jonathan Cape
Random House, 20 Vauxhall Bridge Road,
London SW1V 2SA

Random House Australia (Pty) Limited
20 Alfred Street, Milsons Point, Sydney,
New South Wales 2061, Australia

Random House New Zealand Limited
18 Poland Road, Glenfield,
Auckland 10, New Zealand

Random House (Pty) Limited
Isle of Houghton, Corner of Boundary Road & Carse O'Gowrie,
Houghton 2198, South Africa

The Random House Group Limited Reg. No. 954009
www.randomhouse.co.uk

A CIP catalogue record for this book is available from the British Library

ISBN 9780224081764

Papers used by Random House are natural,
recyclable products made from wood grown in sustainable forests;
the manufacturing processes conform to the environmental
regulations of the country of origin

Typeset by Palimpsest Book Production Limited,
Grangemouth, Stirlingshire

Printed and bound in Great Britain by
CPI Mackays, Chatham, ME5 8TD

for Ian Rickson – inspiration and friend

GARDEN

1

And then just when I thought nothing good or interesting would ever happen again, there he was. This boy. Down at the bottom of the garden behind the big old tree where no one ever went.

In a way I was surprised to see him, but in a way I wasn't. I'd been about to run away, just make myself disappear, but now it was obvious I didn't need to. And straightaway it was like every little thing that had been chewing away at my mind made absolute perfect sense.

I stood there and stared at him. Just stared and stared. I couldn't help it. I didn't want to be rude but it was just so unexpected to see him standing there. And then he saw me and he kind of froze. Like he was deciding whether to stay or go. I waited and held my breath to see which he'd choose.

I knew which he'd choose.

He held his eyes on me. They were endless, the kind of eyes that seemed to go straight in and touch you in a place you didn't even know was there. I felt my heart go up a bit then drop, like when my dad used to drive me over humpback bridges.

I tried to concentrate on what he looked like, because what if someone asked me later?

He had blackish sticky-up hair cut very short and close to his head, almost shaved – much shorter than Sam's. And his skin was whiteish, almost see-through. There was something a bit breakable about it. Even though you didn't want to, it made you think about the veins pumping underneath. He didn't smile. He didn't have to. There was just so much going on in his face.

Looking at him, I felt a bit embarrassed. I kept on telling myself he was just a normal boy, nothing special, but basically I'd never wanted to stare at a boy so much.

It was a loud hot night. You could hear birds calling and now and then a plane going over. You could hear my mum on the phone going on and on about something, I don't know what. There was nothing on TV and I didn't know where Sam was. Actually I didn't care where Sam was. Everything was better when he wasn't around. If you don't know what I'm talking about then maybe you're lucky. Maybe you're an only child or you've got one of those brothers that doesn't help himself to your possessions and acts like a normal person around the house.

We don't usually get anyone coming in our garden. Mostly there's no one except the foxes. Actually the whole reason I'd gone out was to see if they were there. They normally come out when it's about to be dark, but only if they feel like it and quite often they don't. But instead of the foxes here he was, just standing there.

Maybe I should have been scared but I wasn't. I was really, really excited.

★   ★   ★

I glanced back at the house to see if anyone was watching but they weren't. Good. I looked at him again. I wondered what to do. I wondered if he would speak to me. I decided to be the first one to say something.

Hello? I said.

Hi. His voice was soft.

What's your name?

Alex.

Now it was a whisper.

Alex what?

He kept his eyes on me.

Just Alex.

Alex. Part of me had known he'd be Alex. Some names just seem to sound like the person they're for and this one sounded like him. He had a funny voice, almost like a girl's – not low and scratchy like Sam's. Even though the way he kept on looking at me was a bit eerie, still if you'd had to shut your eyes and say what kind of a person he was you'd have gone for gentle and interesting and fairly kind.

But his clothes were weird. Brown trousers that were falling right off him and looked like they'd been got at the charity shop. A shirt that should have been white but was all torn and stained with half the buttons coming off it. Either he didn't have a mum or he didn't have a washing machine, or both.

I asked him how old he was. He said fifteen. This really surprised me. To me he looked way less than that – kind of skinny and underdeveloped for fifteen. I didn't say so though. His accent wasn't from round here either. His feet were dirty and bare and there were scratches all over his legs.

Where do you live? I asked him. Do you live in the town?

He shook his head.

Where then?

He frowned at the sky as if he was trying to think up an answer that would satisfy me. It annoyed me a bit that he would consider lying.

Just around, he said.

Around? What's that supposed to mean? I asked him and he looked at me and just shrugged.

Whatever you want, he said, and looked away.

Hey, no need to be rude, I told him and then I worried that I'd gone too far and he might be losing interest so I bit my thumb and then I stopped myself because he was watching.

Sorry, he said, I didn't mean it like that.

It's OK, I told him, I didn't really think you did.

We were both quiet for a minute then.

When were you fifteen? I asked him. I mean are you just fifteen or are you nearly sixteen or what?

He said nothing.

Well when's your birthday? I said, a bit impatiently. He sighed.

You ask a lot of questions don't you? he said.

Do I? I said, though people had been saying that to me all my life, so I guessed it must be true.

Yeah. Yeah you do.

We stared at each other a bit crossly. I could feel my arms being bitten by the midges and I batted them away. Still he did not take his eyes off my face. I was beginning to find it quite annoying actually.

Why are you in our garden? I said then. I knew it was another question but it was my garden wasn't it? I had a right to ask.

I didn't know it was your garden, he said. Sorry. And he sounded as if he meant it.

It's OK, I said, I don't really mind if you go in it.

I decided to be nice.

I'm Flynn, I told him and I was just about to say my age as well when I heard Anna inside crying her head off and then my mum calling me. If I didn't go in she would come out and see us.

Got to go, I said, but he didn't say anything he just looked at me and seemed quite happy for me to go. He didn't ask if I was coming back or anything. He just kept his eyes on me. I waited for a second, to give him a chance.

'Bye then, I said, but still he said nothing and he didn't move. I knew that if my mum found him she'd tell him to go. I hoped she didn't find him. I hoped he wouldn't go.

As I ran up the steps into the house I turned and checked to see if he was still there and he was. You could just see the dark shape of him against the fat lightness of the trunk.

Yes. There he was. Looking right at me.

You think you know every little detail about your own life – what it feels like to live it and what other people are going to be in it with you and all that. You think you've met everyone interesting that you're ever going to meet and that you already know most of the important and useful stuff in the world that there is to know. But you don't. Because the big thing is, nothing ever stands still. You can never know what to expect. There can always be something else amazing or lovely or terrible right around the corner.

Some days I felt about a hundred years old and full up with trying to know things. Like my brain would heat up and my head would burst, because there was so much I was having to make room for in there. Some days I felt much more grown-up and clever and mature than Sam. But then other days it was like everything unravelled and came tumbling out of me and I was even smaller and stupider than Anna who wasn't even two yet. And then other days I felt like I was this flimsy shivery bubble floating in the air and it would only take one tiny thing to go into me and that would be it, pop, I'd be gone for ever.

Part of me thought that might be good, just to go. To be gone for ever, I mean. I know you're not meant to think that when you're only thirteen and your whole life is stretching out before you and all that, but so what? I did think it. I just did. I liked to imagine the moment. The amazement and shock. People's upset faces.

Ever since I'd managed it that time, my mum was really jumpy. Actually so was I.

Where are you going? she'd snap if she heard me just doing something quite simple like walk through the hall without putting the light on.

Nowhere, I'd tell her, and mostly it would be true. Because wasn't that just exactly what I was doing, spending my whole life going nowhere as fast as I possibly could?

I used to wonder where it had come from, this dangerous out-of-breath feeling. I knew that when I was twelve things had seemed pretty normal. Like I was living at the same pace as everyone else. But ever since I'd been thirteen I'd been waking up in the morning with this panicky idea that I was half a million steps ahead – rushing and chasing. I didn't know where it would take me, where it might make me end up. I worried about it a lot – who it might turn me into, what it might make me do. It was like all the time I was waiting and waiting for something amazing or lovely or terrible to happen and I just didn't know what it was.

And then when I saw Alex at the bottom of the garden, I knew straightaway. He was one of the things I'd been waiting for.

I nearly didn't tell Sam about Alex — part of me didn't want to share him. But another part of me was just dying to talk about him to someone, so in the end I did.

Sam blew out smoke and tried not to look interested. This was how he always looked when I told him something new or exciting. Like he'd heard it all before. It was a big and annoying part of Sam's character that you could never even slightly surprise him.

He stretched out his legs. His jeans were so old and ripped and falling apart, you could see half his legs through them. Big hairy man's legs. Mum had given him money to get new ones but he'd gone into town and straightaway spent it on other stuff I don't know what, drink and cigarettes probably, so Mum said he wasn't getting any more. As far as she was concerned he could live like that — in rags.

I told him the boy was called Alex, and as I looked at Sam's legs I remembered how his trousers were rags as well. Strange, because he somehow didn't seem the type to smoke or drink. But then some people are just poor to start with.

Alex? Sam said and as soon as he said it I felt myself blush. It was just that thing of when a word's been sitting safely inside you and then you hear another person say it out loud.

You could see Sam thinking about this.

What the hell was he doing in our garden?

He didn't know it was ours, I said quickly, I don't know — maybe he just thought it was some kind of a field or something.

Sam flicked ash on the step then rubbed it in with the heel of his foot.

You didn't ask him how he got in?

He probably came in the back, I said, though it was the first time I'd really thought about it. Through the fields I suppose.

Fucking hell, Flynn, said Sam, I can't believe you did that.

Did what?

I can't believe you just started talking to him.

I felt annoyed.

Why not?

I mean you should have come and got me. Or Mum.

But you weren't here, I reminded him.

OK, Mum then.

I put my chin on my knees. I could smell the dirt on my skin. It made me want to lick it.

But what would Mum have done? I said, though actually I already knew. Mum would have interrogated him. She would have asked him all sorts of difficult embarrassing questions and Alex would just have run away. Like any sensible person.

Sam looked at me.

Are you crazy? You're not getting the point are you? He could have been anyone. You had no fucking idea who he was. He could have been some escaped lunatic on the run or something. You are so thick sometimes, you know that?

I sighed. Ever since our dad had gone, Sam was always trying to be the big protector guy in charge of everyone. Which was quite funny as he was the most unresponsible person in the family.

He seemed nice, I said quietly. He didn't seem like a lunatic at all. And I don't see what was wrong with just talking to him.

Sam sucked on his cigarette. It was a roll-up and such a thin little one that he had to suck quite hard. It made these big hollow dimples in his cheeks when he sucked. Sam could look quite handsome sometimes.

What if he'd tried to grab you?

I smiled at the idea.

I'd have just stepped away and run back into the house.

And what if he'd been about to break into the house?

Well I just knew he wasn't, I said. Sometimes you just know things about people and I knew he was a good person.

Sam laughed loudly but it wasn't a real laugh, it was fake.

You think no one who's been murdered has ever said that?

I could have pointed out to him that people who've been murdered never say anything at all because they're dead. But I didn't. Instead I ignored him and began to pick at a scab that'd been on my knee for something like a week. It was a big hard one. I got my nail under the edge of it and a blob of blackish blood appeared. I pushed it straight back down again but the blood still oozed.

There was some blood on my finger and I looked to see if Sam had seen but he was busy rolling another cigarette so I just wiped it on my shorts.

It was after supper but the air was thick and wavy and hot. It had been this same weather all summer, hotter than we'd ever known it – days and days when everyone was cross with everyone else and no one felt comfortable in their skin and nights when you got bitten all over by the insects and couldn't sleep because you were sweating so much.

We were sitting out on the back-door step so Sam could smoke. Mum hit the roof if he smoked in the house. Actually Mum hit the roof whatever, but Sam didn't care. He did what he felt like doing these days.

It wasn't always like this. I could remember a time back

when I was maybe eleven, when he used to take notice of what other people said. But since he started doing whatever he liked, whenever he liked, life had got a bit scary. You never knew what was going to happen next. He shouted and he swore and he kicked doors till they were half off their hinges – and then complained that the house was falling apart. He never put things in the dishwasher or helped around the house. If he felt like frying eggs late at night or playing loud music or going out, he just did it, even if Mum was screaming and yelling and begging for him not to.

In his room were piles of plates with old food going off, old cups of coffee that had gone horrible and green. Sometimes you couldn't go in there it smelled so much. Wherever he went he dropped things. He dropped his hoodie in the hall and his pants on the bathroom floor, his towel on the landing or wherever he happened to end up when he finished drying himself. If he ate a piece of bread or some crisps he just dropped the crust or the packet right there where he was standing, he never thought about who might have to clear it up or anything. Now halfway through last term he'd dropped out of school and so he didn't even have to get up in the morning any more. Mum said he was trashing his whole future and she didn't have any way of stopping him and that was why she always started crying as soon as she had a glass of wine.

It didn't take a genius to see that Sam was out of control. Or off the rails or whatever. Except off the rails never seemed quite like the right words because if a train goes off the rails, then doesn't it stop? And Sam hadn't stopped yet, oh no. If anything he was just going further and further, harder and faster. We were all waiting, Mum and Anna and me, for him to slow down, stop, crash, whatever. And I know it sounds mean, but some days I didn't care any more which of those it turned out to be.

There was another side to Sam though, a side I could never have explained to anyone but it was definitely there. He was an interesting person. He had ideas that were different from other people's. It was like he could walk right around something and make you see it from a different angle and you'd wonder why you'd never seen it like that before, but the thing was, you couldn't have without Sam to show you. There was something about him that made it so easy to get sucked right into his space. Like even though you hated yourself for it, still you wanted to be his friend. Like getting his attention felt so wonderful and made you feel so important that even though a part of you knew better, another part of you so wanted to believe it was real and true.

Sam said he was going to be a famous poet one day. A poet or else maybe a famous song writer, he didn't know which. He needed to learn to play music first though. And he had this journal where he wrote down all his observations about life and all these things he'd done late at night and stuff. Sometimes he let me read it. Some of the pages were smeared with blood, his blood. I don't know how he'd cut himself but he just had. Most of what was written in there was really cool but parts of it made me feel scared. There were things in that journal that I didn't know if he'd made up or not. I didn't want to know. I just really, really hoped he had.

Where we lived was right bang in the middle of nowhere. An oldish house surrounded by a bit of a lawn and then this massive great tangle of garden where no one but me ever went. After that, fields and fields for miles and miles, nothing but fields. Everywhere you looked you saw green or brown or yellow and that was it.

It was wild out there. Part of me liked it and part of me didn't.

For instance I loved that there were foxes in the garden – this whole ginger family who sunbathed in the bracken in the early morning or else slunk around after dark looking for things to kill. Once I found a whole skeleton of some animal just lying there all undisturbed. Its skull was thin as eggshell and there were rows of teeth inside so fine and sharp they made you shudder.

Our mum bought this house for practically nothing because it had been lived in by old people who made it smell. Since our dad left, there was no one around to fix things or do DIY. The pipes were so old and cranky that they made juddery noises if you turned on more than one tap at a time and there were rooms where the carpets smelled of sick. The bath had this great big rusty stain around it. Sam said it looked as if a whole family had slit their wrists in there.

Sam especially hated the house because if you wanted to go into town there was just this one old cronky bus that hardly ever came. On Mondays it didn't come at all. Sam and me wished we could move to a flat in town, a place with a proper shower and good TV reception and near some shops at least, but we knew Mum wouldn't. She said she wanted to be as far away from our dad as possible and that was that.

When she and Dad split up she went a bit crazy for a while. Anna our little sister was born right in the middle of it. When Mum and Anna came out of the hospital, Dad did try to get back together with her, but only for about four days. As soon as he came home they had big fights. One time a neighbour called the police because she heard screaming.

That night I watched Dad put his stuff in a big bag we only ever used for going on holiday and I asked him if he thought he would ever come back and he sighed and said, No, Flynn, probably not.

I waited for him to say something else but he didn't. I waited and waited but he just sat down on the bed in a tired way as if his whole body was a balloon that was going right down because it had lost all of its air.

At first Sam and me used to visit every other weekend and he pretended everything was happy and normal. He let us stay up late and choose what DVDs to watch and what food to eat. We could have fizzy drinks and white sliced bread, we could even have cider if we wanted. Anything, however unhealthy. We didn't have to sit at the table to eat and we didn't even have to all eat the same thing at the same time either, the way we did at home. It was good. The only drawback was you sometimes forgot to eat or sleep and ended up hungry and tired by mistake.

But then Dad got engaged to Carol and the visits just kind of faded out. He didn't exactly say he didn't want to see us, but he was never free, he was always working and he said the arrangements were getting too complicated and that our mum was messing him around and it was doing his head in.

One time he was supposed to be coming to collect me to take me swimming and I got my bag ready and everything and waited and waited for him to turn up but he never did. After an hour of waiting I gave up. He never used to be an unreliable person but it was like now he'd turned into someone who couldn't even remember the simplest arrangements. I wasn't that cross, not really, but I got a stomachache. I always got a stomachache when things I thought were going to happen didn't happen.

When he stopped making arrangements it was almost a

relief in some ways. Though I missed him, still there wasn't any waiting around or expecting things and having all your hopes smashed. Life went all level and normal again. Now he sometimes sent postcards and money on our birthdays but we basically hadn't seen him in more than a year.

I wondered how long it took to forget a person, even if that person was your dad. I wondered how long it took for them to be erased completely from your memory. Because if I shut my eyes I could still just about see the outline of his face and how his hair was and how it felt to have him in a room. But it was hard to remember the little things like the actual shape of his mouth or how his eyes crinkled up when he laughed.

Sam said Carol was having a baby. Actually two babies. They were twins and they were girls. He'd heard Mum telling someone on the phone and saying it was the bitter bloody end. I don't think she knew that we knew. Probably she didn't tell us because she didn't want us to be upset, she thought it would hurt our feelings that he had other children now.

I wasn't upset but I did wonder whether, if a person had brand-new babies to love, they might forget they already had some other old children from before. Babies are so much nicer and more exciting than older kids and I didn't know what I felt really. Though a part of me was quite cross with those twins for being a part of our dad and living with him and all that, there was another part of me that would have so loved to hold them and help dress them and push them in a double buggy and tell people they were my sisters.

But at least we had a baby of our own, we had Anna. And Anna had never known her dad at all, which was funny because of all of us you'd have had to say that she was the happiest. She woke up every day with a smile on her face and went to bed in the exact same way. I thought life must be pretty easy if you were a baby. You could think whatever you liked any time you liked. You could burp and no one minded. You didn't have this great big struggle of always trying to make sense of things.

Sam had gone out somewhere I didn't know where. He'd probably come back in the middle of the night and drive our mum mad by putting on music and leaving all the lights on and acting as if it was the middle of the day.

You always knew what Sam had been doing because he left a trail. You knew for instance if he'd baked a cake in the night because in the morning the floor would be covered in spilled sugar that would make your trainers stick to things. Or there was the time he tried to ring someone at 3 a.m. and when he couldn't get through he just got into a temper and threw the whole phone against the wall so it smashed and Mum cut her foot on one of the pieces when she came downstairs. It wasn't even an ordinary phone, it was Mum's best one, a special black vintage one she got in a junk shop. When she stood there with blood on her foot and yelled at Sam he just shrugged. He never thought anything was his fault. And if you never think anything is your fault, then really you can do anything can't you? Because of this we were all a bit scared of him.

Mum wanted him to move out, she really did. She said it wasn't right to have him living here with a baby as small as Anna. I didn't really want him to go, I didn't want it to be just me and a baby in the house, but I could see why she worried. She thought that one day something terrible would happen – that he would cause a fire and the house would burn down or something. I thought she had a point. I could just see Sam sitting among the ruins of this burned-down house and rolling a cigarette and shrugging and saying it was all someone else's fault and what was he meant to do about it?

I went back outside to look for Alex.

Except I didn't want him to think I was actually looking for him so I just stood on the step and breathed in the dark for a moment as if I was just looking at the sky. It was still hot. Mum had run the hose on the flower beds and you could breathe in the wet soil smell.

I looked around but there was no sign of him.

Hello? I said, half loud and half soft.

I couldn't see anything. I stared into the darkness so hard it went fizzy. Then I heard a noise of leaves being moved.

Hey, said a voice and even though I wasn't scared I jumped.

Is it you? I said. I looked all around me but I still couldn't see him.

Yeah.

Where are you?

Not there, he said. Over here.

And I turned and there he was, by a different tree, not the one where I first saw him. All I could make out in the dark was the whiteness of his face and his arms. I don't know why but looking at him just then gave me the out-of-breath feeling. I shut my eyes and opened them again. I tried to get myself steadier.

Have you got the time? he said.

Time for what?

No. I mean d'you know what time it is?

I felt myself go red.

No, I told him, I don't have a watch.

What do you do if you want to know what time it is then?

I tried to think.

I suppose I look at my phone, I said.

Well look at it now will you?

I don't have it. My brother's taken it.

Sam always took my phone when he ran out of credits on his.

Your brother? said Alex. Is he here?

And he took a step back. Straightaway I realised I didn't want him to go.

No, I said quickly. No, he's out. Why?

He was still moving, backwards. Hey, I said, don't go.

It's all right, he said, as if he'd just decided something, I won't. Not yet.

We looked at each other a moment. There was so much I wanted to know but I didn't dare ask.

Well how do *you* know what time it is if you don't have a watch? I asked him.

I did have one, he said, but it was taken off me.

Who? Who took it off you?

I can't answer that, he said, but he was smiling. But you can ask me something else if you want.

I bit my lip.

OK, I said. Have you been here all this time?

All what time?

While I was inside.

What, in the garden? he said. No. I had to go somewhere. I came back.

Why?

Why did I go somewhere?

No, why did you come back?

To see if you'd come out again.

Really?

I felt myself go red again.

Yes, he said, and I hated that he seemed to be laughing at me, Really.

I tried to look at him but it was hard. Those eyes that went on for ever. They gave me a trembly sick pain in my stomach like before an exam only nicer.

What did you say your name was again? he asked me then and it felt a bit like he'd just properly noticed me.

Flynn, I said.

Flynn?

Yes. Flynn.

Funny name.

No it's not.

I mean funny in an interesting way, he said.

Oh, I said, though I didn't really believe him. I pulled the neck of my T-shirt up over my nose. The smell of my own warmth always calmed me down. He seemed to be thinking.

Do you have any food, Flynn? he asked me then.

Not really, I said, thinking of the fridge inside and wondering what he might want. Why? Are you hungry?

He shrugged.

We'd both moved a bit and were standing right by the far wall now, the dark sad part of the garden where Mum tipped the wheelbarrow. There were slugs here and nettles and dead leaves even in summer. All the plants had these gooey spiders' webs hanging off them. Sam and I once saw a rat.

Suddenly Alex grabbed at the wall with both his hands and got himself up. I watched him. He did it in a slightly showy-off way, as if he was perfectly aware that I was watching. He put his two bare feet in the cracks of the brick and his fingers on the ivy that grew everywhere all over it and he pulled himself up. Then he squatted on the wall, smiling. His trousers were so worn that his dirty knees poked right through.

Hey, he said.

He was looking down at me and kind of grinning.

What? I said.

You have a great face, he told me.

No, I said, feeling embarrassed.

What do you mean, no?

No, I mean, I don't.

He looked confused.

I wouldn't say it if I didn't mean it, he said. Seriously. I like it. Your face. It's good.

I didn't say anything. I didn't know what to say. I wasn't stupid. I knew I wasn't pretty. I was so thin my ribs showed through and my hair was only to my shoulders because my mum would never let me grow it really long and in September I was getting train tracks on my teeth. On top of that my nose was bumpy and my nails were always bitten and one of my knees was wonky and pointed the wrong way. I didn't really care though. It wasn't as if it was a big ambition of mine to be pretty. I was much more keen on being clever. Or adventurous and interesting and brave.

But Alex carried on.

And you've got incredibly blue eyes, he said. Seriously. It's almost spooky how blue they are.

Spooky?

I've never seen such blueness.

Well don't go on about it, I said, because I wasn't used to having my eyes stared at. But Alex didn't seem to mind. He was still looking at me in a thoughtful way.

Come on, he said then.

What do you mean come on?

Up here. Come on up.

And he stretched out a hand that was just as thin and scratched and dirty as his foot.

I shivered.

I can't, I said, I'm sorry but I've got to go in.

It was half a lie and half true. But even though I knew I might be sorry later I just couldn't stay there any longer with his eyes going into me like that. And before he could say anything else I turned and ran.

Mum was upstairs. You could hear her stomping around, picking things up and putting them down. As soon as I went inside she started going on about everything that had to be done. All I could hear was her voice coming down the stairs going on and on. I was fed up with it. She never went on at Sam like that, not these days anyway. She said it was because she'd given up on him and maybe that was true but it still wasn't fair. It meant he just kept on getting away with murder.

I stood in the hall and listened. Well half of me did. The other half was still in the garden with Alex. I wondered if he'd gone now. I wondered if he could hear my mum yelling at me. I really hoped he couldn't.

She was telling me to unload the dishwasher. Put away the clean dishes. And then put the dirty stuff in. To make sure I rinsed the plates. Especially the ones that had rice on. To cover up the food that had been left out. To put away the butter . . .

I let some spit fall out of my mouth onto the hall floor. I wanted to see if I could make it land on the line between the tiles. And I did. I hit it. My spit was frothy. I wiped it in with the toe of my trainer. Then I did it again.

Upstairs Mum's voice was still going. Was she never going to stop?

OK, I said. OK, I'm doing it.

★   ★   ★

Much later, I stood at the landing window looking out into the dark garden.

He wasn't there. He'd gone, I just knew he had. I didn't even need to see the whole garden to know it. I could just tell by the ordinary way the moon was shining on Mum's old white garden chairs and how the shadows were all knotted together under the trees. No one there. No Alex.

I belted up the next flight of stairs as fast as I could so the blood swished in my head. It was a horrible feeling but I was used to it and if I held onto my skull and pressed down with my fingers, I could make it stop. Then, with my hands still clamped on my head, I looked out of the top landing window but he was still gone. A cat was standing on the wall but it wasn't ours, we didn't have a cat.

I cleaned my teeth in the dark I don't know why. Sam's underpants were all over the floor so I picked them up and put them in the basket. Then I went into his room and sat on his bed for a bit. The moonlight made the mess in there look beautiful and eerie – his tobacco spilled all over the floor, bits of paper, a sweatshirt with holes in, a bag of chips from days ago.

I sat on his lumpy messed-up bed and wet my finger and picked up a wisp of tobacco and put it on my tongue. It tasted of old men. It made me feel sad. I spat it out again. I heard the phone ring downstairs and for a moment it was ringing too fast and the room went hard and tight. But it was only for a few seconds and then my breath came back and everything was normal again.

I once asked Sam if he'd ever had the out-of-breath feeling and he just gave me this look like I was crazy. I didn't really blame him. It wasn't something you could begin to get your head around if you'd never had it.

When it came, it was like every normal everyday noise went all extra-loud and speeded up. So for instance just an ordinary tap dripping would sound like this mad gallop going through your head. Or a few birds tweeting outside would sound as if someone had gone and turned the volume right up. Or if a radio was on somewhere, the voices would be all strange and snappy and quick.

I always knew when I was about to get it because suddenly the texture of everything would change. Just before things speeded up and I got out of breath, everything would slow down. Like having mud oozing in slow motion in your shoes or a handful of velvet shoved between your teeth.

I woke up and the light was on and Sam was in my room going through my stuff. I tried to speak but only a groany sound came out.

Go 'way, I said.

He turned round and stared at me as if he was surprised to find me asleep in my own room.

You were talking, he said. In your sleep. It was weird. You were laughing, you really were, I swear.

Go away, I told him again even though I was still too fast asleep to talk. Please, Sam. Just get out –

I wonder what was so funny, he said, and he laughed to himself.

I mean it Sam, I said a bit louder. Get your hands off my stuff and turn out the light.

Hey, he put his hands up in the air and I blinked. Hey, it's OK.

It's not OK. Just shut up and go away, I said again.

My hand was over my eyes. I was so sick of him waking me up. He sat down on the bed and I felt the heaviness. I could smell burning. He was flicking his lighter on and off. He was sitting half on my legs. I tried to shove him off.

Have you got any money you can lend me? he said.

I sat up and rubbed my eyes. I was getting furious.

Please, I told him in a louder voice, it's the night-time. Go away and leave me alone.

He looked at me. The pupils of his eyes were all small.

I need baccy, he said. I need a bit of money.

No, I said.

I'll pay you back, he said. Please, Flynn?

I lay down and shut my eyes. I put my hands over my ears. He looked at me and I said no again and then he got up.

OK then, he said, and he looked like he was going to kick the bed but he didn't. Fine. Have it your way.

Where are you going? I asked him and I don't know why but a part of me felt anxious.

Out, he said, and he turned out the light but even though the room was black my thoughts were moving around too much to let me sleep.

Anna had started walking. It was a pain. Her first steps had been about three weeks ago when Mum was out at work.

I was getting some squash at the sink and something made me turn around and there she was standing swaying in the middle of the floor.

Wa! she said.

I laughed. She looked completely different when she was standing up. So much more like a real human person. She took three whole steps, swayed again, then sat down with a bump.

Mum was a bit upset not to have been there at that important moment. She said she could still remember Sam's

23

first steps and how she'd been so excited she'd actually cried. In fact she looked like she might be about to cry all over again at the memory of her horrible selfish son once being a dear, sweet baby just like Anna. I waited for her to say something about remembering my first baby steps, but she didn't. Maybe she wasn't there, or else maybe she was and it just wasn't all that exciting the second time around.

But now Anna was really walking, she couldn't be stopped. And it was a pain because it meant she had to be watched for every second of the day. You couldn't any longer just dump her in the corner of the room with a few toys and know she'd stay there.

She didn't even want to sit in her rocking chair any more. If you tried to put her in, even if you peeled her an apple or gave her a biscuit or a bunch of keys to play with or something, she stuck her arms in the air and struggled and screamed till you lifted her out again.

Mum had this temporary job in the doctor's reception, filling in for someone who was having an operation. No one knew how long the person would be off – it might be a few days or it might be longer. But Mum said it might eventually lead to something permanent and she needed to start bringing in some money now our father had wheedled our maintenance down to nothing.

She was gone every morning from half-past eight till half-past one and Sam wasn't even up by then and anyway he refused to have anything to do with looking after Anna, so it was always me. Actually I didn't mind all that much. I liked being with Anna. And it was the holidays and we lived in a place where nothing ever happened. It wasn't as if I had anything else so very fascinating to do with my time.

Every morning was the same. I fed her breakfast and then I played with her a bit if I could be bothered and then I changed her and put her down to sleep. The only thing I did different from Mum is if she cried when she went down, I didn't go to her, I ignored her for as long as I could. Even if I had to block my ears and turn on the radio, I stuck to it. Sometimes I felt a bit mean, but I'd always thought that Mum was way too soft, making rules then caving in on them, and I wasn't going to make the same mistakes with Anna as she had with us. Who knows whether Sam would have been a whole different person if she hadn't always gone running to him when he was a baby?

Sometimes I looked into Anna's happy face and wondered how long it would be before she realised she had no dad. I thought of all the things our dad used to do with us like taking us to the swings or kissing us with his stubbly cheeks or chasing us around the room at bedtime pretending to be a monster. I supposed he would do them with his new babies now.

Of all the things we used to do with him, I missed going swimming the most. Sam was always a really good swimmer but when I was young I was scared of water − I didn't even like having my hair washed − and it took me ages to get the confidence to swim without armbands. Once I did though I really loved it. I couldn't believe I'd ever been so stupid and scared. Dad taught me to dive, sitting on the edge at first, but then later standing up, off the diving board. Last time he'd taken me I'd dived off the highest one and gone straight in without a splash. It was such an amazing feeling. But that was more than a year ago. I worried that I might have lost the knack by now.

It was blazing hot outside. It was nearly lunchtime. Mum wasn't home. Sam was still asleep in bed.

The garden was buzzing. I carried Anna out and we sat

together in the big wooden chair under the apple tree. I played with her hair, seeing if it was long enough to plait yet, and then I kissed her and put on her hat. She smelled of honey and warm fingers and baby soap.

I let her go and watched her walk around. She had bare feet. She was holding out her arms and looking at the air in a delighted way as if it was full of fairies which maybe to her it was. Babies always act as if they can see things other people can't see.

I thought how sweet she looked in the clothes I'd dressed her in. Red-gingham romper suit and sun hat, like a baby in a book of nursery rhymes. I liked dressing her. I couldn't understand why Mum always put her in the same old stained things. When I dressed her I liked to look through her drawers and find outfits she hadn't worn in a while and see if they still fitted her. I hoped that when I had a baby it would be a girl and then I could spend all my spare time shopping for her clothes, or making them if I didn't have the money to buy them.

I don't know what happened then. I don't know if I just closed my eyes in the boiling-hot sun or if I actually went to sleep for a few seconds or what. Because suddenly there he was, standing right there in front of me holding Anna in his arms.

I gasped. She was laughing and taking big breaths of enjoyment and kicking her legs but he wasn't holding her quite right. Her arms were too far up and her legs dangled.

You should watch her, he said as if it was perfectly normal for him to be standing there holding my baby sister. She was almost over there by the fox hole. She could fall in or something.

I was about to grab her back but I didn't want him to think I was worried. Instead I shaded my eyes.

26

Thanks, I said, and I reached out and took her back on my lap. She snuggled against me. She was OK with strangers for a bit but not for long. She stretched out a hand and pointed to Alex.

Da! she said. It didn't mean Dad. She said Da for everything.

Yes, I told her a bit crossly, Da.

He looked at me and I looked at him.

Hi, he said at last.

Hi, I said.

He sighed a little frowny sigh then and I saw the wetness of sweat on the side of his face.

I'd never been this close up to him and it felt weird. I saw again how thin he was, really skinny. Nothing like Sam who ever since he was about fifteen had made a kind of man-shape under his clothes that you couldn't ignore.

Have you been here all night? I asked him.

No, he said vaguely. No, I was – somewhere else.

Where?

Just – off – you know, in another place.

What place? Where? I said, because I didn't know.

He smiled in a long-suffering way as if I was being annoying and indicated beyond our garden with his head.

Over there somewhere, OK?

I thought of the tangle of garden and the secret shadowy trees and the fields that went on for miles and miles and my heart jumped.

Is that where you live? I asked him.

He seemed to be about to answer but then suddenly he looked really tired. He sank straight down on the grass where he was standing and sighed. His knees were very black and scratched and his feet were still bare. He was lower than me now and I could see his hair that was so short it was like an animal's fur.

I don't live anywhere just now, he said. If you really want to know, I'm kind of on the run.

I stared at him.

On the run? What does that mean?

He shrugged.

Exactly what it sounds like, he said.

But – do your parents know?

He smiled at the sky as if this was a stupid question and he pulled up some tufts of grass in his hands and let them drop.

What parents, Flynn?

You don't have parents?

He shook his head and kept his eyes on me, smiling.

But – what, are they both dead? I said, trying not to sound too shocked.

He looked like he was used to that kind of question.

I don't know, he said. Maybe. Why?

I couldn't tell if he was cross or embarrassed or what. He gathered up the bits of grass he'd flung down, then he let them go and pulled up some more.

You don't know? But hasn't anyone told you? Haven't you ever found out?

He blinked in the sunshine.

No.

But – I was trying to think what the next question was – so, I mean, who do you live with then?

I told you, he said rather impatiently this time. I've run away.

But – run away from who? I said. He sighed and flung himself flat on his back.

It doesn't matter, he said, and he shut his eyes against the sun and then as if that wasn't enough, he laid his whole arm across his eyes. It's my business, OK?

No need to be like that, I said a bit crossly. I was only asking.

He took away his arm and lifted his head and looked at me.

You're always asking, he said. You do nothing but ask questions, do you realise that?

Thanks, I said, because what else could I say?

Maybe he realised he'd been a bit hurtful because he sat up again. He sucked in his breath and bit his lip.

Look, he said, and he spoke in a careful voice, the truth is, it's difficult. I'm not trying to be mysterious or anything. It's just there's not a lot to say.

I said nothing.

I don't care what you think of me, he added, though I wasn't sure why. I hadn't said I thought any less of him had I?

I went silent for a bit then. I wanted to say that I thought he was very interesting, but I didn't quite dare say something as big as that. And I didn't want to be the type who was always asking questions but really I didn't know how you found the important stuff out about people if you didn't.

I took a breath to start talking and then I stopped myself. Shut up, Flynn, said a voice in my head. But I obviously wasn't listening to it very hard because then I immediately gave in and said, but look, if you're not there, I mean wherever you were before, well I mean, doesn't someone worry about you?

This time he just laughed.

No, he said, they don't.

Anna was getting bored. She wriggled and fussed in my lap. She was trying to get down. I looked around me. I wished I knew what time it was. I was worried Mum might be about to come home. I tried to listen out for the crunch of the car on the drive.

Then it's not really running away, I pointed out. Is it? I mean if no one's worried about you.

Alex gave me a look.

I don't mean it like that, I went on. I just mean if you say you've run away then you have to have run from something don't you?

Or someone, he agreed.

Yes, I said, glad he was getting the point. Or someone.

I held Anna tighter and waited to see what he'd say to that.

He frowned at the grass and pulled up a few more bits. He watched a ladybird go slowly up his arm and then he blew it off.

Well maybe I have, he said.

Have what?

Got someone looking for me, I mean.

Who then?

It's not straightforward, he said.

I wondered what he meant.

Da! said Anna and slid off my lap onto the grass. I kept my eyes on her. She stood staring at the air again.

A minute went by. I hoped he wouldn't go. Something occurred to me.

Are you living in our garden? I asked him, thinking of how many good places there were to hide.

I wondered whether he'd seen the foxes. I thought of them as my secret. Though I'd never touched them or even dared to go very near them, still in my head they were my very own pets. A mum and a dad and three babies. One of the parent foxes, I didn't know if it was the man or the woman, had a stiff thin tail with hardly any hair on it which drooped down at the end and made you feel a bit sad.

No, he said. There's a shed I found to sleep in. Not on your land, he added, as if he suddenly thought I might mind.

I felt a bit disappointed. Part of me had rather wanted him in our garden, like the foxes. Then maybe he could be mine too.

Why've you gone red? he said.

I haven't, I told him and I tried to change the subject by asking him what he was going to do now.

Now this moment or now in life?

Both, I said.

He laughed to himself.

Is that the very last question? he said.

Hmm, I don't know, maybe.

I don't know, he said, and it sounded almost like he was saying it to himself. I don't know what I'm doing.

But what's your plan? I said, hating how I sounded like my mum.

OK, is that the last question?

I laughed.

I don't know, I said.

I don't know what my plan is, he said. I mean, do I need a plan?

I shrugged.

But – I mean – aren't you hungry?

He took a big breath and looked at me.

Yes, he said.

At half-past four Sam stood in his underpants scratching himself and staring into the fridge. He asked me where all the food had fucking well gone. I knew he'd ask me this so I was ready.

I gave it to Alex, I said. The boy in the garden. I had to. He's run away.

Sam blinked.

Well what the fuck am I supposed to eat? He said.

I sighed and folded my arms. I knew there'd be a fight about this.

I've had nothing today, he said. Absolutely nothing.

You've only just got up, I pointed out.

Exactly, he said. And so where the fuck's my breakfast?

It was just like him not to ask if Alex was all right or anything. I suppose I had hoped that even someone as selfish as Sam might be just a tiny little bit interested in Alex. If for instance Sam had come and told me he'd given half our food away to a runaway girl, I knew I'd have forgotten all about my hunger and wanted straightaway to know about the girl.

I pulled myself up onto the kitchen counter and sat there with my legs hanging down. Because I had shorts on the toast crumbs from breakfast felt scratchy on my thighs. I tried to brush them away but they stuck to the hotness of my skin. Plus the scab on my knee had just bled freshly and I saw that there were brownish streaks of blood all the way down to my ankles. I spat on a piece of kitchen towel and began to wipe them. I tried to ignore Sam staring at me.

He's living in a shed, I said, trying to get Sam slightly curious. Sleeping there and everything. I don't know when he'd last eaten. He was really starving.

Fucking hell, said Sam, but you could see he wasn't thinking about Alex at all. He was still staring into the fridge as if something to eat might magic itself up from nowhere.

Far away in the house one of Mum's grandfather clocks was striking way more times than it was meant to. Twenty-five, twenty-six, it might have been that many. Everyone was sick of that clock. It went off all the time, even in the night. Mum said it was an antique as if that made it OK. Mum loved antiques, junk, old stuff. Sometimes I thought there wasn't a single thing in this house that hadn't once been owned by some dead person or other.

Even further away, probably beyond our land, a dog was barking. Not viciously, just lazy sloppy barks one after another. It made me wonder where Alex was and if he could hear it too.

Where's all the milk? Sam went on in a really upset voice. And the cheddar?

I stayed calm.

I told you. I gave it to Alex.

And the half a loaf of bread that was fucking well here yesterday?

I said nothing, just carried on wiping at my leg. I felt almost happy.

There's some eggs, I pointed out.

I don't want eggs.

I shrugged. Shrugging made me feel a bit like Sam. I liked it. It was good.

Fucking hell, he said again and kicked the fridge door so hard that a dish fell off the top and smashed on the floor. I didn't flinch.

You'll have to clear that up, I said.

Fuck off. Do it yourself.

Oh come on, Sam, I said, what'll Mum say?

'What'll Mum say?' Sam copied my voice in the way he knew I hated. I don't give a flying freaking fuck what she says, he said.

He sat down in a chair and looked suddenly depressed.

I'm hungry, he said in a babyish voice.

I shrugged again.

You can't go giving our food away to strangers, Flynn. I mean it. How in fuck's name am I meant to feed myself?

Part of me was sorry for Sam but another bigger part of me peeled neatly away from that part and stayed cold as a piece of ice.

You'll be OK, I said.

That night in the night I heard shouting. Shouting and screaming. It was downstairs. It was Mum and Sam.

I lay on my back in the dark and took deep breaths. The breaths were to stop myself trembling. I hated trembling but it was what my body seemed to do when it heard shouting coming from people that I loved. The shaking would just start up and it would be so fierce I couldn't stop it, not even if I held myself tightly. It made my teeth bump together. It meant I couldn't speak properly. It happened even if I didn't think I was all that upset.

When I was scared or upset I talked to myself to calm myself down. Sometimes it worked and sometimes it didn't.

Don't, I whispered to myself. Don't do it. Just don't. Keep still, keep still, shut up, Flynn, shut up.

But I obviously wasn't listening to myself because then my stomach started to hurt.

Practically my first ever memory was of my mum and dad fighting. Some people remember parties and balloons or Christmas or their first snow or whatever but I just remembered people fighting. I hated it. I hated the shouting (Dad) and I hated the crying (Mum), but what I hated most were the gaps in between. The terrible silences where even if you shut your eyes and pushed your face into the pillow, the pictures in your head just kept on coming.

Mum and Dad and now Mum and Sam. What was happening? Why did people always need to fight around me?

I wondered if I should go downstairs. I decided not. What

was the point? Instead I put my head under the sheet and breathed in the warm smell of myself.

I put my hands between my thighs where it was soft and hot because that always made me feel safe and then I took some more breaths and tried to think about how it would feel if I had a fox cub as a pet and it was here on the bed with me. A little baby cub that had been abandoned by its parents. I would feed it from a bottle. When it had finished drinking there would be a bit of milk in the short fur around its lips. I would wipe it off with a hanky and it would think I was its mum and follow me everywhere. It would love me, I would love it back.

I imagined him, my little fox cub, curled up at my feet and then I imagined him further up the bed so I could put my hand on him. I felt the warm feel of him under my hand, the little wriggle as he made his body into a circle and put his nose on his paws. I wondered if you could really have a fox as a pet if you tamed it right from when it was a cub? Though I didn't know what I'd do with it when I was at school . . .

I was nearly asleep when I heard a door slam. Quickly I knelt up at the window to see if I could see anything but there was nothing and no one but the moon shining down all innocently in the lane.

I wondered whether Alex was OK out there, whether he was in his shed right now at this moment, asleep I supposed.

When I'd given him the bread and milk and cheese he'd been so starving he'd done nothing but stuff himself for about ten minutes. Literally. He didn't talk or even look at me. It was like seeing a wild animal eat and it made me feel a bit strange and upset, to watch someone being so starving that they didn't care who watched them or what they looked like.

When he couldn't eat any more, he'd looked at the food that was left and asked if he could take it with him.

For later? I said, and he nodded. I got a bag and put it in. When we said goodbye he looked at me and said he'd see me soon.

In the garden?

OK.

I asked if I could see his shed sometime and he said yes maybe. I asked him where it was and he thought about it for a moment and said it was exactly four fields away from our house.

Four fields?

I tried to think which four it could be and he saw me thinking and laughed and pointed.

See that field there? Well after that one you go through three more. There, you've got my address now. Alex, Black shed, Four fields.

It's a funny address, I said.

Yeah, he said, it is.

Later, I don't know how much later, I woke up and Sam was in my room. This time he hadn't put the light on. He was just crouching by my bed and his hand was on my face.

What? I said, trying to push him off.

Shh, he said, and he put his fingers on my mouth to stop me talking or making a noise. Flynn, shh, be quiet. Listen. I came to say goodbye. I'm going.

What? I tried to sit up but my face was full of sleep.

I'm going. I've got to get out. Mum's going to call the police on me.

What? I said, and this time I had no trouble getting awake. I rubbed my eyes and stared at him. What d'you mean? What police?

Sam nudged me across so he could sit on the bed. I saw he had two jumpers on and the piece of tatty old red rag he always wore as a scarf was knotted round his neck. His face looked hard. He seemed to be thinking about what to tell me.

Look – can you listen for a moment without saying 'what'? Can you? Are you fucking well capable of that?

I nodded. I felt scared and my teeth were chattering but still I nodded and tried to say nothing.

OK, he took a breath and licked his lips. She found out about something I did.

What? I almost said but instead I just pulled the covers up around me and waited.

She found out that I – acquired – something from a shop.

What shop? I said before I could stop myself.

The petrol station by The Plough, OK?

I nodded again and kept my mouth shut. I knew that place. They sold hot pasties and magazines as well as petrol.

Acquired what? I whispered.

Sam looked impatient.

It doesn't matter what, just some stuff. Some baccy and some milk and a sandwich, OK?

My hand went up to my mouth. I couldn't help it.

You stole it?

Sam looked at me as if I was stupid.

I can't go on telling you this story, Flynn, unless you stop being a baby and shut the fuck up, he said.

OK, I said, but my heart was turning over so fast and squeezing all the air out of my lungs so I could hardly breathe.

Sam waited for a moment as if to test me. I said nothing. Part of me hated him. I looked straight in his eyes and he looked straight in mine. His were black holes in the darkness.

There was – some other stuff too. Look, Flynn, it was only food really. And cigarettes. And a bottle of something.

I tried to keep my shock right down. I tried to keep my voice from squeaking.

A bottle of what?

Tequila.

I thought for a second. The pictures flicked through my head. This was serious. My brother had stolen a bottle of tequila. And cigarettes. And other stuff. My brother was a shoplifter, a thief. But it was odd because all the time I was thinking all these things and my heart was turning over and over, still I felt strangely calm and strong and not really surprised. Why? Had a part of me just been waiting, expecting this to happen?

I took a breath.

She won't do it. She won't call the police, I said, though even as I said the words I realised I had no idea whether I really believed them or not.

Sam rolled his eyes as if I was the biggest idiot.

Oh, he said, believe me. She will.

But –

It's not the first time, Flynn, OK? OK? Do you get it now? Because I'm getting a bit fucking sick of explaining.

It was typical of Sam to tell you bad stuff about himself in a voice that made it sound as if it was all your fault not his. But still I nodded. Because I was beginning to get it, yes I was. And though I was sick of him, though I hated him for all his stupidness, still a small stupid part of me just wanted to save him. Maybe it was just the thing of him being my brother, linked to me through blood and all that. I'd known him all my life, right since I was a baby. He was part of me, simple as that. Whatever he'd done, I couldn't let him go to prison now.

Moonlight was coming into the room and lighting things up. It really was the strangest, brightest night. Because of this Sam seemed to remember something and looked around.

She won't call the police at night, I said.

I don't care, he said. I'm not hanging around here like some moron and waiting for them to come. I need to go. Do you have any money?

I sighed.

I promise, I absolutely swear, I'll pay you back.

I looked at him. His eyes were all glittery with lies.

I swear it on Anna's life, he said, and for a second I was really angry with him.

Don't say that, I told him crossly.

What?

Just don't, OK.

He looked upset and then a bit sulky.

I can't leave without cash, he said.

My eyes automatically went across the room to where my money was. Straightaway I knew I'd made a mistake. He saw where my eyes went.

Sam, I told him, why should I give you money when I don't even think you should go? Please – I mean it, please don't go.

He stood up.

It's not like that, he said, I have no choice. Can't you see? It's not just this – situation. I can't take living here any longer either. It's doing me in, it's fucking up my head. That woman, she's so – fucking insane.

She wouldn't be if you were nicer to her, I said before I could think about it. If you just tried behaving like a normal person instead of a selfish idiot, I wanted to add.

But Sam ignored this. He shut his eyes and flicked his

fingers through his hair. When someone said something he didn't want to hear, he just let it wash over him.

Have you got any money or not? he said.

I thought for a moment and then I slipped out of bed and crossed the room to my bookshelf. Between two old creased books that I'd kept from when I was a baby, was a small plush cow. The cow was hollow – Sam didn't know this – and inside the cow's head was a sock, a grey school one. I pulled out the sock and tipped a whole lot of coins on the bed.

It's all I have, I said, feeling a bit upset that he knew my hiding place now. Though if he wasn't going to live here any more, I guessed it didn't matter. This thought was so sad that I pushed it away.

Sam was sweeping up the coins in his big hands. Something about the relaxed way he did it annoyed me.

It's almost seventeen pounds, I told him to save him the trouble of counting. Sixteen pounds seventy-two pence.

All in change? he said as if that was a problem.

Yes of course what d'you think?

OK, thanks, he said, but not in a very grateful voice.

You have to pay me back. I mean it. You have to absolutely swear to God, Sam.

He looked injured.

What do you take me for? he said.

I was going to say I took him for a thief but decided against it. There was no point turning him against me right now. Suddenly the whole situation felt so horrible.

But where are you going to go? I asked him in a smaller and sadder voice than I meant.

No fucking idea, he said, and suddenly he looked all shabby and tired. I'm just going, all right?

I tried to think. I pulled my T-shirt up over my nose and

breathed it in as deep as I could. My mind was working so hard. I felt some tears prickle my nose and I sniffed them away.

I suddenly saw myself left here all alone with Mum and Anna. First my dad gone and now Sam. How could I be so careless as to somehow manage to lose a whole half of my family? Who would it be next? Would Mum abandon me? Would Anna get an illness and die?

I must have let out a little sob because Sam tutted.

You're not making this easy for me, you know.

Something about the soft way he said it made me look at him. It felt like the nicest thing he'd said to me in years. I tried to think what his options might be.

Could you go to Kara's? I said.

Kara was an old girlfriend of Sam's.

You must be fucking joking, he said. I'm not going anywhere near that girl. She's cracked.

I sighed. I wasn't so sure about Kara either but Sam always thought anyone who didn't see things exactly his way was cracked.

Then out of practically nowhere I had a brilliant idea. I didn't know why I hadn't thought of it before, it was so totally obvious and perfect it almost made me jump out of bed.

Alex's shed, I said.

What?

The shed. You can go there.

Go where? What shed?

The shed where Alex is. Don't you remember, I told you he's run away and he's living in a shed?

Sam laughed.

Well, at least it's somewhere to sleep, I told him as I pushed back the covers and swung my legs out of bed. For tonight I mean.

For a second or two Sam seemed to think about this.

He really is sleeping rough?

In a shed, I said again, wondering as I said it if that counted as rough. He's run away. Just like you.

Sam snorted. Maybe he was thinking of his missing breakfast.

He's just a kid.

He's fifteen, I said quickly. I'm sure he's nearly sixteen. Nearly as old as you, I added.

I was pulling on my jeans and a jumper over my T-shirt.

What are you doing? Sam said as I pushed my feet into my trainers.

I'm taking you there, I told him and I didn't care what he thought or said because suddenly everything had changed and I felt strong. It was like the world, which had been blurry and upsetting, had suddenly become clear and obvious to me. If Sam was running away then I was going to go a little of the way with him – just as far as Alex's shed anyway.

You're not coming out, Sam said and he took a step back from me as if to prove it. Not in the middle of the night, no way.

I didn't listen to him. I gulped the water on my bedside table.

You don't know where the shed is, I told him. And I do. So I'll take you there. After that, well, we'll have a think about what you're going to do next and then, well we'll see.

I listened to myself and I was shocked. I sounded so in charge, so grown up and certain that it made me want to laugh. I waited for Sam to disagree, to tell me to shut up and go back to bed, but amazingly he didn't. For once he needed me.

My heart was bumping with excitement.

OK, he said slowly as if he was beginning to see that I could be of use to him. But don't imagine this is a chance for you to run off somewhere. As soon as it's light you're coming back here and getting back into bed. Promise me that, Flynn?

I smiled, but I didn't say anything. I wasn't going to promise. I suddenly knew that I wasn't going to promise anything to Sam ever again. But I didn't need to tell him that now.

We'll see, I told him, and that was all I said.

I tried not to look too happy. I tried to remember that this was serious and the police might actually be after my brother and it could all end badly, with him in prison and me living on my own with Mum and Anna. But I couldn't help feeling it was also the beginning of the most wonderful beautiful adventure too – me and Sam and maybe even Alex, though of course he didn't know he was a part of it yet.

I couldn't imagine what he'd say when we turned up at his shed and because I couldn't, I decided it was best not to think about that bit yet.

Together Sam and me crept downstairs and into the night.

FIELDS

2

Alex's shed was surrounded by the highest cow-parsley you'd ever seen. Higher than us, higher even than a man. In the moonlight it looked eerie. Like these great big bony monster hands grabbing at the sky.

Sam looked at me as if I'd brought him to the maddest place.

This is it? You're sure this is where he said?

We both stood staring at the shed which was just a piece of blackness in the black of the night. There was a wiggly blackish metal roof and the wooden walls were painted black on the outside too. All of it was black.

The night was so silent and still around us you could almost hear our own breath going in and out. Sam pulled a cigarette out of his pocket and put it in his mouth. I saw that it was a real one, not a roll-up.

Where'd you get that? I whispered but he just frowned and shook his head at me.

I looked at the shed again. It was the right one, it had to be. First, it was exactly where Alex had said it would be – we'd walked across four bumpy fields in the dark with our path lit up by the moon and stars. And second, I just had this feeling.

My feet are so fucking wet, Sam complained as if it was my fault.

So were mine. My trainers were completely soaked from the long grass and even my jumper clung to me with dampness as if I'd been walking through a blanket of fog.

So – what now? Do we wake him up or what? Sam demanded to know, as if from now on all the decisions were mine.

He was trying to get his cigarette to light but it wouldn't. Even though it was a still night, the flame kept going out. After a couple of times of trying, he gave up and put it back in his pocket. Ever since we'd left the house it seemed like he'd been getting slowly sadder and smaller, as if some key part of him had been mysteriously shrinking.

I don't know, I said, feeling a little nervous and realising I hardly knew Alex and wondering if I really dared wake him.

Well I'm not standing out here all night, Sam said, thinking about himself as usual.

Is there even a door? I said then, suddenly realising I hadn't seen one.

Maybe on the other side? he said, but he seemed to be waiting for me to go round there. I hesitated for a moment. Something about the shed was worrying me but I didn't know what it was.

Stop biting your finger, said Sam.

I'm not, I said and I took it out of my mouth.

The shed looked bigger from the other side. There wasn't a proper door – just a piece of wood propped up, with some rusty metal thing attached to it. It didn't fit the doorway properly either, so there were great dark gaps all around the edges. Basically if it had been light, or if we'd had a torch, you'd have been able to see right in.

But even in the darkness, you could see that someone had been going in and out quite a lot because a path had been completely trampled through the grass and leaves. Some of the giant cow-parsley was flattened too and sprawled on the ground in the silvery light.

There was a strange smell in the air like – I didn't know what.

Well someone's been here anyway, I whispered to Sam, who had followed me round. My heart was banging hard in my chest, but I told myself there was no point waiting any longer. We were either going to do this thing or we weren't.

So I took a big breath and knocked on the piece of wood with my knuckles but the first sound it made was way too quiet. So I tried again only with my fist this time. That was louder. I wanted to be loud enough to be heard but at the same time I didn't want to scare Alex too much. I thought it might be an awful shock to be woken with something or someone banging on your shed in the middle of the night.

Alex? I called. Hey, Alex?

My voice sounded shaky and stupid in the darkness.

Hello? I said.

I looked at Sam. He looked at me. His face said nothing. He was waiting. There wasn't the slightest sound or movement from inside the shed.

Alex? I went a bit louder. Are you there? It's me. It's Flynn. From the garden.

There were another two seconds of nothing – blackness, silence, waiting – and then everything happened at once.

There was a scuffling sound and a clattery bang and the sound of something falling inside the shed. But then, even before we had a chance to wonder if Alex was coming out or not, something we could never have dreamed of happened.

A baby started screaming in there.

The sound flew at us out of the darkness. Great gusty screams. No. It wasn't possible. We stared at each other and then we stared at the shed. We were frozen up with shock.

Fucking hell, said Sam – and he began to half run, half stumble away from the shed as if it was on fire or something. Straightaway I grabbed onto the sleeve of his jumper and told him not to be so silly.

It's a tiny baby, I said. Listen. You're scared of a baby? Come on Sam, it's fine, it's –

But he carried on trying to pull away.

You don't know what the hell it is, he said, a bit crossly because he didn't want to look like the scared one.

Shush, I said and I tried to shake him out of it. Stop it. I mean it. It can only be a very tiny baby. Can't you hear?

The screams were louder now and closer together. The kind of young animal noise Anna used to make that made you think she was going to forget to breathe and suffocate with crying.

Sam just stared at me as if he still couldn't take it in. He blinked and turned his head back to the shed.

It's really small, I said as it turned into one long wail with almost no gaps in between. Really newborn, you can tell.

But – then who the fuck is in there? whispered Sam.

I hugged myself. I realised I was shaking even though I wasn't cold.

It must be him, I said. Alex. He must be in there. He's got to be. He must just – I don't know – he must have a baby or something.

Sam stared at me. All right, even though I said it as if it was obvious, still in my heart I knew it made no sense. But there was definitely a baby in there and I certainly wasn't going to run away now.

I grabbed his sleeve again.

We have to go in, I told him. Come on. We just have to.

It occurred to me anyway that if it wasn't Alex in there with the baby then it was actually possible that the baby was alone. And if it was alone then that was serious. We had an absolute duty to save it. Maybe even adopt it. It could be a little brother or sister for Anna, I was already thinking. Secretly I really hoped it was a girl.

Come on! I said again, a bit impatiently now.

But before Sam could answer me or we could even get near the propped-up door, the whole thing fell forwards onto the ground because someone had shoved it hard and then jumped right on top of it with their two bare feet. Not Alex or the baby, but a very small girl of about five or six years old who was standing and staring at us now with furious eyes.

Yeooow! she screamed and we both flinched and took a step back because she had a great big stick in her hand which was sharpened to a point at one end and looked like a serious weapon. She thrust it straight at Sam as if it was a gun or a knife. She looked like she wanted to hurt him.

Whoa! went Sam and he put out his hands but she kept on coming forwards.

She was small and light as a fairy with snaggly black hair knotted on top of her head. It wasn't curly and it wasn't straight, it was just kind of wiggly and tangled up. Her skin was light brown. She had on a pair of dirty purplish leggings with holes in the knees and she had no top on and her nipples and tummy were all smudged with dirt and mud almost like she'd done it on purpose.

She glared at us. She was skinny but her tummy stuck right out the way babies' tummies do. She was only little but she actually looked quite scary, like a bad little elf in a book. She took another stompy step towards Sam, showing small pointy baby teeth and still waving the stick.

Now look what you've gone and done, she shouted. You great big stupid fuck!

It was a bit surprising to hear such a small girl use words like that. Sam tried to laugh, but she just stayed very still and made her eyes go narrow and licked her lips as if she would have liked to eat him.

Are you deaf? she said. Are you? Can't you hear that the baby went and got woken up by you? None of us will be able to get any sleeping done now and all because of you, you great big —

Is Alex here? I started to say, but she just turned and snapped at me to shut up and then went on talking to Sam who she seemed to be obsessed with.

Now you, say sorry! she demanded and she jabbed at him again with her stick. Do it now!

He said nothing just laughed again, but it was the kind of laugh he does when he's unsure about things. And she carried on waving her stick and I actually thought she might be about to hit him with it. She was stupid enough to do some damage. Sam seemed to think so too because he flinched and stepped away from her. She came after him.

Hey, he said. Cut it out. I mean it.

He put out a hand and tried to grab the end of the stick.

Say it! She practically screamed it this time. Her scream was so loud it seemed to go up into the air and hit something and come right down again.

Sorry, he said, and he held out both his hands in the air in front of him. Look, I'm really sorry all right?

You could tell he still thought it was quite funny but I felt suddenly cross.

Hey, that's really dangerous, I told the child and I wondered if her mum knew she went around trying to hit totally innocent strangers with sticks. I thought Sam was being much too nice with her.

Get off! she yelled, swinging round at me. I mean it. Go away from me! And even though her face stayed fierce I could see there were all these tears just stacked up and waiting behind her eyes.

There was a lot of noise going on what with the baby still screaming and all that. And now you could hear other voices in the shed as well. Someone was calling to the child and I didn't think it sounded like Alex. It seemed to be a girl's voice. I glanced at Sam. How many people could be in there?

But before anything else could happen, there was a shout and some more scuffling inside the shed and someone said 'OK' and two slim white hands came out and pulled the child back inside. You could hear her answering back loudly in a rude and complaining way and someone else saying things back to her.

And then next thing we knew, there was Alex standing there right in front of us, yawning and rubbing his eyes. He picked up the heavy piece of wood which the little girl had pushed over and calmly propped it back in the doorway.

That was Mouse, he said. Sorry. She's in a foul temper right now because she's tired. And don't worry, it's not just you. She's like that with everyone.

We'd expected to find just Alex in the shed, but it actually contained four people. All of them sleeping there in the middle of the night in the middle of that quiet dark field.

They'd made the place quite comfy. They'd made themselves a kind of a den. They'd piled up jumpers and blankets to make some kind of a bed. And there was a bottle of Diet Coke and a box of crackers and some candles in jam jars, and a torch which someone had hung from a nail so it shone down on everything and was just about bright enough to act as a light.

I recognised the very milk carton I'd given Alex out of our fridge, and a lump of cheddar wrapped in foil that someone had taken a bite out of. Nothing else was in there except for some dusty old sacks and a pile of what looked like old farm machinery strung with cobwebs in the corner. It wasn't exactly luxury but they had four walls and a roof. And a door – until we came along.

I say people but they were all of them just kids no older than us really. There was Alex and then there was the angry little girl. And then the baby we'd heard screaming and the baby's mother, who could really only have been about Alex's age or maybe even younger.

The baby was wrapped up in a towel and the girl was holding it tight against her. She must have had it by mistake, I thought, and the idea made me want to go red but I didn't. I could tell the girl was the mother because of how pink her cheeks were and how she looked like she'd been running a race that was taking place in another world. She looked exactly like Mum looked when we visited her in the hospital after Anna was born.

That's Diana, Alex said when he saw me looking at her.

Hi, I said. I was trying to be friendly, but she didn't seem to hear me. She just did a cough and blinked and said nothing back.

She had very long straight blonde hair that was parted at the side and fell forwards over her face. She had round glasses and was wearing baggy old jeans and a long stripy man's shirt with a pale pink T-shirt underneath. She was kneeling on a blanket and shushing the baby by joggling it on her shoulder. I noticed there was a little tattoo on the inside of one of her wrists. I didn't know if it was a real one. It was too dark to see what it was of.

The baby had quietened down now and was just making a snuffling noise. It must have been very young because it still looked all sticky on the top of its head like it had just come out. I really wanted to ask if it was a boy or a girl, but it didn't seem the moment.

Diana was quite pretty. She was thin even though she'd just had a baby. Without the glasses she could easily've been a model. I wondered if she ever wore contacts and if she was Alex's girlfriend. Then I had an awful thought – a thought that had only just occurred to me. I wondered if Alex could be the father of the baby. Could boys have babies when they were only about fifteen? I decided I wouldn't think about that right now.

Alex had borrowed Sam's lighter and was lighting the rest of the candles calmly one by one, just as if we were going to have a party or something. Once they were lit the shadows of their flames wobbled on the walls of the shed in a ghostly way. I saw that the shed was actually way bigger on the inside than it had looked from the outside.

I was surprised that Alex didn't seem all that surprised to see us.

You remembered my address, he said even though that was kind of obvious. He gave me a quick shy look then looked away again. Then the little girl called Mouse started trying to get the lighter off him but he wouldn't let her. She jumped up and down and started pretending to cry, but he held it right above her head and passed it back to Sam.

Don't let her have it, he said to Sam, who put it back in his pocket. I didn't tell him that Sam never let anyone have anything if he could help it. He just took other people's stuff instead.

Now we were here I didn't know what to say to Alex.

It's nice, I said, looking around the shed.

Yeah? he looked for a second as if he cared what I thought.

I mean it's bigger than — many sheds.

I heard my stupid voice and decided to shut up.

Well, Alex said with a shrug, it'll do.

Sam had been just standing there with his hands in his pockets.

Flynn thought it was just you here, he said. I mean you on your own.

Alex flicked a look at me.

Did I ever say that?

No, I said slowly, I suppose you didn't.

He smiled as if he was sorry to have tricked me. I tried to remember the stuff he'd told me back in the garden which suddenly seemed a very long time ago. I looked at the small angry girl and Diana. Now I knew who the extra food had been for.

Are they your sisters? I asked him then.

For some reason he seemed to think this was very funny.

My sisters? He screwed up his face as if it was an awful thought. No, he said. Not really, no.

Not really?

He shook his head and breathed out some air.

They are not my sisters, no.

Who are they then? I said, realising as I said it that I was asking more questions.

He didn't seem to mind. He seemed to think about it.

I suppose they're my mates, he said.

53

We're his mates! said the one called Mouse and she came and put one hand on Alex's shoulder and, keeping her black eyes on me, started jabbing at the ground with her stick. I'm his mate, she added, more quietly and the way she said it made it sound a bit like a threat. I smiled even though I wasn't sure if I liked her.

Have you all run away? I said. I mean you too?

I said this bit to Diana, but she still would not speak to me. Instead she just stared at the corner of the shed and yawned. If I hadn't been so excited I would have thought she was quite rude.

Diana's a bit out of it, Alex explained.

Mouse was jumping up and down trying to get Alex's attention. Have we runned away? she said. Have we, have we?

He looked at her and then at me.

You know we have, he told her and he frowned a bit and she looked suddenly upset.

Why? I asked him.

Why what?

Why did you run away?

He hesitated.

It's a bit complicated, he said.

I was about to ask him why was it complicated but I stopped myself and tried to think. So many things I wanted to ask and tell but I was worried they'd all come spilling out at once and I was afraid I might be pushing my luck. What if Alex decided he'd had enough of my questions and asked us to leave? I suddenly realised I could not bear to go.

At that moment Mouse let go of Alex and went over to Sam.

Can I have your lighter? she asked him in a bright little voice.

Alex looked up.

Please? said Mouse.

Tell her no, Alex said quickly.

No, said Sam, and he shrugged at Mouse as if it was out of his control. He still looked a bit nervous of her as if she might lurch towards him at any minute. He pulled out a cigarette and put it in his mouth. Mouse stared at him.

Are you going to smoke? she said.

Sam said nothing.

Can I have it when you've finished smoking? she asked him.

Have what?

The lighter.

Mouse, Alex said sternly, I already told you no. Now stop it. I'm not telling you twice.

Suddenly I remembered something.

Sam's running away too, I said. From the police.

Straightaway Mouse cheered up.

What'd he do? she said. Did he kill someone?

No, I said, He −

Shut up, Flynn, said Sam, who had got his cigarette lit. He offered it to Diana who, a bit surprisingly, took it, sucked on it and gave it back to him without a word. He offered the cigarette to Alex then but he just shook his head.

He can't smoke, said Mouse. She said it proudly almost as if she was his mother or something.

I gave up, Alex said.

Because he was really really sick! shouted Mouse.

No, Alex said a bit irritably, nothing to do with that, actually. Calm down, Mouse, and don't say so many stupid things. She gets the wrong end of the stick sometimes, he added.

I like sticks, Mouse said quietly. Actually I love them.

We all looked at her.

Why's she called Mouse? I asked Alex.

He smiled.

Because she used to be very quiet, believe it or not, he said.

Then one day I started talking and I never stopped! said Mouse, and she let out a big fat laugh and her black eyes lit up.

Mouse was laughing and so was Alex a bit and then I saw that Sam was laughing too. He was being quite nice but only because he was nervous and he wanted to impress Alex. Mouse didn't seem to mind being laughed at. She didn't seem to mind anything as long as people were looking at her. She put her hand on Alex's shoulder again and fixed her eyes on Sam in a slightly triumphant way.

Have you got any kids? she asked him.

Sam laughed again as if he didn't know what to say. It was funny to see him lost for words with such a small child.

Don't be so nosy, Alex told her. He wouldn't tell you if he had.

No I fucking well haven't, said Sam.

But you might, said Mouse. Want some, I mean?

Nope, said Sam and he shook his head. I definitely don't.

One day, continued Mouse firmly as if she knew.

I never ever want to have kids, Sam told her. Never. I would rather die than have to look after some stupid fucking child.

Mouse stared at him as if he was wonderful.

I'd never given any thought to the idea of my brother having children or not having them, but now I heard him say it I realised it was true. He wasn't the type to be much of a dad. I couldn't see him looking after someone or taking them swimming. All the same it was strange to hear him discussing it with some small muddy girl who'd been trying to beat him with a stick just a little while ago.

Lots of people don't want children, Alex tried to tell Mouse. But already she wasn't listening. It was like she'd forgotten all about the question and gone on to the next thing. She tiptoed over to where Diana was and now she was bending very carefully over the baby.

Is he sleeping now? she asked Diana in a whisper.

Yeah, said Diana softly.

We won't wake him up will we?

No, Diana said, and I saw her and Alex look at each other.

Is it a boy? I asked Alex.

Yes, of course a boy, said Mouse.

When was he born? I asked and for the first time Diana looked up and spoke to me.

Yesterday, she replied.

Alex took me and Sam outside into the field. It can't have been more than 2.30 a.m. but because it was the middle of summer, the sky was already turning pink between the blackness of the trees. The outlines of things were getting sharper and clearer. You could hear the faint twitter of birds starting up.

Alex explained that he and Diana and Mouse had already been in the shed a week and would have to move on soon. They just hadn't decided where yet.

But why? I said, and this great cloud of disappointment went thudding over me. Why can't you just stay here?

Alex looked at me and then at Sam. His eyes were careful.

There's a situation, he said. Someone we need to avoid.

Police? said Sam. Alex shook his head.

Trickier than that. Like I said, it's complicated. I'm not being funny. I just can't tell you about it now.

Sam asked him where they'd been living before and Alex hesitated and said they'd lived with lots of different people.

How d'you mean lots? asked Sam and for once I was glad it was him asking the questions.

Alex shrugged. Foster-parents mostly.

What, none of you have real families?

He shook his head. Mouse kind of did. For a while. But not any more. I don't think anyone will want her again. You've seen what she's like. She's too hard to cope with.

He hesitated as if he was trying to decide how much to tell us.

The two of them, he said, her and Diana, they're kind of like my family. We all need to stay together, especially now there's the baby. Otherwise, if they find us, we'll all be put in different places and I just don't think Diana could take that right now. Certainly I know Mouse couldn't.

Sam sucked his teeth. It was very unusual to see him with such a polite and concerned look on his face. I realised it was the first time in ages I'd seen him show any respect to anyone.

Jeez, he said, it sounds quite tough, what you've been through. But is it even legal, what you're doing?

Alex looked as if he didn't know what he meant and I guessed Sam didn't know himself.

How d'you mean? In what way legal?

I dunno. I mean can't they force you to go back by law or something?

I'm nearly sixteen, Alex said, and his voice was quiet. Soon they can't force me to do anything.

But he looked quite pale when he said it.

But – how come she had a baby? I heard myself ask before I could stop the words coming out.

Alex blinked.

How does anyone have a baby? he said.

For fuck's sake, Flynn, said Sam as if he wasn't wondering the exact same thing. What a question!

Sorry, I said, to Alex not Sam. I didn't mean, you know, like that.

I didn't care a bit what my stupid brother thought but I didn't want Alex to be annoyed with me.

I'm sorry, Alex said, It's just — well it's really hard for me to answer so many questions right now, OK? It's like — well we don't even know what's happening ourselves.

OK, I said. He smiled at me and then turned to Sam.

Look, I don't really know where we're going but if you want to hook up with us for a while, that's fine by me.

Sam didn't look especially grateful or happy, not the way I would have done.

Yeah, he said. OK yeah, I think I will. I'll come along.

What about me? I said quickly.

You're going home, Sam said.

I stared at him.

I am not.

You promised me, Flynn.

I never promised anything, I told him, and it was the truth even if he didn't know it.

It's me who's got to leave, he said. It's me who can't go back home again. Don't be so fucking stupid, Flynn. You're fine.

I am not fine, I told him. I'm leaving too.

I stood there with my arms folded and I could feel Alex staring at me in confusion and I suddenly could see how it looked. Sam was right, of course. There was nothing to stop me going home. But suddenly I only knew one thing: that if I couldn't go wherever these particular people were going then my heart would burst with frustration and I would die.

I'm leaving too, I told him again, even though the words were beginning to sound more and more babyish.

Sam looked at Alex. He dug his trainer into the ground in an irritated way.

I'm fine with her coming along, Alex said. But Sam ignored him.

Don't be so fucking stupid, he said again. You can't. You know you can't. Think about it, Flynn. Mum will go completely fucking crazy if neither of us is there in the morning. But especially if it's you who's gone. She won't worry about me. She's been wanting me to go for ages.

But what will I tell her about you? I said. Where will I say you've gone?

He shrugged.

Tell her whatever you like, he said. Make something up. Tell her the truth even. Whatever you say won't make any fucking difference.

I sat down on the ground and put my head on my knees.

I don't know how you can be so horrible, I said, and I felt the tears starting to come.

I knew Alex was listening but I couldn't do anything about it. I was just so furious – with Sam and his selfishness but also with myself for being so stupid as to bring him along here and introduce him to my only friend, my only adventure. I'd even given him the money that was in my sock, I reminded myself now. What an idiot I was. Would I never learn?

Alex gave me a look like he was on my side. But he didn't say anything. The baby had started crying again. A shivery hungry sound coming out of the shed.

Suddenly I had an idea.

I could come back in the morning, I told Alex as I swallowed to get rid of the tears. I could bring you some stuff. I mean for the baby?

You could bring us some food, said Sam slowly. I saw I'd been clever. He was always worrying about having enough to eat.

If I brought a whole load of stuff then I could come and hang out here a bit, I added hopefully. Maybe stay for the day?

Alex seemed to be thinking about this.

I think there's something Diana needs, he said slowly as if he'd only just remembered and he wasn't sure what words to choose. He touched the sleeve of my jumper lightly and steered me back towards the shed. Do you mind? he said. It's just I think it's maybe best if she tells you herself.

I didn't mind. I was intrigued to know what it was a person like Diana might need. I realised at that moment that I would be happy to get her anything – anything at all. Also the feel of Alex's fingers on my sleeve made my heart speed up in the maddest way.

It was completely light by the time I went to bed and the birds were loud but I slept straightaway. It was like my body was exhausted but had been pretending not to be because of how exciting everything was and now it had given in and let go. For once I didn't dream of anything.

I woke up with the phone ringing. I didn't know what time it was but I went downstairs. By the time I reached it, it had stopped, but luckily it started again. I picked it up and it was Mum and because I was still half asleep it took me a second to wonder why my Mum would be ringing me when she was here in the house.

But it turned out she wasn't in the house. She was ringing from a long way away, about a hundred miles, in the town where our gran lived. She asked me if I was awake and I said yes obviously I was. She told me then that Granny Jane had been taken ill and was at the hospital and she had left in the night with Anna and not wanted to wake us. She said Granny's condition was pretty serious but the doctors hadn't told her very much yet.

Mum sounded upset. She wasn't exactly crying but her voice was all wobbly and broken. She loved Granny Jane. Granny Jane was Hungarian and had been a refugee and used to have a foreign name but she'd changed it to Jane, which I always thought was disappointing. I mean, if someone said you could change your name to absolutely anything, would you really choose Jane?

Mum always used Granny Jane as an example to Sam and me, to make us realise how greedy and spoilt we were. It was a famous fact that Granny Jane had once had to live on dry bread for a week, hidden with priests in cabbage fields and had had an outdoor lavatory all of her life. Once Granny had gone to the toilet in the night and a rat had popped his head up, which I thought was gross. I never used Granny Jane's toilet if I could help it, not even if I was bursting.

I asked Mum how long she was going to be away and she said she didn't know. Not too long, she said. She hoped we could cope. She said there was food in the fridge and she'd left a twenty-pound note on the kitchen table to go to the shop with, but we weren't to buy any rubbish. She said I was to be in charge of the money and not to let Sam use it for cigarettes.

OK, I said. I told her I hoped Granny would be OK and to send her lots of love and then I put the phone down. It only occurred to me when I'd stopped talking to her that she'd said nothing about calling the police on Sam. Was it possible that he'd made the whole thing up?

I went and got the twenty-pound note and stuffed it in my pocket. Great, I thought, now I could buy stuff for Alex and Sam and the others. I had four people to feed. Four people and a baby. I felt like a mum. I could go to the Spar and buy whatever I wanted.

★   ★   ★

Outside there was a dead bird on the lawn. It lay on its side in the hot blue morning with its claws all drawn up. Shiny greenish-black flies moved over it.

I nudged it with my foot and saw that its beak had a rim of blood which made the ends of my fingers go funny. I hoped that Granny Jane was not going to die. Because she lived so far away we didn't see her that often but there was something relaxing to me about the idea of her in her flat, putting the biscuit tin away, watering her spider plants and all of that.

I kicked the bird into the flower beds so cats wouldn't get it, then I got a bag and picked some damsons and some apples. You had to be careful not to get the ones with holes in. They might look the sweetest and reddest from one side but the other side would be brown and rotten and completely crawling with wasps.

I thought I'd see what we already had in the house or garden and then I'd go to the Spar for the rest. Even if Mum hadn't said about me looking after the money, I still wouldn't have dreamed of telling Sam I had it. We'd all somehow got used to not trusting him which was sad if you thought about it.

I packed up one basket and one carrier bag with food. They were already quite heavy and I realised I couldn't take too much. Just as much as I could manage to carry over four fields.

The last thing I had to get was the thing for Diana. I knew where Mum kept them.

I need some pads, she had whispered to me. The big ones. Super or maxi or whatever. As many as you can get.

Pads? I didn't know what she meant, so she showed me that her jeans were only half pulled up because she was sitting on what looked like someone's swimming towel. It was folded over lots of times and it was soaked bright red, brownish black at the edges. She blinked.

I can't even get up, she said, I can't even do up my jeans. I never knew there'd be so much blood.

When she said it, I blushed. Not because I was embarrassed but because I really felt for her. I thought how awful it would be to be sitting in a shed in the middle of a field with a new baby with all that blood coming out and people like Alex and Sam around to see.

Now I went up to Mum's bedroom and straight to the big old drawer where she kept her underwear and private stuff. I'd looked in this drawer loads of times before when she was out. There were lacy knickers and packets of pills in there even though she didn't have a husband any more. There was a card with a doctor's name on it. There was a pair of Anna's baby bootees and an old curling picture of Sam and me from another time with shiny red cheeks and paper party hats on. Every time you opened the drawer this smell came out, a kind of powdery, responsible smell. I breathed it in and even though it was stupid and pointless, for a second I really missed my mum.

In there at the back just as I'd hoped were three packs of Super Plus. Only one of them had been opened. I took them all. I hoped they would be enough. Then I looked through Mum's piles of knickers and found a couple of pairs that were plain and black. I thought Diana might need them and even though her bum was a lot smaller than Mum's still I thought they would probably at least stay up.

I looked around the room to see if there was anything else I should take. Mum's bed was all rumpled as if she'd left in a hurry and Anna's pyjamas and a fleecy blanket were flung on it. I picked up the pyjamas but they'd be way too big for the baby. I'd forgotten how huge Anna was, not a baby any more really but the beginnings of a child. I thought it might be worth taking the blanket though, so I stuffed it in the bag along with the knickers and the pads.

Then I went over to Mum's dressing table and had a look at her make-up and bottles, I don't know why. I rubbed a bit of her cream onto my face but it just melted the dirt into streaks and made me look worse. I stared at myself in the mirror. I looked so horrible. I wished I had long blonde hair like Diana. I wondered if there was an operation to get rid of freckles. If so I might save up and have it when I was older.

I made a face at the girl in the mirror and then I stuck out my tongue at her. Then I sprayed on a bit of Mum's perfume, the one in the tall blue bottle that smelled like cake. I jumped down the stairs in a haze of sugar.

In the kitchen I wrote a note for Mum.

Dear Mum, I wrote, *Because you and Anna are away, Sam and me thought we'd go and stay with friends. You don't know them but they're very nice people.*

I stopped a minute and read this back and tried to imagine what her reaction would be, or what mine would be if I was someone as edgy and fussy as Mum. Straightaway I knew she'd be worried that we'd gone off with some men in a van or something.

They're not men, I wrote because after all this was completely true, *in fact one of them is a mum with a lovely young baby, a little boy. They're very responsible so don't worry about us we'll be fine. Hope Granny Jane is OK. Please tell her we are thinking about her. See you soon, love FlynnX.*

PS I don't know when we're coming back but please don't worry. You can't call us because I'm afraid my phone isn't charged so I'm leaving it here.

PPS I love you.

★   ★   ★

When I wrote that last bit I had to swallow back a tight feeling. Years ago, I don't know when, Mum and I used to say those things to each other all the time, like they were just natural. But not any more. Now just even writing those words down felt like using a language I didn't speak any more. Thinking this made me feel all shaky inside. Like Granny Jane who had burst into tears in the middle of a cabbage field when she was little because she suddenly couldn't remember what language she spoke or what the words for anything that mattered were.

It was almost the middle of the day by the time I'd been to the Spar and bought some bread and cheese and lemonade and chocolate and trudged back over the four fields to the shed.

I was so boiling hot there was sweat all down my back. I knew now that the chocolate was a bad idea but I had really wanted to bring them something nice. I wanted them to be pleased to see me. I wanted them to beg me to stay.

But I'd forgotten there wasn't a fridge and now the chocolate had turned bendy then floppy and soon it would be nothing but liquid. I didn't want to look stupid so I took it out of my bag and threw it into a hedge. I hoped a dog wouldn't find it and get sick. Chocolate is poisonous to dogs. I love dogs.

I reached the shed. In the boiling yellow heat of lunchtime it all looked different. Then I realised it really was different. Something was wrong. Very wrong. Part of it had gone. At least half of it in fact. I dropped my bags and ran towards it.

Sam! I called out and my heart was thumping in my chest. Sam? Alex?

No answer. I stared at the shed. One of the side walls had

been smashed or torn into, like an axe had been put through it. Huge splinters of wood stuck out like sharp black teeth. The wiggly metal roof was at an angle, half sliding off. It was obvious no one was in there, you could see right inside now. The blankets had gone but I could see the place between the sacks where Diana and the baby had been.

My knees felt shaky as if they were going to give way and my heart was banging so hard that every time I breathed it hurt.

Hey! I shouted. Hey, where are you? It's me, it's Flynn.

My voice broke off. I sounded stupid in the bright hard silence. It sounded like I was going to cry which I definitely wasn't. Far away I could hear a machine going putter putter, maybe a tractor or something.

Hey! I shouted again, less loudly now.

And then some branches snapped and suddenly there was Alex, pale as a ghost. I took a breath. Every time I saw him it was like I'd forgotten how he looked and had to get used to the sight of him all over again. His quiet careful face, his black black eyes with their long lashes. Right now, maybe because I was glad to see him, I thought that even though he was just a boy, he had the most beautiful face I'd ever seen on anyone.

I licked my lips. They tasted of sweat.

Here, he said.

What?

We're in here, he pointed into the thickest part of the bunch of dark trees which ran along the edge of the field. Sorry, he said. It was just – we had to get out.

I stared at him.

As you can see, he said.

But what happened? I asked him and my stomach hurt so much I felt I was going to be sick. Where's Sam? Is everyone OK?

It's fine, said Alex, and he reached out and touched my arm. Hey, don't worry. It's cool, OK? Everyone's fine.

He walked over and picked up the two bags I'd dropped.

Come on, he said, and you could tell he wasn't desperate to talk. We shouldn't hang around here too long.

I followed him and I said nothing else.

They'd spread the blankets under the tree and Diana was lying curled on her side with the baby. Her head was leaning on her arm and the baby was snugged up in the crook of it and her hair fell like a light yellow curtain over both of them.

At first I thought that they might both be asleep but when I got closer I saw she had her T-shirt up and her nipple out and the baby was sucking. I tried not to stare. The towel was still folded up between her legs. I wondered if she needed the pads right now this minute and I nearly said something but then I thought it would be wrong in front of the others.

A little way away and not looking at them at all, Sam sat slumped against a tree with his knees up, smoking a cigarette. His wrist was dangling on his legs and he had his head back and his eyes half shut in his typical Sam way and he was blowing out big lazy smoke rings one after another as if he hadn't a care in the world. To anyone who didn't know him he looked bored, but I knew Sam always looked bored when he was feeling insecure about things.

Right bang next to him though, I was surprised to see Mouse, squatting and busily doing something with a pile of twigs and stones.

I was surprised because it looked like she and Sam were chatting to each other in an easy way, making little remarks here and there whenever they felt like it. Sometimes Mouse would go over and say something right in his ear and instead of pulling away, he'd open his eyes and hold his cigarette away from her so the smoke didn't go in her face and say something back. This was weird. Sam never normally took any notice of younger kids. He never even bothered with Anna, his own sister.

Seeing him and Mouse together, I felt a little pinch of jealousy. Maybe it was the idea that he'd already had so many more hours than me to get to know these people. I wondered if he'd spoken to Diana yet. I wondered if he knew her whole life story. I wondered if he'd seen the baby up close and even knew who its father was.

Alex saw me looking at Sam and Mouse.

She likes boys, he said. Mouse does, I mean. Big boys. She's really obsessed. I think she likes to play a game that they're her dad or something.

I didn't know what to say.

Hasn't she got a father of her own? I asked him quietly and then I felt bad because I remembered what he'd told me and Sam.

None of us has, he said. Not Diana, not me. Have you?

Lots of possible answers went through my head.

Not really, I told him and as I said it, I realised with a little bump of sadness that it was true.

Alex and I walked over to the others. As soon as she spotted us, Mouse jumped up and started hopping from one leg to the other so her raggedy curls bounced. She held a stick in the air, but I was glad to see it was a much smaller one than before and she didn't seem to be considering it to be a weapon.

He came! she yelled and even though she sounded excited her eyes looked dark and upset. He came to get us and this boy your brother, he was really really scared!

Sam gave me a look.

Like hell I was, he said, stubbing his cigarette out on a stone.

OK, said Mouse, still hopping up and down as if a new thought might come each time she lifted up into the air. OK, I didn't mean it, you weren't scared, not really. I was scared, she added and she looked at Sam in a careful way as though she badly wanted to stay friends with him.

Who came? I asked Sam and then I looked at Alex and a cold lump of worry formed inside me. What happened? Who came here to get you? Please – you've got to tell me –

Look – Sam began but Mouse interrupted.

We're OK! She sang the words as if she'd just been taught them. It's OK, we're all OK. The man went and gone away now.

Then she noticed my bags which Alex had put down on the ground.

Hey, what you got? Something to eat? I'm hungry, oh I'm really hungry!

She clutched her stomach in a dramatic way.

Shut up, Mouse, said Alex but in a gentle voice. Just be quiet a moment, will you? I mean it. We need to talk to Flynn.

OK, OK, Mouse muttered and she frowned to herself and, still looking at my bags, sank down onto the ground next to Sam. She scratched at her knee and I saw that her mouth was stained all purple as if she'd been stuffing berries into it. I hoped she knew what was poisonous and what wasn't. As she sat down her body touched Sam's legs slightly and he didn't move away. She put her thumb in her mouth then pulled it out.

Is her name Flynn? she said, pointing her wet, sucked thumb at me. Alex nodded and told her to shush.

He sat still on the ground and thought for a moment. He seemed to be trying to find the right words. I waited and so did Sam. One of the things about Alex was that people always seemed willing to be quiet and wait for him to speak.

He took a breath and looked at me and Sam.

The person – the man she's talking about – who came and did that to the shed, well, he's sort of the same person we've been running from.

Sort of?

One of the people. Well, yeah, the main person, I suppose.

I nodded. Without exactly realising it to myself, I'd kind of already worked that out. I waited for him to go on. He hesitated a moment. Something occurred to me.

But are you sure he's gone? I said. I mean you don't think that he's, well, still around and will find us here?

Alex shook his head.

No, he said. No it's not like that. That's it for the moment. We know him. We know what he's like. He's done all he wants to do for now.

He got a look at the baby! whispered Mouse in a shrill naughty voice but keeping her eyes on the ground as if she knew she wasn't supposed to be talking but just couldn't help herself.

Mouse, said Alex in a sterner voice this time, if you can't be quiet I'm going to have to make you go and sit further away.

Mouse said nothing.

You'll be all on your own, Alex warned her.

No I won't, said Mouse. That boy will stay with me.

No I won't, said Sam quickly and he looked like he was getting sick of her after all.

Mouse scowled but she didn't look at him or Alex. She just kept her head right down and stayed where she was and scratched her stick on the ground.

But who is this man? I asked Alex. He sounds horrible. I don't get it, why would anyone want to hurt any of you?

Mouse looked up quickly and with an anxious face to see what he'd say.

I'm not sure he wants to hurt us, Alex replied slowly. He wouldn't dare do that. More like threaten us. He definitely wants to scare us. He wants us to think he might do something. He wants to make his point, that's all.

He's got a great big axe! squeaked Mouse but Alex gave her the fiercest look and straightaway she got up and walked over and went and sat down on the other side of Sam. Then she did a big showy thing of sticking her whole fist in her mouth as if that way she might be able to stop herself talking.

Alex gave Mouse a fed-up look.

Have you got anything you could give her? he asked me.

To shut me up, said Mouse, who seemed almost proud of the idea.

I felt around in the bag and pulled out an apple from our garden and a pack of digestive biscuits I'd bought at the store. I handed them to Mouse who took them in exaggerated silence. While we all watched, she took one big slow bite out of the apple then put it carefully on the ground the right way up so it wouldn't get dirty. Then she fiddled with the biscuits trying to get them open.

Here, said Sam and he opened the biscuits and took one himself and handed two to Mouse.

Give me that one! she immediately said, grabbing at Sam's biscuit.

No, he said. Fuck off.

You fuck off! she said, and Sam turned his back on her, you could tell he was getting sick of her grabbiness. Actually it wasn't hard to see that Mouse was just like him, with her annoying rudeness and wanting attention all the time.

She still had a mouthful of apple but she held the two biscuits together and bit into both at once like a sandwich. Crumbs sprayed everywhere, all down her bare chest and into her lap. Sam put the packet down beside him but Mouse stretched out a hand impatiently.

Me hold them, she said.

Don't talk like a baby, Alex said. But Sam wasn't looking so she picked the packet up and put it in her lap while she got on with eating both the biscuits and the apple together and separately.

Alex turned back to me. His eyes were serious.

The thing about this person is, we know stuff about him that could get him into trouble. Big trouble. And he knows it.

What stuff? I said, but Alex just shook his head.

It's – I'm not trying to hide anything but it's a long story and –

I'm scared, said Mouse, and her voice sounded like she was. Alex turned to her with a slightly impatient noise.

It's over, Mouse. Nothing's going to happen, OK?

She kept on eating biscuits and watching him and she didn't look like she believed him.

Sam looked at Alex.

But look, he comes after you with an axe. You know stuff. You've got to tell us who he is. He's fucking dangerous.

Mouse gazed at Sam.

Fucking dangerous, she said, but her eyes were happy.

Look, said Alex, I'm not trying to be mysterious or anything –

He sighed and shut his eyes for a moment. I thought he looked incredibly tired and pale, as if someone had emptied all the blood out of him.

I know you're not, I told him, because I wanted him to know I believed him and was on his side.

Alex took a breath.

OK. He's Diana's brother. Not her real brother of course,

73

she doesn't have one. But she was brought up with him since she was about, I don't know, eight or nine.

Her brother?

I stared at him and my stomach turned over. Somehow I wasn't expecting the axe person to be anyone's anything.

He shot another look at Mouse but she was concentrating on her biscuit and looked like she'd gone into a place in her own head and wasn't listening to us any more.

Foster-brother, not real brother. The son of her foster-parents. He's a lot older than her. He's about twenty-five or something now. I mean at least twenty-five.

He hesitated and glanced over at Diana. She looked like she was asleep. Or at least her eyes were closed and her hair fell over her shoulders and her legs were pulled right up. Her jeans were still halfway down her knees but I thought that even with the blood-covered towel between her legs, she looked pretty amazing and special, like a princess in a film or something.

Alex looked at the ground. He pulled up some blades of grass where he was sitting, threw them down and pulled up some more. It was a habit of his. He put a blade of grass in his mouth and bit on it. He did not look at me. His feet were so black with dirt and so completely still that they looked as though they were rooted to the earth and not a part of him at all.

He did stuff, he began, and then he stopped and looked at Sam.

Stuff?

He did a lot of stuff he shouldn't have done, he said at last.

I looked at him and I still didn't get it.

What, you mean to Diana?

I looked at him and then a terrible thought crawled into my head.

74

The baby –

Alex nodded.

Yes, Flynn, the baby.

I felt myself gasp and I blushed. Even my ears felt hot. Either Alex didn't see, or he pretended not to. I was grateful.

We all sat in silence for a bit then, listening to the sounds of the wood. Wind pushed gently at the trees and birds called and every now and then a branch crackled for no reason. Even though it was peaceful, still the air was lonely. You felt that there might not be another human anywhere in the world, just the five of us all alone in this uninhabited place. Maybe because of this, I felt suddenly sad. I wondered if Alex loved Diana. I thought from the slow and careful way he talked about her he probably did.

How long have you known her? Sam asked as if he was thinking the same thing.

For ever, said Alex with a sigh. Well since we were quite young kids, I suppose.

And me, said Mouse through a mouthful of crumbs. Me too since I was a kid.

Mouse and me were in the same home, said Alex. She was almost a baby when she came in.

I was two! shouted Mouse.

OK, you were two. Well, Mouse was in and out of it. She'd be gone for a bit and then she'd be back. They wanted to find her a proper family but – well, no one was able to have her for long.

Because I talk too much, whispered Mouse as if it was something to be proud of.

You also set fire to things, Alex reminded her in a slightly sharp voice. Mouse looked happy again.

I do that too, yeah.

75

Sam laughed and you could see that he was partly impressed.

Are you serious? he said, and he must have been remembering about the business with the lighter. What things?

Mouse flicked a look at Alex and then shut her mouth tight as if she wasn't going to say.

Just don't give her matches, Alex said, and you could see he didn't think it was very funny. I mean it. Or your lighter. Just don't let her get her hands on it, OK? I'm serious.

Mouse smiled and looked at her dirty feet and shook her head calmly as if he was talking about someone else and she completely agreed.

We were all silent for another minute.

And was Diana in the home? I said.

Only to start with. She was fostered when she was quite young and the second family kept her. Diana's easy. Everyone loves Diana.

Everyone loves me, said Mouse, but Alex ignored her.

The thing is, he said then, she had no idea she was having a baby – not really, not till it happened.

No? My mouth was open.

It's not possible, Sam said as if he knew.

Alex shrugged.

She didn't look like she was having one. I mean she always wears quite baggy clothes so it didn't show. Then a couple of days ago she didn't feel very well and she got this bad pain but not so bad that we thought it was anything and then well, suddenly she was on her knees and there was this baby coming out. It was quite unbelievable – I can't tell you – it was the biggest shock.

Mouse stood up as if she was excited just thinking about it.

His head was all wet and sloppy! she said. And we were all crying and crying.

You were screaming, Alex said. Which didn't help at all. Diana was very quiet, actually. She hardly made a noise. I think she was in shock.

Christ, said Sam, I'm not surprised.

But, I said, suddenly feeling like my mum, wasn't it dangerous? I mean shouldn't you have called an ambulance?

Alex gave me a look.

How, Flynn? We didn't have a phone or anything. How could we? And anyway it all happened so quickly. I had to cut the cord with my penknife. That was the worst bit.

Then there was some meat stuff coming out, said Mouse excitedly. It was, oh it was yuk.

The placenta, I said, because we'd done it at school.

Secretly I was thinking how I would adore to see a baby born. Mum hadn't let me see Anna. She'd said it might shock me, to see the pain and blood and all that. But she was wrong. I'm good with pain and blood. It's being shut out of things and waiting behind closed doors that frightens me more.

That's right, Alex said. The placenta. Diana wouldn't look. She couldn't. She doesn't like blood.

Even though it was just shooting out of her! said Mouse.

But shouldn't she go to the doctor? I asked Alex again because I remembered how Mum had been visited by the midwives every day after she had Anna and how she stayed in bed for ages and we brought her drinks and stuff.

Alex looked a bit worried at the mention of doctors.

Well – I don't know. The thing is if she does that, then that's it, they find us, it's all over, we go back.

Not going back, said Mouse quickly.

We stayed in the cool shadowy part of the woods till late afternoon. But once the air changed colour and the tractor noise stopped, Alex said we should wait as many hours as we could bear, till the beginnings of real darkness fell, and then we should get going.

But get going where? I asked him, while slapping madly at my arms and my legs because of the midges that were suddenly all around us.

Alex seemed to be thinking.

We need to get away from here, he said. As far as possible. We need to walk just as far as we can manage once it's dark enough and before Mouse starts complaining. At least it will be cool. I think Diana's feeling a bit stronger. We'll get as far as we can then we'll try and find some place where it feels safe to sleep.

You think we'll find another shed like before?

Alex put his chin in the air as if he had lots of thoughts going round and round and he was trying to make at least one of them stop still for a moment so he could get a look at it. It was a habit of his I was getting used to.

Something like that, yes, he said.

I wondered how easy this would be. I wondered whether there were empty sheds dotted all over the country just waiting for people like us to come and sleep in them. It seemed unlikely. But since I'd met Alex, all the unlikely things seemed to be getting likelier.

Sam came over to me. The sun had burned his nose and cheeks, making him look like he had shadows under his eyes. This was probably the longest time he'd been out of doors in years.

Flynn, he said, you know you have to go home.

I shook my head and smiled and for once I felt superior.

Come on, he said, you know you can't come with us. Stop talking as if you can.

I am coming, I said, and I waited, just for the satisfaction of seeing his annoyed expression. He bit his lip and looked around him as if hoping for support from the others.

For fuck's sake, Flynn, he said.

And that's when I told him – about Granny Jane and Mum and how I'd left a note. Everything I told him was perfectly true, I didn't tell any lies. It's just I left some other bits out, some bits that might have slightly changed the true bits I'd told him. I told him I'd spoken to Mum on the phone.

I said we were going away for a little bit, I told him.

He looked amazed.

You really said that to her?

Kind of, I said.

He carried on looking at me as if I was mad.

And let me guess. She said yeah go on, go right ahead?

Kind of, I said again, and I tried not to blink.

Flynn, said Sam.

What?

Now tell me what she really said.

I was feeling cross now.

I told you, I said. I've told her we're with friends and that we're fine and we'll be gone for a few days.

Sam narrowed his eyes.

She would never have said yes to that, Sam said. Not in a million fucking years. Not after what you –

Shut up, Sam, I told him, because I didn't want him embarrassing me. Just shut up. Don't say anything to anyone about anything, I mean it.

I glanced around to see if Alex was watching us. He wasn't. He was sitting with Mouse. She'd changed out of her purple leggings and now she had a dress on, a pale-blue kind of old-fashioned pinafore dress that looked a bit big for her and hung down in a strange way over her grubby legs. Her hair had been let out of its top-knot and brushed

79

a bit too but it still stuck out all over the place and was just as wiggly.

Alex was counting out stones for her. Grey stones in a row, one two three. Arranged in different sizes, large, medium and small. Mouse was standing with her hands behind her back and watching with her tongue hanging out like she was going to eat them. If I hadn't been so cross with Sam the sight of her doing that would have made me laugh. I wondered how everyone managed to be so patient with Mouse.

Alex looked up then and saw me and smiled. He looked tired. He had deep shadows under his eyes. But the smile lit up his whole face and made everything feel happy again. Maybe he saw me feeling that because he got up and came over. Mouse followed him, trying to grab at his legs.

She'll kill me, Sam was saying. She'll fucking kill me.

Just leave me alone, I said, because I was so sick of him trying to interfere with my life.

Who? asked Mouse and her eyes had a half-excited half-fearful look. Who's gonna kill him?

Not literally, Sam said. As if she'd know what literally meant.

What's going on? asked Alex.

Nothing, I said. Don't listen to him. He's talking rubbish.

Is the man going to come? Mouse said in a slightly yelpy voice. I'm scared.

Shush, said Alex. Just stop it, Mouse. No one's coming.

You can't just run away again, Sam said. Tell her she can't run away.

Why not? I said. It's what you're doing.

I'm not thirteen, I'm not a girl and I've never done it before.

Alex looked interested.

Have you done it before? he asked me.

Has she done it? What's she done? asked Mouse.

I kicked at a patch of dirt on the ground. Sam looked at Alex and Alex looked back at me.

Shut up, I said again, because I knew what Sam was doing. He was trying to act like he was the good and sensible and reasonable one so as to get everyone on his side.

We have to get her to go home, Sam told Alex, and the way he said it you really would think he cared about me.

Please, I said to Alex, don't listen to him. I want to come with you. My mum says it's OK to come with you.

Alex looked at me.

Does she? he said. Did she really say that?

She's lying, Sam said. She's a real fibber when she gets going.

I glared at him.

Shut up, Sam, I said. Just shut up, I mean it. I don't like to be talked about.

Alex looked at me. He looked like he wasn't used to arguments between brothers and sisters and as if he was trying to decide who to believe and what to say.

Then suddenly Mouse went calmly over to Sam and took hold of both his hands and looked up into his face.

Don't talk about her, she said in a small anxious voice, but she said it like she had no idea who or what she was talking about or why. Sam tried to let go of her hands but she wouldn't let him, she hung on harder and wouldn't let go. When he finally managed to push her off he did it too roughly and she fell backwards onto the ground.

Straightaway she burst into screaming tears.

Hey, said Alex, and he gave Sam a look and went over and picked Mouse up. She clung to Alex but kept on crying.

He hurt me! shouted Mouse. Make him say sorry.

Sam didn't say sorry.

Alex tried to pull Mouse's fingers from around his neck. He looked at me.

Maybe you should just let her make up her own mind, he said to Sam and you could tell he was more on my side than his. Sam looked sulky. Even though Alex was younger than him you could see he wanted his good opinion. He couldn't help it. It was one of the many strange effects Alex had.

I went over to Diana to give her the pads. I wasn't sure if she was asleep or not and I remembered what Alex had said about being careful not to ask her too many questions, so I just touched her lightly on the shoulder. Her skin felt hot.

She didn't have her glasses on and she opened her eyes and looked at me as if she wasn't quite sure who I was. Her eyes were blurry and dark with some of her eyelashes stuck together, like she'd put on some make-up a few days ago and never got around to taking it off. I guessed I'd be the same if I'd been busy having a baby. There were little specks of black all down her cheeks as well and she had a whiteish spot beginning on her chin but she was still just so burstingly beautiful I couldn't help staring at her.

I got them, I whispered, and then when she said nothing, I shoved the pads towards her and said, here, look.

She seemed to be trying to think what I meant for a moment. Then she blinked.

Ah, she said.

She sat up carefully, screwing up her eyes as if something hurt her a bit. Somehow with one hand she kept the baby against her shoulder. He looked like he was asleep. He looked like a little animal, all flopped over. One of his ears was folded the wrong way and a part of me was desperate to put a finger in and straighten it out, but I didn't.

Thanks, she said as I put the pack of Super Plus on the ground next to her and she moved the baby to the other shoulder. Hey, you're a star.

It was funny but when she spoke to me, even though she said nice things, it sounded all distant like she could have been speaking to anyone. As if she might forget it was me the moment she stopped speaking.

No one had ever called me a star before.

As she moved her arm I saw that the tattoo on her wrist was of an insect. Long thin blueish wings and a thin, blue body. It wasn't quite like a butterfly. I badly wanted to ask her what it was and where she got it but it was too much of a question. All my thoughts seemed to be questions these days. I wondered if it was something you just grew out of eventually or what?

I got you these as well, I whispered and I gave her the two pairs of my mother's black knickers. They were shiny stretchy satin with a little bow at the top. In Mum's drawer they had looked quite ordinary but suddenly now out in the open air they made me feel a bit weird. Diana looked at them. She seemed very pleased indeed.

They're my mum's, I told her and she frowned.

She won't mind?

No, I said, she doesn't mind things like that.

I wondered if this was true.

Oh, I said, and this.

I'd almost forgotten Anna's blanket that I took off Mum's bed. I held it out and Diana touched its blue fuzzy edge.

For him, I said.

Hey, she said, and she bit her lip, that's really nice of you.

She unwrapped the baby from the old bit of towel that was round him and put the blanket under him instead. As soon as he was uncovered he flung his long arms out in a startled way, but he stayed asleep. She snuggled the blanket up round his head and over his body. He looked sweet wrapped up like that. He looked suddenly more like a real baby. I wondered if she was going to wash the blood and stuff off the top of his head or if it would just come off by itself. I was longing to be the one to give him his first bath.

Are you OK? I asked her, hoping that didn't count as a question.

Oh, she said, blinking into the distance as if she wasn't sure who'd asked her. Oh. Mmm. Yeah.

And that was all. She just sighed and yawned. As she stretched her arms out the insect on her wrist moved with her. I wished I had one of those. And maybe a baby too.

What was all the fuss about? she asked me then.

What? What fuss?

Your brother. Why was he shouting at you?

Oh, I said, he's being stupid. He wants me to go home. But I'm not.

You're not?

No. No way. I'm coming with you.

She gave me a strange careful look out of the corner of her eye. I did a little gulp.

Don't you want me to come? I asked her because suddenly it was a bit important to me that I was welcome.

Diana shut her eyes a moment and her face was like a closed white circle. Then she opened them again.

It's up to you, she said slowly. But if I were you, I'd go home.

I didn't know whether she meant she didn't want me around, or whether she just meant she envied me. That if she had a home to go to, that she'd go to it.

It's up to you, she said again.

Then she laid the baby on the ground and the blanket fell open and because he was completely bare you could see the thing sticking out of his tummy that meant he really was newborn. There was a piece of string tied tight around it. Or at least I thought it was string at first and then I realised it was actually someone's hair elastic that had been cut in half and used like string.

Anna had a clip on hers. Mum had to clean it and dust it with special powder till it fell off. It looked so weird at first that you couldn't believe it would ever end up looking normal like everyone else's, but it did. I wondered what would happen to this one, whether it would manage to fall off without all the powder and stuff.

I wondered if Diana was at all worried about it. I badly wanted to ask her. I wanted to ask her so many things like how did it feel to feed your own baby milk from your own nipple and was she scared the first time she did it? But I didn't ask any of this as I remembered what Alex had said about too many questions.

Just then the baby opened his eyes and looked at me. His eyes were blackest black just like his hair. In some ways he looked a bit like Alex. His gaze was like Alex's too – proud and careful, as if stuff was going on in his head that you couldn't possibly know about but would be really interesting if you did.

The baby sneezed and his eyes closed tight shut for a second but when he opened them he still kept them on me.

Can he see me? I asked Diana but she just looked at me sleepily as if she didn't really know. She didn't seem like the kind of person who was really interested in babies, except for her own of course. I knew she must love her own. Unlike me who loved them all.

But the baby seemed to know he was away from his mum

because he began to throw out his arms and legs then in a breathless and panicky way as if he'd been dropped and was falling. I saw that some bright yellow poo had come out of his bottom but just like Anna's poo when she was small, it didn't smell bad. It smelled almost sweet like honey or grass. Diana didn't seem bothered. She took the old towel and just wiped it.

He needs a nappy, I told her. The baby wasn't crying yet but he was taking big furious breaths like he was about to.

Diana looked at him thoughtfully and then she took a piece of her long blonde hair and stuck it in her mouth and sucked on it.

Yeah, she said, he does.

We'll get him some, I told her, trying to think how much change I had left from the twenty. I wondered whether Sam would give me back some of the money I'd lent him. He'd have to. We had to get nappies, that was definite. If I got some nappies then Diana would realise I was useful and that it was good to have me here. I didn't like the idea that she might want me to go home.

She glanced away towards the trees. Then she pulled the bloody towel out from between her legs and, without looking at it, scrunched it up and put it to one side. She pulled her jeans up a bit and picked up the pads and the knickers.

Can you stay here with him – while I go and do this?

I said yes straightaway. I was so pleased that she was trusting me with the baby. I told her she could take her time. She got to her feet a bit awkwardly, holding the top of her jeans with one hand. I realised she probably hadn't stood up in ages.

I cupped my hand over the baby's soft head, just to feel it.

Can I pick him up? I asked her.

Yeah of course, she said, as if it was a weird question to ask.

I know how to hold babies, I told her. Supporting their heads and that. Because I've got a little sister.

I thought she might be glad to know this but she didn't seem all that interested. Instead she looked at me and hesitated a moment.

Sorry, she said, I've forgotten your name.

Flynn, I said, and she nodded and yanked her jeans up a bit higher.

Thanks, Flynn, she said. Thanks a lot.

As she walked away the baby started to take more big gulping breaths as if he really did mean to cry this time, so I gathered the warm blanket up around him and very carefully lifted him against my shoulder the way Diana did.

Shhh. It's OK, I whispered and I kissed the top of his head which because of the dried blood still smelled a bit hot and sticky, of people's insides. I realised I didn't even know if he had a name.

Even though I didn't know who he was really or what to call him, even though I'd only known him for less than a day, still I held him tight and breathed him in. And maybe it was because he wasn't my sister or anything but it was entirely different from holding Anna, even when she was newborn. He had a different smell perhaps from not ever being in a house or touched by a doctor. Plus the weight of him was different somehow. He felt so bouncy and un-decided and alive.

He must have had a strong neck because he kept on trying to twist his head around to look at things even though he was so tiny and he couldn't really do it. And I don't know why – maybe because there were no grown-ups around and it was beginning to feel like we were the parents now – but just thinking about the fact of holding him made tears come rushing into my eyes. It was so unexpected and so lovely and so magic.

I swayed him back and forwards in my arms and I blinked a bit to get the tears away.

It's OK, I whispered to him. I love you, I love you, it's OK.

DARK

3

I don't know how many fields we crossed in the dark that night. It felt like a hundred but it was probably only nine or ten.

The ground was bumpy and smelled of rotten cabbages and hot dry earth and we could only see our way because luckily there were so many stars. Zillions of them. When you first looked up at the sky, the stars seemed tiny and not that lit-up. But if you gazed at them for long enough then it was like someone had turned them up to full brightness. They dazzled so hard it made you dizzy.

Wooo! shrieked Mouse, staring up at them with her head flung back. She turned around and around until she wobbled and fell over.

Mouse, please stop it, Alex said. We haven't got time for this. Please just walk like everyone else.

But Mouse wasn't listening. She was lying on the ground gazing up. Her blue dress was already as grubby as her body from falling over so much.

But it's so lov-erly, she said, and you knew she was saying it partly to be irritating.

I know, Alex said. I know it's lovely but we just haven't got time.

Mouse would keep on walking for about two minutes then fall over again. Every time she fell over everyone had to stand still and wait while she got up. Even though we all tutted and sighed she didn't get the message. I guessed it was just her way of getting people's attention. Now she gazed at Alex with big wide eyes as if she was trying to make herself into a baby who couldn't understand.

Not got time for it to be lov-erly?

You know what I mean, said Alex in a slightly annoyed voice.

Even though it was the middle of the night, the air was strange – hot and thick like daytime. It was lucky because most of us only had jeans and T-shirts on, we'd tied our jumpers round our waists. We didn't have a lot to carry because the food had all been eaten but Alex and Sam and me each carried a blanket over our shoulders and Diana had the baby and Alex also carried a bag belonging to Diana which I guessed contained the pads and other stuff. She seemed to have changed into another pair of trousers which was good because the first ones were so covered in blood.

Mouse wasn't much help. She was too unreliable to carry anything except one little tiny stick. She insisted on carrying it. I didn't know if it was the one from before or not. I thought it was smaller. She seemed to have a thing about sticks.

I used to have a raggy that I sleeped with, I heard her telling Sam as if it was the most interesting news in the whole world. She seemed to have forgiven him for pushing her over, or maybe she'd just forgotten all about it.

Mmm, said Sam not really interested.

But now instead I have this beautiful cool stick, look!

Sam laughed.

You sleep with a stick?

She did a solemn nod and waved it.

It's my raggy.

OK, said Sam slowly even though he had no idea at all what she was talking about.

I'm thirsty, Mouse said then. I want a drink.

You just had a drink, said Alex.

I want another one.

Well you'll have to wait, he said.

We'd all drunk all the water before we set off so we wouldn't have to carry it. Water is the heaviest thing in the world unless it's inside you. And Alex was going to bring the torch they had in the shed but it had stopped working and we had no more batteries so there was no point. We left it. It meant we had no light except the candles and we couldn't very well walk along carrying them.

Now Alex led the way holding Mouse's hand to try and hurry her up and Sam dropped to the back. And I walked as close to Diana as possible so I could see the baby and in case she might get tired and let me take a turn. I thought she must get tired in the end. Even a little baby that weighs almost nothing starts to make your arms ache after a while.

I thought of all the books I'd read and the films I'd seen where people have to travel across the countryside on foot for some reason or other – usually running away from something like a war – and how they nearly always had a horse. And the weakest or the sickest or the smallest person would be put up on the horse and someone else would lead it. Sometimes they even managed to sleep with their arms around the horse's neck as it bobbed along. I thought how good it would be if we could put Diana and the baby on a horse. I wondered if she'd be able to sleep. I thought I could be the one to lead it and I'd make sure it walked along very gently so as not to tip her off.

If only we had a horse, I said, surprising myself by thinking aloud.

Or a helicopter, said Sam.

Can we get one? said Mouse quickly.

What, said Alex, a helicopter?

No, a horse.

No, he replied and you could hear him smiling a bit. But it would certainly be useful.

Or a little donkey, Mouse pointed out in a hopeful voice.

A donkey would be good, Alex agreed.

I had a donkey once, Mouse told him.

No you didn't, he said.

I did, said Mouse. It was my mum's. Ask Diana.

But no one bothered to ask her and Diana said nothing.

But – do you have a mum? I asked her after a few minutes, because I'd thought she didn't.

She used to, Alex told me. She lived with her mum till she was two.

Not used to! said Mouse. My mum's still there but now she's just only in the letters.

Her mum sends her a letter every year, Alex explained.

Except I can't read, said Mouse sadly.

Only one letter? I said, a bit shocked.

It's the law, said Alex. She's only allowed to do the one.

Does someone read them to you? Sam asked her, and you could tell from the gentle voice he was doing that even he was thinking it was a pretty sad situation.

Diana does, said Mouse. She reads 'em out loud. Very loudly.

No I don't, said Diana with a little laugh. Someone else reads them for her, she added quietly.

And what kind of things do they say? I asked Mouse because I couldn't really imagine what a mum might write if she was only allowed to do it once a year.

Mouse took a breath.

She says . . . that I can eat as much sweets as I want and ride on tops of buses and I mustn't smoke and I can have a donkey or a horse or maybe a dog if someone will do the mucky stuff for me like cleaning it out, Mouse said but she sounded as if she was making it all up.

Alex laughed.

And – and she says she's gonna come and get me one day to go shopping to buy some pink clothes. Or on holiday.

No, said Alex, she's never said that.

I think she has, Mouse insisted. I really think so.

She didn't, said Diana in a slightly hard voice. Stop saying things that aren't true, Mouse. You're kidding yourself.

Fuck off, said Mouse.

Look, we just don't want you to be disappointed, Alex added kindly.

She sounds OK, your mum, Sam said then, and I thought it was funny that he could be nice about someone else's mum but not his own.

Well, the thing is, her face is all black, said Mouse in a thoughtful voice.

What d'you mean? I asked her.

Alex laughed again.

No, he said, she doesn't mean black like that. She just has the same skin as you, Mousie, only darker.

Was her dad white then? Sam asked Alex.

I guess, he said. No one knows. He was never really on the scene.

Mouse seemed to be thinking about this.

Wasn't my dad brown, then? she said.

Don't know, said Alex, and you could tell he didn't want to go on with this. Does it matter?

Can I see my dad? Mouse asked him, though she must have already known the answer because she gave a little sigh and didn't seem to mind when Alex said nothing.

Eventually after a lot of walking we came to a road. A real road. It was grey and hard and flat and went winding on into the distance. It looked so flat and smooth it was almost like water – more like a river than a road in the moonlight and you couldn't tell where it went or how long it went on for or whatever. Alex and Sam started having this little argument about whether it was more or less risky to stay on the road.

Why would it be risky? I said.

Sam gave me a look as if I was even more stupid than he'd thought.

I never said it would, he said. It's me who wants us to go on the road.

Oh.

It'll be so much quicker, said Sam.

But we don't want to be picked up, Alex explained. There might be people out looking for us. And we'd be so easy to spot. Especially with Mouse.

It's because I'm young, Mouse pointed out. They'd be able to see me. In the light shining out from the cars.

That's right, Alex said.

I thought it was funny that, although she wasn't exactly clever, Mouse seemed to be quite quick when it came to realising how the world worked. Maybe it was because of having to make do with one letter a year instead of a mum.

How old are you? I asked her as we all stood there in the dark by the side of the road.

I don't know, she said, and she turned to Alex and pulled at his trousers. Am I six or seven?

Six, Alex said but in a not very interested way because he was still worrying about the road.

Mouse seemed to think about this. She looked like she was counting something out on her fingers, but she might have been pretending. Now she tugged at Alex's shirt.

But when I had a birthday, I mean the last one not the one before when I set the cake on fire, well was that me being seven? she asked him.

No, Alex said, that was six. You were six.

You set a cake on fire? said Sam.

Mouse ignored him.

But I was six before, she told Alex rather impatiently.

No, you weren't, you were five. But we can't talk about this now, Mouse.

What are we doing? I asked the boys. I mean are we taking the road or what?

It's nearly my birthday now, said Mouse to no one in particular.

No, it's not, Alex muttered.

It is! Ask Diana.

But Diana shook her head.

No, Mouse, she said, it's not. It's ages away. Your birthday's not till June, remember?

You just had it quite recently, Alex said. Now please, Mouse, for goodness sake shut up and let us think.

Oh, said Mouse, and she sounded like she might cry with disappointment.

I wondered how she could possibly have forgotten she had a birthday quite recently. I felt suddenly sorry for her.

You're quite grown-up for six, I told her.

Shut up, she said. You just fucking shut your mouth. I'm trying to think.

All right, I said. Fine, I will.

And I decided I wouldn't bother trying to be nice to her again.

Alex said he thought it was safer to keep on through the fields but Sam insisted we try the road. When Sam insisted on something he had this high-up way of talking as if he was the only person in the world whose opinion could possibly count. It was really annoying. It made you want to hit him or shake him or wish he'd trip over or something. I wondered whether Alex had realised this about him yet. Usually it didn't take people long to work out.

But Alex was so patient. There was something very still about him, as if a part of him was always about to leave and go somewhere else. You could see him looking calmly at Sam and weighing up whether he could be bothered to fight or not. Sam didn't realise this. Sam just thought he was winning.

Part of me just basically wanted to be on Alex's side but another part of me wasn't sure about the fields. They were so dark and bumpy. There could be cows or maybe bulls in them. I was sure it was mostly laziness and the fact that he wasn't an outdoors person that made Sam want to be on the road, but all the same I did think we might actually move quicker if we didn't have to deal with twigs and branches and stubble under our feet. Plus there was the fact that Mouse and Alex had no shoes.

I looked at Diana but she seemed in another world, a world of tiredness. She didn't seem to care what we did. And Mouse was still grumbling about her birthday.

I don't want it to be ages away, she moaned. I want it now.

Sam gave her a look as if she was really getting on his nerves. Alex looked at him.

We'll try the road, he said. But one glimmer of a car light and we're back in there.

He indicated the woods. Sam said nothing. You couldn't help feeling that even though he had got his way, Alex still seemed to be the one in charge.

So we walked a little way down the road and the hard smoothness of the ground felt all surprising. Because it was man-made I supposed. Even though it was only that morning that I'd last been on a normal road, still real life was somehow fading. Even this morning and waking up at home was beginning to seem so unlikely and far away.

Some bird, probably an owl, hooted in the trees and Mouse squeaked loudly with surprise. Straightaway Sam clapped his hand over her mouth which was a stupid thing to do because it only made her cry louder. She yowled and yowled.

Mouse, Alex hissed angrily. You can't do that. I mean it. This is really serious, you've got to be quiet.

Sam took his hand off Mouse and straightaway she started to cry but more softly this time.

It's not a game, Alex said rather sternly.

She's scared, said Diana. Can't you see that?

I know she's scared, Alex said. But one more sound like that and she'll start the baby crying and then someone will find us, is that what you want?

Diana glanced away into the darkness.

Well is it? he said again quite roughly.

Diana said nothing. She kept her eyes on nothing. She was just brilliant at keeping her whole self somewhere else.

The whole thing's pointless if we get caught, said Alex. We may as well just give up now and hand ourselves in at the next village.

Diana gave him a look.

I was only saying, she muttered.

But Alex just shrugged. It was the first time I'd seen him be annoyed with her. But it wasn't really Alex's fault. It was only because he was trying to take responsibility for everyone.

Mouse carried on crying but very softly. She kept rubbing her fists in her eyes and lifting her feet up and down off the ground like she was walking on the spot.

I thought – I thought it might be the man, she said. And that he was coming after us.

It was an owl, Diana whispered, bending down to her. Not a man, an owl. A nice big friendly brown owl, OK?

Mouse took her fists away from her face and looked at her.

A brown one?

Diana nodded.

Yes, she whispered. Yes – and you couldn't help feeling she was slightly sending Mouse up for caring so much about the colour – a brown one. Brown, yeah?

Mmm, said Mouse slowly as she thought about this. But – but I thought the man was in the shape of the owl, she said, and she shot a quick glance at Alex as if she suspected that what she was saying was a bit silly.

I saw Alex smile. Then he stopped smiling and he crouched down in front of Mouse on the road and held onto her bare thin little arms. He looked into her upset face for a moment, then he took her chin in his fingers. His face was hard.

He's not. It's not him. He's not in the shape of an owl or even a man. He's not in the shape of anything because he's gone, OK? He's not going to come now, have you got that, Mouse?

OK, said Mouse slowly but she sounded like she didn't believe him one bit.

98

It's the middle of the night, Sam said, trying to join in the game of reassuring Mouse. He'll have gone home, won't he?

Gone to which home? asked Mouse rather fearfully but Sam didn't have an answer to this.

We don't know which home, Alex said, still looking into Mouse's face. It doesn't matter, we don't care. But, Mouse?

Yes?

If you make any more noise at all, any more shouting or crying, any more yowling, we're going to have to leave you behind. Do you want that?

Mouse's face was frozen. She stared at Alex.

Well do you? he said again. Do you want to be left alone here on this road in the dark?

Mouse whimpered but her body was completely still.

Without anyone to look after you? said Alex.

Very slowly and with one tiny little sob, Mouse shook her head.

Good, he said.

He stood up. Mouse kept her eyes on him. Her head was still but her eyes followed him. Everyone was silent. Maybe everyone was a bit shocked at what he'd just said to Mouse. He didn't seem to care.

Let's get going, he said.

Diana was staring at him and biting her lip.

That was just so mean, she said. She said it half angrily and half with admiration in her voice. Alex said nothing. He pressed his lips together as if he was thinking.

I stared at them both. It was the first time I'd seen Alex be really tough with someone and I didn't know what I felt about it. Maybe it was that right from the start I'd had this idea of him as this nice soft gentle person. I couldn't have imagined him saying what he'd just said to Mouse. I wondered if he meant it about leaving her behind. Could he really have done that? Thinking about it gave me a strange feeling in my stomach. I didn't know how tough I really wanted to think he was.

OK, Alex said, I think we have to get off this road now.

I noticed that this time Sam didn't even try and disagree.

As he spoke we all looked to our left and saw there was a little wooden stile leading into a field. It seemed to have appeared from nowhere. We all stared at it.

There you go, said Sam with only a small bit of disappointment in his voice.

Great, said Alex.

Sam just shrugged in a defeated way.

So one by one we all climbed over. Mouse had to be lifted. She stayed very quiet even when her dress caught on the fence. Alex said the stile meant there might be a footpath but there didn't seem to be one.

Instead we found ourselves in a field of corn or something that had been harvested and all over it were these great big bales standing up like big pale giants in the moonlight. They looked amazing. They towered over us. The ground was cut down to stubble and prickled my feet even in their trainers. I wondered how Alex was going to walk on it in his bare feet. Mouse too.

Wowee! shouted Mouse and straightaway she let go of Alex's hand and ran right out into the middle of the field as fast as she could. I couldn't believe it. After all we'd been saying, after Alex's terrible threats. This was really, really naughty.

Mouse, Alex hissed in a voice that was half loud and half quiet. You come back here right now!

But Mouse didn't hear him. Either that or she chose not to. She'd forgotten all about men and owls and being left in the dark in the middle of nowhere and she was running and running like she couldn't stop. She really was being very bad but maybe she really couldn't stop. It was a bit like the moonlight and the open field and sight of those huge bales had made her drunk. And she had her small arms held out and the stick in one of them and she looked really funny, this little crazy person zigzagging across the field from one bale to another.

Sam looked at Alex.

It's OK, he said. I'll get her.

I stared at my brother because why would he volunteer? Was he afraid of what Alex might do to her if she wasn't stopped? But then since when did he care about someone else being punished?

He ran quickly but he didn't need to. You could see Mouse was ready to be caught. She didn't even wait for him to catch her up. She just smiled and ran towards him and went diving diving into his open arms.

I looked at Alex and my heart went tight.

Don't leave her, I told him. You're not really going to do it, are you?

I saw Diana looking at him to see what he'd say. He turned his face to me but I couldn't read it at all. He didn't seem to be thinking about what I'd said, or about Mouse, or about anything. His face was all distant and far away.

Sam brought Mouse back on his shoulders. Like a prize, a special bad lively thing he'd captured. She kept her own hand over her own mouth but her face was cheeky and smiling. She really was the naughtiest person.

She's promised to be good, Sam said, if we give her another chance.

OK, said Alex, but his face was closed.

Sam lifted Mouse down and as I watched how carefully

he let her feet slip to the ground I thought how different he looked – almost like a nice person and not like my brother at all.

That was the effect Mouse had. In the same way that Alex seemed to be able to make people listen, so Mouse seemed to make people go all patient and kind.

The countryside had felt very flat and all the same up till now, but as we reached the end of the cornfield you could feel it starting to slope quite steeply down towards something dark and deep and cluttered.

It's a wood, said Sam.

Good, said Alex. We'll go down there.

I saw that he kept on looking at Diana. She walked like someone in a daze, like someone whose body was trying to wake up and do as it was told while the rest of her stayed asleep.

Sorry, by the way, he said to her.

She hardly looked at him. She just blew out some air.

I didn't mean to be harsh, he said.

Still she said nothing, she just coughed. She had the asleep baby in the crook of her arm but she'd taken off her shirt and half tied it around one of her shoulders so there was a kind of cradle to take the weight of him. It was interesting that even though Diana had only been a mother for about two days, it was like she already knew the stuff that mothers know, like how to do practical things and take care of the people who come out of you.

I mean it, said Alex. I'm sorry.

But still Diana didn't say anything back to him so he put his hand out and touched her arm and I don't know why but it gave me a turning-over feeling in my stomach.

He took his hand away and looked at her then and she

looked back at him and just nodded. And there was so much going on in that nod. And even though they were completely separate it was like these two things touching each other, reaching out and touching.

And a part of me wished I had a friend like that. Wouldn't all the difficult and lonely things in life be so much easier if you had someone who could say things to you in total silence?

I saw Sam was watching them too and I wondered if he was thinking the same thing or if he was just thinking that Diana was hot.

Mouse was holding onto Sam's hand now and he seemed to be letting her and Alex seemed quite happy not to have to think about her for a bit. We all walked on in a strange kind of silence.

But something else, not just the thing of Diana and Alex, was making me feel funny. I looked around me and tried to work out what it was and then I realised.

Once we'd left the road and the field behind, that was it, there was nothing, just the five of us – well six counting the baby – in the middle of the darkness under the stars and nothing else. No other human signs – no houses anywhere, not a single one, not even in the distance. Not a chimney, not a swirl of smoke, not a light, nothing to show that anyone but us was still alive in the world. Just the rolling darkness and the hillside and the depths of the woods dipping down in front of us. It reminded me of that feeling when you're the last to be collected from school and slowly the playground empties till it's eerie and quiet and it's just you left standing there.

Something's weird, I said to Sam.

What do you mean? What's weird?

I don't know. It just feels funny. It's like – well where is everything?

Where's what? Alex said. What everything?

I mean – I struggled to think what I meant – there's nothing. Where are all the electricity pylons for instance?

Sam laughed to himself.

She's missing the pylons. Great.

I ignored him.

I mean there's no light anywhere, I said. You can usually see lights somewhere, can't you? Far off in the distance or wherever. But look around you. Look over there. There's nothing.

Alex was silent a moment.

It's pretty dark, he agreed.

It feels like we are the only humans, I said. Even as I said it, just that word 'human' seemed to empty itself till it sounded echoey and strange.

Have you any idea where we are? Sam asked Alex. I mean are we near a village or what?

Alex kept his head still for a moment as if he was listening for a clue.

We could be anywhere, he said slowly.

Or nowhere, I said.

Don't say that, Diana said suddenly.

Yeah, whispered Mouse. Don't say it, OK?

But it felt like Alex knew what I meant. It felt like we'd somehow walked into a place that contained no one and nothing but ourselves. I wondered if there were still places on this earth or even just in England where human beings had never gone, lost places that maybe didn't even exist in a solid way in the day and that you could only find if you walked at dead of night for miles and miles in the right conditions and then –

I shivered.

Maybe it's just that no one lives around here, Sam said.

It was typical of him to think it could be that simple.

I don't like it, Mouse said again. I keep getting a bad feeling –

Shhh, said Alex. It's OK.

No, said Mouse. Shut up! It's not OK. I have a feeling!

Don't tell me to shut up, Alex said fiercely. Remember what we talked about.

Mouse gave a little moan.

What d'you mean, feeling? Diana asked her a bit scornfully. What kind of feeling?

You got the sense that she was a bit sick and tired of Mouse's feelings.

Mouse did one of her little sobs. Then a hiccup.

A feeling like, like, like – like I just really really want to be picked up.

Mouse, said Alex, we can't pick you up. You're just a bit tired that's all. But we can't carry you right now.

We're all tired, said Diana and her voice was heavy.

I'm not tired, Mouse said, but so sleepily that no one bothered to listen.

I could really do with a cigarette, said Sam at last.

Have one then, I said.

I can't. I've only got one left. My last one. I need to save it. Oh God I can't tell you how much I want one.

Stop going on about it then, I said, because I was sick of him always showing off about how much he needed to smoke. I noticed that Diana said nothing but she gave him a hungry little look and I guessed it was probably because she wanted one too. I thought she ought not to have one though as you shouldn't smoke around babies and it really annoyed me that Sam had to go on about it in front of –

Suddenly before I could even carry on with this thought, Alex stopped dead exactly where he was. He stood frozen for a second in that sly, unsurprised way that wild animals freeze and then the very next second he unfroze and took one quick step backwards and crouched himself down low near Mouse and held his hands over her small face.

Mouse gasped. Between his fingers you could see the terror and the big question mark in her eyes but she didn't even struggle. She did nothing. It was like she just knew deep in her bones to give in and be still.

Diana stood rigid as a statue with her baby glued to her shoulder. Sam stared at Alex's face.

What? he mouthed but Alex just kept his eyes down and shook his head. Slowly Sam crouched down and so did I, so did Diana.

We all crouched down keeping our eyes on Alex. His face said what we didn't want to know. Because even though he was quicker than us, we'd heard it too, we could hear it now. Somewhere not very far away, just beyond the place where we were all crouching, was the definite sound of a person walking.

Snap. Snap. Crunch. Snap. Snap. Swish.

Twigs breaking. The movement of grass. You could almost hear the black air bunching up in shock.

We waited. The sound carried on.

Snap. Swish. Swish.

It was coming towards us.

My heart was beating so jaggedly it hurt in my ribs. It felt like my body was so full up with stuff going on that my lungs were going to burst right out of my chest.

The sound came closer. And closer. The snapping stopped. Then started again. I saw Diana had shut her eyes.

Nobody was breathing. No one dared look. But if you did you could just see the blackness of something moving in the trees. Another snap. The sound of a bird or something lifting upwards. Then another. Then nothing.

Still nothing.

The silence pushed at our ears.

The crouching was beginning to hurt so I sank to my knees. Very very slowly Diana moved the baby to her other shoulder. Alex's eyes looked up, then down, then up again. You could hear Mouse daring to take a single small breath.

We waited. Still nothing.

We waited, huddled together on the ground. We waited about five minutes altogether probably, even though it felt more like five years. Alex still had both his hands on Mouse's little head, which was against his chest. He was holding her face, her ears, her eyes shut as if that was the best way to protect her and keep her quiet both at the same time. I really hoped Mouse wouldn't hiccup. Alex looked at me. I looked at him. Our looks went nowhere they just bounced back at each other.

Still no sound came from between the trees. I dared to take a bit of a breath in but I didn't let it out. Sam was so close to me that I could smell his clothes and the smell was of Mum and home and the washing machine, a smell that made me want to give in and put my head down and just sleep.

We carried on waiting. There was still no sound coming and after a few more minutes of listening and hoping, I felt Sam's shoulders relax and he let out the smallest sigh.

Has he gone?

This was Diana. Because she'd dared speak, everyone waited again for a second.

Who was it? I whispered. Was it him?

Alex released Mouse slightly. Still we all listened.

I don't know, he said under his breath. It was certainly someone.

He looked at Mouse who was staring and staring at him as if she could see right through his head to the other side.

You were very brave, he said. Very brave to be so quiet. You hear me? You're a brave good girl.

But Mouse said nothing, she just kept on staring at Alex or at the place where his face was. I saw that every bit of her body was shaking, even her lips, even her face.

Hey, said Sam, and he reached out and put his big hand on her little shoulder and rubbed at it. Hey, are you OK?

Mouse said nothing. She just shook and shook.

Mouse? said Diana. Mouse! Say something!

The person had gone. The air was empty. Whoever it had been was far away and nowhere near us. Actually it felt like no one in the whole world was anywhere near us.

The baby woke up and started crying so we waited while Diana sat down and opened her shirt and fed him and Mouse sat quietly beside her and just whispered things, I don't know what. Maybe she was talking about brown owls or maybe she was just chattering on about nothing at all. It didn't matter. At least she wasn't talking out loud.

Sam looked at Alex.

You really believe that was him?

Alex glanced at Mouse to check she wasn't watching and then he nodded.

Sam looked confused.

But it could have been absolutely anyone, he said. I mean really, how can you know? There's no law saying people can't walk around at night, is there?

Instead of answering him, Alex gave him a look and then got up and walked a little way away towards the place where we'd last heard the sound. We watched him. He looked around carefully. He sniffed at the air.

What is it? I said. What are you doing? What can you smell?

He looked at me and then he looked back at Sam.

Come over here, he said, I want to show you something.

I stayed where I was because I was still a bit scared to go where the man had been, but Sam walked right over to where he was standing. Alex waited.

No, he said when Sam stayed standing about a foot away from him, a bit further. Come right over here.

Why? said Sam. But he did as Alex said and he went.

Alex seemed to be looking for a certain place in the air or something. At last, still sniffing, he found it.

OK, he said. Here.

Here what?

There's a smell. Very strong. I caught a whiff of it when he came close. It's still here in the air, just a bit fainter that's all. There – can you smell it?

He breathed in and then he looked at Sam who sniffed and gave him a funny look, then sniffed again. You could tell by the way his face changed then that whatever it was, he could definitely smell it too.

What the fuck is it? said Sam. It's really – oh it's weird. You can smell it?

Yeah, like kind of flowery only not like flowers. Bad flowers?

It's kind of musky and oily, Alex said. It's – I don't know, it reminds me of something I've smelled before, but I don't know –

Suddenly Diana looked up from feeding the baby and her face was white and empty. She looked sad and frightened and unsurprised all in one go.

Patchouli, she said. It's patchouli. It's horrible. It's what he wears.

After ten minutes or so we carried on our journey. We had to. We didn't dare stay in one place for very long.

Before, there'd been a kind of footpath through the stubble which had made it easier for the ones without shoes to walk, but now that seemed to disappear. Now the grass was long and there was more of the giant cow-parsley we'd seen around Alex's shed.

I don't like this stuff, Mouse said. It stings me and it's nasty and I don't like to walk in it.

She'd stopped trembling and got her calm back just enough to start complaining again. In a way no one minded. Things felt more normal when Mouse complained.

Shh, Sam said. You haven't got to. I'll carry you if I have to.

Mouse looked at him as if he'd just said he was going to buy the whole world and put it on a plate for her.

You'll pick me up?

Yes, but not yet, in a minute. If you promise to try walking a bit first.

We're not going much further anyway, Alex said suddenly. I think we've done enough walking for one night.

Yes, Mouse quickly agreed. Enough walking.

I noticed that Alex had bent over double and was holding his stomach.

Are you OK? I asked him. Do you have a pain?

He straightened up and I saw that there was sweat on his face.

I'm all right, he said, and he blinked. Just I think I have a stitch.

He tried to stay standing up straight but you could see that something was hurting him.

If we can just get into the wood, he said, and find a quiet safe place, we can stop and sleep.

OK, I said but I was still worried about the way he looked. He saw me watching him and he tried to smile.

I'm fine, he said, I need to sleep. We all need to sleep.

I wondered if any place could feel safe enough to go to sleep in tonight but I didn't say so. I could see that what Alex was saying was sensible and we probably just had to get on with it.

Diana must have been exhausted too because she was already starting to sit down just exactly in the place where we'd stopped, but Alex took her hand and pulled her up.

Come on. We just need to get properly into the wood. A bit further then we'll stop. Can you manage a bit further?

OK, she said, but she didn't move, she just stood there all pale and empty and see-through, like a ghost mother with her ghost baby in her arms.

Do we have to go into the wood? she said.

Yes, said Alex and he was looking better now.

Sam looked at her.

He's right, he said. The woods are dark. It's the safest place.

At the mention of dark, Mouse shivered.

Pick me up, she said.

In a minute, said Sam.

No, do it now, said Mouse, and because she was starting to fuss, he sighed and bent down and swept her up in his arms and then lifted her onto his shoulders.

Whoo! went Mouse and she waved her stick around and looked all happy at getting her own way.

No noise, said Alex quickly. I mean it. If you make a noise he'll put you down.

He seemed to have forgotten his threat about leaving her behind. Maybe the fear of the man made us all realise we had to stick together.

We moved through the grass until we got to the very edge of the wood but the trees were so thick and close together and so laced with brambles it was impossible to find a way in.

Can we go under? I asked Alex, though I was doubtful that there was room under the low branches.

We'll get scratched to pieces, said Sam. There must be an opening somewhere. Why don't you three stay here and me and Mouse will go a little way round and see if there's a way through.

It was hard to see how big or small the wood was and how long it went on for. So Sam took a few steps into the long grass with Mouse on his shoulders. But Mouse had other ideas. She grabbed his hair and shouted, No!

Her voice rang out strangely in the darkness.

Quickly Sam slipped her off his shoulders and put a hand over her mouth.

Get off me! she yelled and she tried to hit him with her stick.

Just wait, he said holding her. It's OK. We're just going to see what's there, that's all.

I know what's there, said Mouse through his fingers, and I don't like it.

No you don't, said Diana suddenly. Shut up Mouse. You're really getting on my nerves.

Mouse started to cry again. It was like every little thing seemed to set her off. So Sam left her with us and went alone round the edge of the wood. He was gone for about three minutes and when he came back he was wiping his hands on his jeans.

It's OK, he said. There's a rough sort of track. I don't know if that's a good or a bad sign − it could lead anywhere I suppose, but we may as well see.

We have no choice, said Alex.

So Sam picked Mouse up again and she didn't make any noise this time and we all followed him. The long grass was starting to be damp with dew but it quickly got shorter and flatter and the giant cow-parsley which had scared Mouse so much stopped, and then there was a rough track which led us along the edge of the wood for a bit. The moon shone brightly through the black trees. It looked like a cartoon drawing of a moonlit wood.

In a while we reached a fork in the track where you had the choice to either stay on the outside of the wood or else go right in. Alex said we should go in.

But it's dark, Mouse said, and her voice was getting all trembly and whiny again.

That's good, Alex told her. Don't you remember? Dark is safe.

I don't think so, said Mouse.

Well it is, I told her. Dark means no one can find us.

Don't want them to find us, muttered Mouse.

Exactly, I said. She really could be very boring to talk to sometimes.

Come on, said Sam. We need to sleep and then when we wake up it will be light.

It'll be the next day, yawned Mouse.

Yeah right, Sam said.

The air in the wood was black and thick and smelled of bracken and leaves. It was so dark we could only just barely see the outlines of each other, let alone anyone else.

I didn't think I'd ever in my life been in such darkness. It was like being blind. It was hard to take steps forward and you didn't dare reach out a hand in front of you in case of what might be there. I felt quite scared but I didn't say so. Someone had to set an example to Mouse. And anyway, just because you can't see what's in a place doesn't mean there are bad things there.

But maybe even the baby understood about the darkness

because almost straightaway, having been so good and quiet up till now, he started fussing and crying. Everyone stopped for a moment while Diana moved him over to the other shoulder.

Are your shoulders hurting? I asked her.

A bit, she said.

Do you want me to hold him? I offered.

No, she said.

I thought she might have said no thank you.

Do you think he's hungry? Alex asked her.

Diana shook her head.

I just fed him, didn't I?

Mouse kept getting her face scratched by the high-up branches.

Ow, ow, she said.

I'm going to have to put you down, said Sam. You'll have to walk now and hold on tight to my hand, OK?

OK, she said in a surprisingly quiet voice.

In the dark we kept on nearly losing each other so Alex said it might be best if we all stayed really close and he went first and Sam and Mouse went last and Diana and me walked in between.

Soon the baby stopped crying and started snuffling instead. He'd found this way of putting his fist in his mouth and moving his lips around on it. Babies are clever, I thought.

There were all these sounds. Branches snapping under our feet and big sighs that must have been the wind or the air or something. Sometimes it felt like things were dropping from the trees behind and in front of us and to the sides.

I kept on wanting to turn round quickly just in case. You could almost swear you could hear someone breathing in there. I was worried that someone might suddenly smell patchouli and that would be that. The hairs on my skin were all standing up and I had to concentrate really hard on not thinking about anything but where my two feet were.

I don't li–ike this, Mouse whimpered after a few more paces.

It's fine, Alex said. Come on, do you want to come in the front with me?

No, she said in a voice that sounded a bit close to tears. I want to stay holding onto Sam's hand.

I wondered if Sam was glad about that or not.

Come on, he said in a much gentler voice than I'd ever heard him use with anyone before. You need to think about something else. Have you got your stick?

Mouse said nothing, just made a funny noise.

Have you? he said.

I've got it and it's scared, she replied.

Sticks don't get scared, said Sam, as if he was the world authority on the emotions of sticks.

Mine does, Mouse said. Mine isn't like the others. That's why I had to be its mum.

We all started to laugh, even Diana.

Don't laugh at me, said Mouse.

We're only laughing in a nice way, I told her.

Because you say good things sometimes, Alex said.

I say bad things too, said Mouse.

It's true, Alex said. That's true. You certainly do.

Like, if my stick is bad, I'm gonna break it, said Mouse.

That's not very nice, Sam said.

If it's bad I tell it to shut up and shut up or I'll fucking break you right in two, snap! Mouse said.

Oh dear, I told her, and I didn't know whether to laugh or not, that's really horrible.

Yes, agreed Mouse and there was a bit of pleasure in her voice, sometimes I am a bit horrible. Just like him, she added.

Just like who?

Him. Like him.

Hey, let's talk about something good, can we? said Alex.

Like my mum? said Mouse.

No, said Alex, not your mum.

The baby had started crying again. The cries were getting louder. I wondered what we'd do if someone heard him.

Suddenly Mouse screamed.

Ouch!

What is it? Sam asked her.

Ow, ow, ow, I stepped on something!

We all stopped.

Pick me up! Fucking pick me up right now, do it! screamed Mouse like she was the queen of everything.

Alex picked her up off the ground and Sam took hold of her foot. I could just see the lightness of his hands in the darkness.

Let me feel, he said. It might just be a thorn.

A thorn! repeated Mouse. Or else – or else a thing has bit me?

Nothing bit you, said Alex. There are lots of little thorns. I swear I can feel them too. Really we need to get you some shoes. Now just calm down and let Sam give you a piggy-back.

Mouse said nothing but little sobs were leaking out of her all the time. Alex put her down and I felt Sam pick her up in the darkness behind me and lift her back onto his shoulders.

It's OK, you're OK, I heard him say. I was seriously surprised now. I'd never heard him be so nice to anyone in his whole life.

I did have shoes, sobbed Mouse. I used to. In my other life I mean.

Yeah? Sam said trying to sound interested. So what were they like, these shoes?

Um – Mouse was gulping air between the sobs – um I don't know but maybe – maybe I think red ones.

Red, said Sam. Well that's really nice. It's my favourite colour, red is.

Well it's not my favourite, Mouse said.

What's your favourite?

I don't know, she said, and the sobs turned to sniffs. Brown, she said. Brown like the owls and like my mum.

No one said anything.

I walked close behind Diana. The only good thing about Mouse screaming was it seemed to have calmed the baby right down.

Does he have a name? I asked Diana then, more to change the subject and distract Mouse from her feet than anything else.

But before she could reply, Mouse took a little breath and said, I call him Yes!

Yes? said Sam. That's a funny name.

It's short for Yesterday! Because he was born yesterday.

But he wasn't born yesterday, Alex pointed out. It was the day before yesterday.

But, said Mouse, cheering up hugely now, it was yesterday when I called him Yesterday.

Everyone thought about this for a second or two.

I'm lost, said Sam.

We all are, Alex said, and he half laughed half sighed.

Suddenly Diana spoke and it was so long since she'd said anything that it was a shock to hear her light and gentle voice in the blackness.

I'm calling him Jocy, she said.

What, you mean Joseph? said Alex.

No. Just Joey.

That's what baby kangaroos are called, I told her.

So? she said a bit sharply.

She didn't mean it like that, said Sam.

No one knew what to say for a moment.

Oh, but that's a beautiful name, I told her.

I thought that we might walk all night in that thick dark wood but in the end it wasn't Alex but the place itself that told us to stop.

It wasn't that it got any lighter. More that the darkness seemed to lose confidence in itself and just give up. You began to get a feeling of the outlines of things. It was easier to move and think. It wasn't like treading through soup any more.

I began to see things. The dark curve of the back of Alex's head, then his thin shoulders and then more or less the whole of him, right there in front of me. He wasn't as tall as Sam, but something about the size and shape of him made me feel absolutely happy.

I could see Diana's hair. I could see Mouse's stick. I could see one of Joey's crinkly feet all curled up and purplish, poking out of the blanket. Now and then I could see a leaf, a twig, a shadow. It didn't feel scary, it felt good.

No one spoke, no one said a word. It was like everyone had felt the change but was afraid to comment on it. But it suddenly seemed as if we weren't lost any more, that we knew exactly where we were going, that something good and safe and sweet was waiting for us. So we all stayed quiet, even Mouse. I felt myself relax. I felt my whole body smoothing out and letting go. I realised I'd been holding my breath for what felt like hours.

About three seconds later we came to something a bit

like a clearing. A space between the trees. The air was cooler. I could smell water. Or was it fruit? Something sparkly and refreshing anyway. The ground beneath our feet was soft and even and dry, so nice it made you just want to give in and sink down. Even the trees themselves looked a bit friendlier, polite and careful, lifting their branches up as if to shelter us but not get in our way.

It felt like a good place.

Diana sat down. So did Alex. Then once he had, we all did. Still no one said anything. Sam and Alex spread the three blankets on the ground.

We're here, Mouse said with a little sigh and it was funny because I was thinking the exact same thing at that same moment.

Yes, said Alex. Here we are, we're here.

I need to do a wee, she whispered.

Go on then, he said.

I heard her go over to a place not very far away and lift up her dress and squat down. She couldn't have had any knickers on because straightaway I heard it coming out, a long one that seemed to go on for ever, and then I heard her sigh again, a little sigh of satisfaction. And that was the last thing I heard before I fell asleep.

LIGHT

4

Bright hot sunshine was on my face. My cheeks and nose were burning. I didn't know where I was then suddenly I did. A shadow moved over me. Alex was standing there.

You have to come, he said. Quickly. Now. You won't believe it.

What?

I lifted my head.

Just come, his voice was quiet and steady and kind of happy. You'll see.

I sat up and rubbed at my face. My legs itched all over from the bites and I was much too hot. It was boiling. There was no shade where I'd been sleeping. I looked around me. The grass was bright green and dotted with mauve clover and little pink-and-white daisies. Above it, blue sky like in a picture. All around us in a circle, trees and trees going on for ever.

The night came back to me.

You slept for ages, Alex said. Hours and hours. We all did.

Sam, Mouse, Diana and Joey lay almost in a heap on the furthest blanket which was just about in the shade of the trees, though little bits of sun came through the branches and flickered over their faces.

It was a peaceful sight. They were all very asleep. Mouse had one arm flung up on Diana's leg and the other hand in her mouth. Dribble was coming down her cheek. Next to her Sam was absolutely still with his hair sticking up and his mouth wide open.

Only Joey was awake. It was his third day in the world and he was watching everything from the safe crook of Diana's arm. His eyes glinted at me. He looked like he was waiting to decide something very important and no one was going to rush him into it.

I blinked in the light. It was so bright it hurt my eyes. Alex squatted down next to me. The tops of his feet were literally black with dirt. You would have had to scrub them hard with a brush to get them clean. Or maybe soak them for days. I thought how Mum would've had a fit if she'd seen them.

Listen, he said, and his eyes slipped over in the direction of the wood and then back to me again.

What?

Just listen.

I can't hear anything.

Shut your eyes.

I did. I heard a rushing sound. I opened my eyes. I couldn't hear it. I shut my eyes and it was there again. Alex was smiling.

Is it water? I said.

Alex looked happier than I'd almost ever seen him.

Come on, I'll show you, he said.

★　　★　　★

121

Where we were sleeping it had seemed to us in the darkness that the trees formed a circle all around us that went on thickly for miles and miles, but it turned out that was all wrong, they didn't. You can't tell anything about a place if you arrive there in the middle of the night. In the morning the texture of everything, including what's possible and impossible, changes completely.

Alex had discovered that if you pushed your way through a gap in the undergrowth and then went on a few feet further and followed the rushing noise, you dipped under an even darker canopy of low trees with twigs that crunched underfoot and then you were suddenly in the light again and in a quite quite different place.

I gasped. I couldn't help it. My hand went right up to my mouth in sheer unbelievable astonished amazement. I'd never seen anything so madly beautiful in my whole life. Not in my real life anyway, maybe just in my craziest most fantastical dreams.

We were standing in front of a deep glittery pool. Into it, a waterfall poured – long white ropes of sparkling water coming down, down, down. You couldn't see where it was coming from, it was so high up, way above our heads. And down below, where the water fell, it went all foamy and bouncy but further on it calmed down and became deep and silky and greeny blue and made you want to forget everything and just jump right in.

But maybe most amazing of all was the roaring sight of the water as it came down. If you watched it hard enough it felt like you couldn't breathe. I tried to stare at the sparks of glitter that went flying into the air and I blinked and blinked, I couldn't help it. The water was so blindingly loud and so crashingly bright you couldn't tell if you were hearing it or seeing it.

But that wasn't all.

And look, said Alex, pointing across the water to the other side of the pool.

Over there, on the side furthest away from us was a house, a crazy little – or maybe not that little but actually quite big – house that might or might not have been lived in. I didn't know why I hadn't seen it when I first looked, but I hadn't and now suddenly there it was.

It was perfect. Long and low and pale buttery yellow like the kind of house you get in a fairy tale, with a grey tiled roof and lots of higgledy-piggledy windows and about three or four chimneys that looked like they were about to fall over. A bright-blue front door stood a little bit open in a welcoming way and a cosy little path went winding all the way up to it.

But the longer you looked the more you could see that the house wasn't all that well cared for. One of the chimneys had actually crumbled and slid right off and lay in a sad heap on the ground. The roof was missing quite a lot of its tiles in places, with the wooden rafters showing through.

It's unloved, I breathed to Alex, but he didn't seem to hear me and I couldn't be sure if I'd said it aloud or just thought it.

There was a white rose climbing right up the side of the house but you could tell whoever lived there wasn't much of a gardener as the rose hadn't stopped but had just kept on going until it scrambled across the roof and down the other side as if it had plenty of energy but not a clue what to do next.

At the front of the house, two brown chickens scratched about in the dirt and weeds.

It's perfect, I said, because I had never seen such an adorable house except in my dreams. I liked it so much I almost wanted to cry.

Alex grinned. He just kept on looking at me as if he could only properly believe in the place himself if he knew I'd seen it too.

I had to show it to someone, he told me. I just couldn't wait. I knew you'd like it. It's just − I mean − isn't it just incredible?

Incredible, I said, and I went red with pleasure and surprise at the idea that of all those possible people, the one he'd chosen to show was me.

Did you really?

Did I really what?

Think I'd like it? I said, and I kept my face pointing straight ahead so he wouldn't see that my stupid cheeks were so pink.

Yes, he said and I didn't know why I felt so explodingly happy. Yes I did.

I looked at the house again. But who did the chickens belong to? Who had left the door open?

But − can anyone be living there? I asked him.

I felt suddenly anxious. What if there was a bad person in the house? What if Diana's brother with the axe was in there waiting for us?

Alex shook his head.

I've no idea. What do you think? It looks pretty run-down and deserted to me.

Except for the chickens.

Well yeah.

Should we go and knock? I said, surprising myself with the words.

He looked at me with his chin up in the thinking position.

I don't know, he said with a little bubble of excitement in his voice. Do you want to?

I don't know.

I bit my finger and we gazed at the house for another minute and then I felt suddenly overcome with bravery. Or maybe it wasn't that. Maybe it was just that I was here with Alex and I liked him so completely that in a way anything seemed possible.

Let's, I said.

What?

Let's go.

Over there? You mean now?

Yes now.

What, without waking the others?

I nodded and kept my eyes on his. You could see him thinking.

Well, I suppose it is kind of easier without Mouse, he agreed.

So we walked right around the side of the pool, not the waterfall side but the other side, which was edged with tall orange flowers and strange grass things that looked like they were made of plastic but I thought might be bulrushes. The air felt cooler near the water but the sound of it was so loud you would have had to have shouted, so we didn't talk.

Just above our heads a tiny dark little bird swooped up and down in the strangest sort of flight, climbing and dropping, climbing and dropping. It felt meaningful, like it was a message. I wondered if Alex thought so too.

I used to know what they were called, those birds, he said, and he frowned and looked upset for a moment.

Sometimes he acted as if great big chunks of him had been left behind somewhere, I didn't know where.

As we reached the door of the house, the hens ran away, squawking loudly. If someone was in there, then they were surely going to hear that noise. I felt a bit scared now though I didn't say so to Alex. I just bit the skin around my thumbnail and kept my eyes open, trying to take in the smallest details as a way of calming myself down.

I saw for instance that there were two giant hollyhocks by the door, one pink, one yellow. Or at least I thought they were hollyhocks, though I wasn't an expert on flowers. They were really big, like flowers in a nursery rhyme, with the kind of heads that remind you of people in olden-days' bonnets. They would have been much higher than Sam's head.

And the blue door was a bit faded with the paint peeling off and it had a letterbox but it was hanging right off as if someone had bashed it hard. Whoever lived here didn't bother with much in the way of letters, that was pretty clear.

Alex touched my arm.

If there's someone in, he said quietly, we'll just ask if they can spare some bread or milk or something. Then we'll leave fairly quickly, OK?

OK, I said, and took my finger out of my mouth. It wasn't until Alex said the words bread and milk that I realised how starving I was. My stomach felt hard and tight like it had curled in on itself. I hadn't eaten anything since an apple and a bit of bread yesterday morning and that seemed a million years ago.

Alex rapped quite loudly on the door.

Hello? he called. Anyone there?

His voice sounded very daring in the silence. It reminded me of the moment a million years ago or was it yesterday when me and Sam had done the exact same thing to him, knocked on his shed. Except that was in the dark not the light. So why did this feel scarier?

Hey there! he rapped again.

Nothing. Just the sound of the waterfall crashing behind us.

We looked at each other. Slowly he pushed at the half-open door. Its hinges made a long eerie squeak. I thought of Hansel and Gretel and then I tried not to because don't they get eaten? It was a stupid babyish story anyway.

Hello? Alex said again in a slightly louder voice.

Then we both froze. Because there was a noise coming from inside the room. It was the sound of someone crying quietly. Or whimpering or whining. It started and then it stopped again.

We looked at each other with question marks in our eyes. The door stood open but neither of us dared look inside the room. Instead we stayed there on the doorstep for I don't know how long until the noise came again. Very quiet at first, then louder. A sad beseeching sound, almost a whistle.

Alex's face relaxed.

It's just a dog, he said, and he stepped inside the house with me close behind him.

Not just a dog though. An old man or maybe it was a woman was sitting in a chair with their back to us. You couldn't tell which it was because all you could see was the hair, a stiff fluff of white sticking up over the back of the chair which was old and brown and made of leather and had half the stuffing coming out of it.

At the person's feet lay a large brown dog with its chin on its paws. It stared at us in a very troubled and upset way but did not move at all when we came in the room, not even slightly, not even to lift its chin off its paws. Keeping its head absolutely still and its eyes on us, it just whimpered softly again. Its forehead was all creased up like a piece of brown velvet that someone had folded over and over lots of times.

Alex looked at me. We looked at each other. It was hard to know what to do next. Because the person stayed completely frozen like a stone statue in the chair and showed no sign at all of turning round. Suddenly it felt creepy and I didn't like it, not at all. Plus the room had a smell of old things and old people, a bit like Granny Jane's flat only worse, there was another smell on top of that. Flesh or skin or going-off meat or something. It made me want to cough high up in my throat. I thought I might be sick.

Excuse me? Alex said, and he went a few steps closer.

The dog was quiet. Only his eyes moved ever so slightly as he watched us come near.

OK, boy, it's OK, Alex said to the dog as he reached the chair and went round the other side. I held my breath. I would never have dared go first but I was right behind him as he reached out to touch the man – for now you could see from the stubbly skin it was a man – gently on the shoulder.

Nothing moved. Except –

An awful shocked sound came out of Alex's throat then and I saw why. The man's eyes were wide open and staring but there was nothing in them. They'd gone all thick like a cup of hot milk goes when it cools down and gets a skin on it.

The dog did a long heavy sigh then, as if he'd been trying to warn us and we hadn't listened. And as Alex's fingers came away from the man's shoulder, something dark and wet slid out of his nose.

We ran back. We ran so fast that I forgot even to notice if the chickens were still there or if the dog was following us or if we'd shut the door behind us or anything. Even the sound of the waterfall seemed to have dissolved to nothing in my head and all I could feel was my blood going round and round, bumping through my body in a hot scared way.

The others were awake now. They were sitting around in the clearing on the blankets which they'd pulled further back into the shade. Diana had her shirt undone and was trying to put her nipple in Joey's mouth and he was fighting her, crying and twisting his head from side to side the way babies do when they're hungry and cross both at the same time. Sam was looking the other way and smoking what I guessed was his famous last cigarette.

Mouse was sitting on the grass all alone with her feet out in front of her and rubbing her fists in her eyes and crying loudly like a baby. I noticed that Sam wasn't bothering to comfort her.

As we came closer Mouse struggled to her feet and wiped her face on her dress.

Where were you? You're bad! You shouldn't just go off like that! she shouted in a furious upset voice.

We didn't go off, I told her even though I was right out of breath and still panting. But she didn't listen to me, she just kept on looking at Alex.

I'm hungry, she sobbed, I'm so sta-arving and I thought – I thought you'd gone away and left me behind.

Alex flopped down on the blanket. I could see his face was covered in sweat. He looked at Mouse.

Don't be stupid, he told her between breaths. You know we wouldn't leave you behind.

She stopped crying and sat down again and took a surprised breath.

You would! she said. That's a lie! If I was naughty and loud you said you would.

Alex was getting his breath back. He looked at her in an exhausted way.

That was before, he said, still gulping air. To make you behave.

But I am behaving, Mouse said.

OK, said Alex. Shut up then.

Mouse stared at him. I think she was wondering why he didn't come over and pick her up. There was a line of snot hanging out of her nose from crying so much and the front of her dress was dirty and wet.

Diana was looking at me and looking at Alex. Her gaze flicked backwards and forwards between us as if she didn't know which to look at.

Where were you? she said in a voice that was a little bit annoyed.

Yeah, said Sam, what's going on? Where the fuck've you been? Hey, what's the matter — you look weird.

He held the cigarette out to Diana but she shook her head and kept her eyes on Alex. Baby Joey was sucking happily now. His eyes were closed.

Alex looked at me.

We just went to see something, that's all.

See what? said Mouse, a bit angrily.

Alex looked at Sam and then back at me again.

See WHAT? Mouse demanded again, even louder. She really could be very rude sometimes.

Just something, Alex said. You'll see. It's pretty good actually.

And pretty bad too, I added.

We told them everything. We had to. Even about the man. Especially about the man. Everyone was shocked, even Diana.

Oh my God, she said, forgetting for a moment to be cool. Oh my God but that's really, really awful.

It was the first time I'd seen her look really worked up about something. She twisted a long strand of hair around her hand and stuck it in her mouth and sucked on it then let it go again.

I'd been thinking that ever since she'd woken up she'd looked a bit miserable. She'd taken off her glasses and she kept on rubbing her eyes which had these great dark shadows under them and she was doing one big yawn after another. It was like none of the yawns satisfied her.

Joey had fed and gone sleepy again and she held him against her while she tried to pull her shirt closed with the other hand. She kept on licking her lips and yawning.

Are you OK? I whispered. I had this feeling of wanting to help her but somehow I guessed that if she was going to accept help from anyone, it wasn't going to be me.

I was right. She turned and looked at me politely as if it was the first time she'd ever set eyes on me. Then she seemed to shake herself awake and remember who I was.

Really thirsty, she whispered. Feeding him – I don't know – it makes me die of thirst.

I thought of how Mum used to insist on having a glass of water right next to her whenever she fed Anna and I was suddenly worried. None of us had drunk anything for hours now, but Diana was feeding Joey. She had to make enough drink for two.

We need to get her some water, I told the boys.

I couldn't help thinking of the cool green stillness of the pool and how badly it made you want to jump into it. I wasn't sure, if I saw it again, that I'd be able to resist just throwing myself in, splash!

Diana needs water, I said again.

Me too, said Mouse. Or Fanta.

But the boys weren't listening, they were still on the subject of the man. They were still trying to work out how he'd died.

A heart attack probably, Sam was saying as if he really could know. He probably didn't even know it was happening – old people can drop dead just like that, can't they?

Mouse was listening with her mouth open.

He'd stubbed his cigarette out halfway through so he could finish it later. He was holding it between his finger and thumb like it was the most precious and valuable thing and Mouse was staring up at it as if it was too. Sam had a very annoying way of smoking as if he was the first person in the whole world ever to do it, and Mouse was the perfect audience for him.

Well he did seem fine, Alex said. He was just sitting there in the chair very peacefully.

Peaceful and dead, I pointed out.

Mouse laughed loudly. It wasn't the moment to laugh but she was only six so what could you expect?

He definitely died of old age, I heard myself say, though something about the easy definite way I said it made me feel I must be making it up. I didn't want to talk like Sam. How did I know what he died of? I tried not to think about the bad smell in the room and what had come out of the man's nose.

We need to get Diana some water, I said again.

Now Mouse was doing a funny thing. She was walking up and down very slowly with big exaggerated steps, lifting each foot quite high off the ground, and her finger was on her cheek as if she was deep in thought. Or as if she wanted us to think she was.

But if someone killed him, she said slowly and in a big grown-up voice, then what I'm wondering is, how come they didn't do the dog as well?

I realised what she was being. She was being a detective.

We didn't say he was killed, Alex said, but Mouse wasn't listening. She had gone leaping from that thought onto an even more exciting one.

Hey, can we keep him? she said, and her voice was suddenly normal again. Can he be my very own pet dog? Please can he? My mum said in the letter that it was really OK for me to have a dog of my own.

No one said anything. Everyone knew she was lying about the last bit.

We'll see, Alex said, only half listening. He picked a piece of clover out of the grass and sucked on it.

What kind of dog is he? Mouse went on, as if she couldn't let go of the subject now. Is he a great big one? Can I touch him or will he bite me?

But Alex wasn't listening.

We should really tell the police or a doctor or someone about this, he said to Sam and me.

I don't mind if he bites me just a little bit, Mouse whispered even though no one was listening to her.

There was a bit of silence as we all thought about what Alex had just said. We were wondering who you were supposed to go and tell when someone quite old who was a stranger just died in their chair like this. But our faces looked like we were all thinking something else as well, the exact same thing in fact. Even Diana bit her lip and looked at Alex.

Fuck that, Sam said. We need somewhere to sleep, don't we?

Mouse sucked in her breath and sat down next to him so she was leaning against his leg.

You're always saying that word, she told him.

So are you, Sam replied.

Yeah, she said with a little sigh. Yeah, I am.

She put her thumb in her mouth and sucked for a second and then she took it out again.

I'm gonna sleep with the dog, she said.

In all the worrying about the poor dead person and what to do about him, it wasn't surprising that the amazingness of the pool and the waterfall had been completely forgotten. Alex and I had told them all about that too but it was the kind of thing you couldn't really believe in properly till you saw it for yourself.

Now we were right there standing in front of it.

Fucking hell, said Sam as we all watched the water come rushing and crashing down.

Diana took a step back and shielded her eyes as if she'd never seen such brightness. Mouse just jumped up and down on the spot in total silence. As if all the words were knocked out of her for once.

Pretty crazy, isn't it? Alex said.

It's fucking wild, said Sam.

It's wild, it's wild, it's wild! It's fucking fucking wild! said Mouse, and everyone laughed at her.

I bit my fingers. I was glad it was still there. Part of me had secretly worried that it might not be. The whole shape of the morning so far, ever since Alex had woken me, had been hazy and unlikely and strange.

I could see the two brown chickens still scratching away. And the door was still ajar. I wondered if the dog was still lying in his same sad place exactly where we left him.

I just − I do wish there wasn't a dead person in there, I said to Alex.

In some ways I'm glad there is, said Sam. At least we know who the place belongs to.

I thought how easy it was for him to say that when he hadn't even seen the poor old man, or had to touch him, or seen what happened when Alex did.

Can you still be trespassing if a person is dead? I asked Alex. On their property I mean?

He looked at me thoughtfully.

Depends if he owned it or not I suppose, he said.

But if he did?

I don't know.

Does it matter? Sam asked me. We're not going to do anything we shouldn't do, after all.

Except maybe stay here, I reminded him.

Can we stay here? Mouse asked quickly.

I don't know, Alex said again.

We all stood there for another moment. No one said anything. It was very hot, unbelievably hot, so hot that sweat burst out on your face even if you did nothing at all. Just standing there breathing and thinking felt like an effort.

My T-shirt felt sticky on me and my stomach hurt. I was still so hungry. I'd been hungry for so long that it was like the hunger had started to move onto the outside of me instead of the inside.

Suddenly without saying anything, Diana passed Joey to me and then she threw herself down at the edge of the pool and cupped her hands and scooped the water into her mouth. Scoop, scoop, scoop. She drank and drank like an animal who was falling over with thirst. We all watched her and I used the opportunity to put my mouth on Joey's hair. It smelled of hotness and sunshine.

Can I do it? Mouse asked going over to her. Can I get a drink?

Diana turned around and cupped her hands and let Mouse

drink. Mouse wanted to do it herself but Diana wouldn't let her.

You might fall in, she said.

I won't, said Mouse.

But you might, Diana said.

So Mouse put her little hands around Diana's bigger ones and lapped at the water. When she'd finished she made Diana get some more but I don't think it was because she was thirsty, I think it was more that she liked drinking out of Diana's hands.

There were these orange lily-type flowers around the edge of the pool. A bit like the bulrushes they were so perfect they almost looked like they were bought ones not real. They had tall sharpish leaves and they seemed to be growing right out of the water. Suddenly Mouse stopped drinking and looked up.

Look! she shouted, pointing to a bright-blue blur that was jerking about in the air above the flowers.

A dragonfly, Alex said.

Hey, said Diana and she held out her bare arm. Just like this one, look.

Yeah, cried Mouse. Like your butterfly!

No, said Diana, dragonfly.

So that's what it is! I said, looking at her tattoo.

Yes, she said glancing at it fondly. It's a little dragonfly.

It's lovely, I said. But I've never seen a real one before.

A real tattoo?

No, a real dragonfly.

I didn't want Diana to think I'd never seen a real tattoo. Though I wasn't sure I had.

Neither have I, she said as we watched it dart around.

Why'd you have it done then? I asked her. I mean if you'd never seen one?

She shrugged.

I don't know, she said, I just felt like it.

Did it hurt?

She looked at me for a second and I couldn't see what the look meant.

Not much.

I stared at her a moment and thought how mysterious she somehow always managed to be. Mysterious and beautiful and somehow – just in control. No wonder Alex liked her. The one thing I knew I could never be was mysterious. All the stuff that was going on inside me always showed. I couldn't stop it, couldn't help it. It just came flooding out of me all the time, spilling over the edges, however much I tried to stop it happening. It was stupid really.

The real dragonfly was huge, not really like an insect at all but almost the size of a tiny bird. The wings were going so fast they looked all fizzy. Except for the fact that it was blue, it wasn't actually that much like Diana's tattoo. I thought that when I was older I might get a tattoo.

Catch it catch it! Mouse shouted, trying to cup her two hands as it darted through the air.

No leave it, Diana said. Hey, Mouse, don't go too near the water.

Why? Why can't I?

Because we don't know how deep it is, Sam said.

And you can't swim, added Alex.

Yes I can, said Mouse, but her voice trailed off as if she wasn't very sure.

No you can't, Diana said. Don't tell lies, Mouse. You know you can't.

Mouse came back and sat at our feet while we all stood and gazed at the water.

This place, said Alex after a moment. Why does it give me such a weird feeling?

How do you mean? asked Diana.

Alex glanced at her, then at the ground.

I don't know, he said, and he rubbed his face in a baffled way. I don't really know what I mean.

It wasn't a very nice thing to feel, but I was quite glad Diana didn't know what he meant. Because I did. I knew. I knew exactly what he meant. I'd been thinking the same thing ever since we got here, ever since he woke me up this morning with the light dazzling me, so bright in my face. I just wished I could find the words to explain it back to him.

There's something – a bit wrong with it, I said, trying.

Yes, Alex glanced at me. Yes, there is. But what?

Well I just think it's fucking incredible, Sam said.

Yes exactly. It's too incredible, I heard myself say. It's almost a bit too – beautiful.

Diana stared at me as if she hadn't a clue what I was talking about, as if I was off another planet or something.

How can something be too beautiful? she said.

I know what she means, said Alex.

It's too perfect, I said slowly, trying to explain. It's like – it's like it all just came out of our own heads, like we imagined it. Or we are imagining it right now.

I keep thinking I'm dreaming, Alex said almost to himself.

I saw Diana look at him.

Me too, I said. Ever since we woke up this morning. All this. It's like a part of me can't quite believe in it.

I wanna see the do-og, Mouse moaned. Everyone ignored her.

What crap, said Sam. What utter crap. You've just never seen a waterfall before, that's all.

Diana laughed but you could tell it was a slightly put-on laugh.

It's not a dream, she pointed out, because we can all see it. All of us. We're all here, aren't we?

Unless we're all dreaming the same dream, Alex said, and Diana rolled her eyes and looked at Sam.

Me too! said Mouse not wanting to be left out. I'm dreaming it too!

Diana started to laugh again.

Maybe it's her dream, she said. Maybe we're all just people in Mouse's dream.

Mouse looked confused. Sam shook his head.

Don't listen to them, Mouse. Flynn just gets these ideas that's all. She makes things up as she goes along.

But that's exactly what I mean, I said. It almost feels like that – as if we're making it up.

Sam laughed and so did Diana but I could feel Alex looking at me carefully.

I carried on looking at the house across the pool. It was still bothering me. We'd never seen it before and it didn't belong to us, so why did it already feel like ours? And why was that such a worrying idea?

But if it's real then I wonder where we are, I said. This place, I mean. Where is it exactly?

No one had an answer to that, not even Sam.

Can we go and paddle? Mouse asked after a few minutes. I mean right now, can we?

She looked at Alex to tell her yes or no. She always looked at Alex. Alex said nothing.

Well? said Mouse.

I'm thinking, Alex said.

Can you swim? I asked Mouse then because no one seemed to have answered the question before. I mean have you ever?

She seemed to think about it.

You mean in the sea? she asked me carefully.

No, I said, not necessarily the sea. I mean anywhere. In a swimming pool for instance.

I don't know, she said.

Well, I told her, even though I felt a bit mean saying it, I think what that means is you can't.

But – I don't know where the swimming pool is, she said as if that mattered. And then she asked me, can *you* swim?

I laughed and that made me feel even meaner.

Of course I can.

When did you learn? Mouse asked.

I don't know. I don't really remember. When I was little, about your age – five or six I guess.

I'm six.

Yeah. Yeah I know.

And who teached you?

I hesitated. I saw my dad's hands reaching out to me from the pool as I dripped and shivered on the side.

No one, I told her. I just learned.

We're all going to swim, Alex said. But not yet. We need to decide what to do about everything first.

About what? said Mouse.

Just everything. Sam and I need to go in the house.

Me too! Mouse shouted, scrambling to her feet. I'm going to see the dog!

No, Alex said, I think you should stay here with Flynn and Diana. Just for a few minutes.

Stay here with us, Mousie, Diana said and she yawned and before I could even think what was happening, she passed the asleep Joey to me and stretched herself out in the sun.

Mouse and I watched the boys walk round the edge of the pool towards the house. Mouse made a little impatient noise.

They're not going fast, she said. Why don't they go faster?

They're just walking at a normal pace, I told her.

No, said Mouse. They're not, they're all slowed down.

I smiled.

That's just because they're far away.

Mouse shook her head.

No it's not, she said.

Well how fast do you want them to go? I asked her.

She said nothing.

Tell me what you mean, I said. How fast do you think they should go?

She took a little breath.

I don't know, she said, and she put her thumb in her mouth then took it out again. She looked at me.

Don't be silly, she said.

I laughed and kissed Joey's head.

I'm not the one being silly, I told her.

She was silent for a moment, then.

What are they saying? she asked me.

What, Alex and Sam? How do I know?

I could see that the boys were talking. Or at least Sam was mostly talking and Alex turned his head once or twice to listen.

Joey woke for a second then settled against me with a little sigh. I felt his wet mouth nuzzle my shoulder. I put my face against his soft head.

Do you think Alex is saying I can have the dog? asked Mouse.

No, I said, I don't think that.

Diana was still lying down. The sun was high in the sky. None of us had any way of telling the time, but it must have been around midday. I sat with Mouse at the edge of the pool and we let our feet dangle in the cool water.

Why oh why are they taking so long? grumbled Mouse even though the boys had only been in the house maybe five or ten minutes. Fifteen at the most.

They've hardly been any time at all, I told her. Just be patient, OK?

But I'm hungry.

I know you are. We all are.

Except for baby Joey, said Mouse looking at him rather crossly.

Yeah, I said, patting him. Except for him.

Mouse turned and looked down at Diana. Her eyes were shut. There were freckles starting on her nose. Somehow they weren't like my freckles. They were sexy woman freckles not stupid babyish ones.

Could I drink your milk? she asked her.

Diana kept her eyes shut but she laughed. When she laughed you saw her teeth which were very straight and white except for one little pointy fang on each side. She had a little gap between the two front ones. She didn't laugh all that often, but when she did you saw that her face was a funny mixture of very grown-up and very young.

No, she said, shading her eyes to look at Mouse. You can't.

Why not?

Because it's not for you, is it?

Isn't it? How do you know it's not?

I just know, OK?

OK.

Mouse sighed deeply and looked so gloomy I suddenly felt quite sorry for her. I patted her dirty little leg and for once she let me.

We'll get you something to eat, I told her. There might even be something in the house.

I tried to remember what I'd seen in the morning. Was there even a kitchen? If so, then the man must have some food. It had been hard at the time to take everything in. I only remembered a dark and gloomy room with a chair, a fireplace, a dog, a man. My thumping heart.

I hope it's cheese and biscuits, Mouse said, and she crossed her legs and lifted up her stained and dirty dress then pulled it down tight over her knees.

Haven't you got any pants on? I asked her as I caught a glimpse under her dress.

No, she said, and lifted it to show me.

But Mouse, Diana said in a sleepy voice, where are they?

I don't know. I just never had them.

That's not true.

I must've just forgot to put them on.

What happened to your purple leggings? I asked her.

I don't know.

She sighed again.

Cheese and biscuits or else maybe a tin of Hoops, she said to herself and then she made a greedy face and licked her lips.

Just don't keep thinking about what it might be, I told her.

Why not?

Because that will just make you hungrier.

OK, she said, and she opened her mouth wide and stuffed her knuckles in and squeezed her eyes tight shut as if that might help.

Then it was later. We were in the house, in the room where the man was. The room was grander and prettier than it had looked when Alex and me first walked into it in the morning. The lampshades all had flowers on and the wallpaper was a leaf pattern. The sofa was big and saggy and velvety with pink–and–purple striped cushions.

We weren't thinking about the furniture, though. We were talking, trying to figure out a plan. Sam and Alex were trying to convince us that the best plan would be to just dig a grave and bury the old man.

Just? I said, because part of me couldn't quite believe what they were saying.

It's either that or tell the police, said Sam. And if we do that then it's all over. We might as well just give ourselves up right now.

I looked at Alex to see what he thought of this, but his face was all tight and he wouldn't look at me.

Well? Sam said. It's true, isn't it?

We all tried to think about this. I wondered how Sam could be so practical and calm, like he was suddenly this person in an adventure story or something. Alex seemed to be agreeing with him but he still kept his eyes on the ground.

But where would we do it? I said. And wouldn't it be hard, I mean to dig the hole and all that?

I wondered how deep the hole would have to be. I'd buried pets before. I'd buried a goldfish and a hamster. Actually the biggest thing I'd ever buried was the hamster and even then I couldn't get it deep enough and in the end a fox dug it up.

Alex took a breath. He didn't seem as keen on the idea as Sam. Or maybe he was keen but he was also feeling a bit sad about the old man. This was real live death we were talking about after all.

I don't know, he said. I mean it would obviously have to be here on his land. We'd have to find a discreet place. And we'd have to try and do it, I don't know, with respect.

And if someone finds out we did it? I asked him.

Yeah, Diana lifted her head and looked straight at Alex. She's right. What then?

Sam flicked at a hole in his jeans.

Then we tell them the truth, he said as if it was all so simple. That we found the man dead and we thought we were doing the right thing and so on.

And you think they'd believe that? I said.

Sam looked at me and you could see from his face that it all seemed so simple to him. Maybe he just wanted the house. Maybe to him it was just another way of taking something that wasn't his.

Why shouldn't they? he said.

Part of me felt mean for thinking what I'd just thought because he was only being practical and anyway wasn't it true that I wanted to stay in the house too? We all wanted to.

The thing is, Alex said, I don't see that we really have any other options.

We all thought about this and realised it was true. No one was going to come up with a better plan.

I'll tell you one thing, Sam said. He's beginning to stink.

We all looked at the old man. The boys had put an old bedspread thing over him so you couldn't see his face but it didn't help much. You still knew he was there. The smell was terrible but it was funny how after a short time you almost got used to it.

I don't like him, said Mouse, eyeing the bedspread from across the room. I'm worried he's going to get up and chase me and play monsters and do bad things to me.

Well stop thinking that because he can't, I told her a bit crossly. He's not a monster. This isn't one of your stories, it's

real. He's just a real live poor old man who died. He's dead,
OK?

Mouse looked upset.

I know what dead means, she said in a small voice. And
then I felt bad because I'd forgotten for a second that she
didn't really have a mum or a dad and although they maybe
weren't dead, still what was the point of parents you could
never touch or see? A picture of my own mum – crying,
shouting, worrying – flashed through my head and I pushed
it to the very back of my mind.

Shall we go and look for the dog? I said, trying to be nice.
Straightaway Mouse brightened up.

Ever since Alex and Sam had come back in the house, the
dog hadn't been around. He'd vanished and there was no
sign of him.

Maybe he's hiding, Mouse said. Maybe he's scared that
we're gonna hurt him or eat him or something?

Why on earth would we eat him? Alex said.

Well, Mouse scratched at her arms, we are very very very
VERY hungry.

That reminded me that I was hungry too. I took her hand.

Come on, I said. Let's explore. Let's look for the dog and
for some food as well.

And whichever you find first, you eat, Sam said. Only
joking, he added. But Mouse just glared at him.

Even though it was a mess and even really quite dirty in
places, the house was every bit as adorable on the inside as
it had looked on the outside when Alex and me first set eyes
on it.

It really was like an enchanted house, a house in a fairy
tale. Not that everything in it was exactly perfect or shiny
or new or anything – quite the opposite really. It was better

than that. In some ways it was a bit like Granny Jane's house, only more interesting. A house full of worn-out, old-fashioned things that had been used an awful lot a long time ago then put away in cupboards.

Everything in there made you wonder, everything made you want to touch it. I couldn't work out why every object, every curtain and carpet and corner felt so strange and so normal at the same time. Everything felt ready for something. Everything felt like it was waiting. It almost felt like the house had been in the middle of telling some amazing story which had got interrupted and it was now just up to us to get on and finish it.

Just as I'd hoped, the room next to the one that contained the old man was a kitchen. I held Mouse's hand and pulled her in after me. We stared around us. It was nothing like our kitchen at home. Everything seemed to be made of wood and there were no shiny things anywhere.

The door wasn't a real door but a strange swishy curtain of red, blue and yellow plastic ribbons. You got a smell of teatime when you pushed your face against them. Mouse shrieked and ran in and out of them, letting them flap around her. The windows had blue and yellow squares of glass in them and the curtains that hung there were made of crinkly material and had pictures of pots and pans all over them.

This is a funny, funny room, said Mouse.

I know, I said. The funniest.

Funniest of them all, Mouse said, stretching her arms in the air and wiggling her hands with a kind of excitement and delight.

No one seemed to live here except spiders. Beautiful complicated webs were stretched in all the corners of the room and a fly was buzzing angrily on the windowsill just ready to be caught. I flung the window wide open and he lifted off into the bright air. Straightaway the room got lighter and you could hear the rushing of the water outside.

There was a big old wooden table and on it a loaf of bread half cut into with the knife still sitting by it. As soon as she spotted it, Mouse raced straight over and began tearing big pieces off and cramming them in her mouth.

I was about to tell her to slow down because I thought maybe I should check it wasn't mouldy or anything. But then I realised that she was probably so starving that she'd have eaten it even if it was.

I felt my stomach twist and water came into my mouth.

Give me some, I told her, and I took a big bite. It was soft and delicious, it melted on my tongue – it tasted as if it had just come out of the oven that very second.

I didn't stop to wonder how that was possible.

Do you want me to see if there's some butter? I asked her, but she didn't even answer, she was too busy stuffing in the bread. I looked around me.

There didn't seem to be a fridge or anything but a little door to a tiny room was standing wide open and in it there were cool narrow shelves with more food on them. There was a lump of yellow cheese on a dish and some brown stuff in a pot with the spoon sticking out that smelled half of jam and half of onions.

There was an enamel dish with some grey jelly and bones in it that smelled much nicer than it looked – cold roast something, chicken probably. There were some big and small onions and a pile of ripe red tomatoes. There were lots of tins too. They looked very old and some of them were rusty but it didn't matter. I knew that tins could last for ever, through wars and things.

I thought I shouldn't give Mouse the chicken jelly in case it was bad and made her sick, but I rubbed a tomato on my

T-shirt and handed it to her. She bit straight into it so the juice ran down her chin. She grinned. She didn't care. She just stuffed the rest of it in.

Then I sliced some cheese off and put some of the onion stuff on it for her. She reached up to grab it and she ate it keeping her eyes on me all the time in case I came up with something else. I laughed. Her eyes were huge. It was fun feeding her.

You're like an animal in the zoo, I told her as I threw her another piece of cheese and ate one myself.

Let's play that you're the keeper, she said, still gazing at me seriously. And I'm your pet.

You're not my pet, I told her. You're a little wild animal. You're a tiger.

She liked that.

Grrr, she went, grr, grr.

She made claws with her hands.

Aren't you full up yet? I asked her. But she just shook her head and sat there on the floor still reaching up for food with her pretend claws and eating and eating in perfect happy silence.

Do you like beetroot? I asked her.

Yeah! she growled. There didn't seem to be a single food she didn't like. So she wouldn't get beetroot all over her dress, I sliced it and fed it to her one bit at a time on the end of the fork, but in the end she got impatient and grabbed it from me with her fingers.

After a while she forgot to be a tiger. Bits of juice and food crumbs fell into her skirt and she just lifted it up to her face and licked them off. Her fingers and her face were stained pink. I hoped she wouldn't get a stomachache from eating too fast.

Go and see what else there is, she said, so I did.

Every single shelf of the little room seemed to be laden with some kind of food. There was a jar with 'greengage jam' written on it in curly writing and next to it, on a higher shelf, there was a big tin, black with reddish roses all over it. I could only just reach it and I had to get on tiptoe to pull it down.

Is there ice cream? shouted Mouse.

No, I said. But I've found something else.

What?

Something heavy slid around inside the tin. I got the lid off and there was a big sultana-type cake with only one slice gone. Home-made it looked like. The top was golden and smelled of syrup.

Cake, I said. I think it's cake.

Is it a birthday cake? shouted Mouse.

No, I said as I came back into the room. It's just a normal cake but it smells good. Look.

I took the bread knife and cut a piece. Mouse said nothing, just reached out again with her small dirty hands.

On another shelf there was a big brown jug. I brought that in and sure enough in it was milk. Cold fresh white milk. I held it up to my face and breathed in the cold creamy cow smell and wondered why I'd never understood the pure white glory of ordinary milk before.

Here, I said, and I poured some into a cup for Mouse and she glugged it straight down. I had some too. It went well with the cake. Of all the things I'd tasted so far it was the best – milk and cake, crumb and cream.

Mmmm, said Mouse. Nice.

I thought about calling the others but felt suddenly sleepy like my legs had gone weak. I sat down on the floor next to Mouse. It was a cool brown tiled floor and there were crumbs everywhere but they weren't ours. Or maybe some of them were ours but who was going to tell us off now?

All around us were the black and brown legs of different bits of furniture – table, chairs, a dresser thing – twisty and wooden and spindly, a whole forest of legs. And right across on the other side of the room, between two of these legs, a pair of eyes was watching us with an expression of such concentration and sadness. Very quietly and slowly I pointed them out to Mouse.

Dog! she shouted and crumbs from her mouth sprayed out everywhere.

Does stuff come out of you when you're dead? I mean out of your mouth and nose and everything?

I was asking the question to everyone so I was rather surprised that it was Diana who spoke.

Mmm, she said quietly. Yes it does.

Why? Mouse asked straightaway. What comes out? Why does it?

She had her hand on Dog's smooth brown head. He was sitting next to her – well half sitting, half lying. The look on his face said he was feeling kind of relaxed but not quite sure whether to trust the feeling or not. He looked like he might jump up at any minute. Not so much that he wanted to, just that he might. Because of this, Mouse kept on patting and patting him as if just by not stopping doing it for one single second she might persuade him to stay.

She looked around at everyone.

What stuff? she said again.

Mouse, said Alex, and he reached out a hand and stroked Dog's silky nose, shut up, OK? It doesn't matter. Flynn didn't mean to say it. Just don't think about it, all right?

Mouse reached out and rather rudely lifted Alex's hand off Dog's nose. She'd already decided that Dog belonged to her.

Nothing's gonna come out of me, she said crossly. 'Cos I'm not at all leaky.

Diana giggled and so did I.

It was almost night, our first night in the house. Outside the darkness was getting thicker by the second. You could still hear the waterfall but there was no moon and hardly any stars and it felt like someone had thrown a velvet sheet over us. It was hotter and stickier than any night so far.

We were sitting all together in the room with the man, but only because it was the coolest place to be. It was dark and hushed in here with the leafy wallpaper. There were two big armchairs with ears as well as the brownish velvety sofa which we now saw was coming apart in places. On the floor was an old Indian-looking rug. As well as the stripy cushions there were lots of squashy ones all sprinkled with little flowers – mauve and pink and orange, not really what you would have expected a man living all on his own to choose.

Speaking of the man, it was odd but even though we could still see the shape of him there under the bedspread, the bad smell of him had completely disappeared and now all you breathed in was old leather and dust and the hot night air coming in from outside.

We'd had a feast in the kitchen. Everyone had eaten as much as they wanted and then Sam had found a bottle of something that tasted a bit like wine only browner and sweeter and we were sitting all together on the floor now and passing it round, everyone having some apart from Mouse who wasn't allowed.

You wouldn't like it, Alex said.

I would, she said. Why wouldn't I?

Because it tastes sour.

Mouse made a face and tried to lie.

But I like sour.

152

No, you don't, you like sugary stuff.

No I don't.

Yes you do.

Every time the bottle went past her she tried to reach up and take it but we wouldn't let her however much she fussed. I thought it was just as well because it was magical stuff. Just one sip made the air go wavy and you felt as if the bones might burst out of your body because they'd gone all sparkly. It made me feel chattier, it made me want to ask everyone all these questions. It made me a bit like Mouse in fact, only a more grown-up version or I hoped so anyway.

When my nan died, Diana said, and I noticed the wine stuff was making her talk more too, they had to stuff her with cotton wool. Her nose and mouth and – you know . . .

What? I said.

Well, you know – other places.

She laughed again even though if you looked at her face, it was quite sad. Her mouth wobbled. I sat up and tried to focus on her but she kept going far away.

Your nan? I didn't know you had a nan, I said. I mean was she your real nan?

Diana looked like she was holding her breath and I thought for a minute that she was going to cry but actually it was a sneeze. She sneezed and then because she didn't have a hanky or a tissue she wiped her nose on her sleeve.

She had me till I was seven, she said. She was great. She never shouted or lost it or anything. She was just great. She lived in a caravan, you know the type that stays still and is in a park? Yeah, she was my real nan.

This was a lot of information to get out of Diana in one go.

Did she write you letters? asked Mouse. Diana gave her a look.

She didn't need to, silly. I was with her.

Yeah, said Mouse, but afterwards when you weren't with her, did she?

She couldn't write then, because she was dead.

Mouse laughed.

What did she die of? asked Sam.

No idea. Can't remember, said Diana, and she yawned a big yawn to stop herself looking upset. I think she had a stroke or something.

Mouse sat up in amazement.

Someone stroked her?

Now we all laughed. Mouse was so stupid sometimes.

A stroke is an illness, Alex explained. Something you die of like a heart attack.

Or smoking, said Mouse, looking at Sam.

Yes, said Alex, or smoking.

Or a fire, said Mouse.

Yes or a fire, said Alex. That's why you don't play with matches.

And why did they stuff her? Mouse asked steadily.

I rolled my eyes.

Because of what we were just talking about, I told her. Don't you ever listen? Because stuff comes out.

I knowed that, said Mouse even though she didn't.

Dog was trying to get up. Very patiently, because Mouse was holding onto his ear. Sometimes having anything at all to do with Mouse was a struggle that could drive anyone mad, animals or humans.

But what stuff? she said as she pretended she wasn't holding too tightly onto Dog.

Just stuff, I told her.

You don't need to worry about it, Alex said.

Sam had gone out of the room and now he came back.

Hey, look what I found, he said — and he tossed a squished-up pack of cigarettes to Diana.

Cool, she said, and she pulled one out.

I looked at Sam. He looked so pleased with himself, so clever to have gone and magicked some cigarettes out of nowhere, but I wasn't that surprised. I was already beginning to realise that this house seemed to contain everything we could possibly need. Or, in the case of the wine, stuff we didn't even know we needed.

I thought of Mouse on the floor growling and being a tiger and taking beetroot and cake and I smiled.

What's funny? said Alex, who was on the rug next to me.

He said it quietly in my ear so no one else could hear. Something about his face and his voice so close to my ear made me feel strange and all the words were knocked out of me and I couldn't think what to say.

I felt myself begin to blush.

What? he said again in a low voice. Flynn? Tell me —

I shook my head and looked at Mouse, Dog, the room — anyone but him.

Sam bent and struck a match to light a cigarette for Diana. She shut her eyes as she sucked in the smoke. She had her glasses off and I noticed how mauve her eyelids were.

Do you want me to hold Joey? I said, and she shook her head.

I thought that I would never smoke if I had a baby. It wasn't something you could say to Diana of course, but I really thought it.

Hey, keep those matches away from Mouse, Alex said, but he needn't have worried because Mouse was still frowning and thinking about what might come out of dead bodies.

Is it like what Baby Joey did in the bath? she said as Dog at last lost patience and started growling at her.

No that's different, Diana said.

Hey, Mouse, Alex said, let go of the poor dog. If he wants to go, he wants to go.

Joey just pooed in the bath, I told Mouse. All babies do that.

Earlier we'd gone upstairs and found a strange wonky bathroom with tiles all covered in little flowers. In there was a big old basin with enormous jutting-out taps, perfect to wash Joey in. Mouse had watched while Diana let me hold him carefully in the water, which he seemed to like. His small bendy arms went out and his hands hit the water like it was a toy. Then we found a clean pink towel to dry him. The towel had roses all around the edges and he looked like a little angel when we wrapped him up in it.

How do you know? Mouse asked me as Dog finally managed to shake himself free and hurried across the floor to sit by Sam's stretched-out legs. How do you know they do it?

Because my baby sister used to do it, I told her. In fact she still does.

And I shut my eyes for a second and prayed that Anna would forgive me for letting everyone know that.

Not one bit of me was touching Alex, but it was like something had happened to the air between us. I could feel it pressing against me as if it wasn't just ordinary air any more but something solider and warmer and more real.

We were leaning back against the big brown sofa, across from where the others were – Dog and Sam, Diana, Mouse, the baby – and his long legs were next to my skinny dirty ones and his bare feet were bang next to mine as if they were getting to know each other. And his head and shoulders were close to where I was, the space where mine were.

And even though we weren't touching, my skin kept going fizzy just with the idea of him.

Part of me liked feeling this and another part wished I didn't because for some stupid reason it seemed to stop me thinking properly about anything else in the room. It was like I couldn't get a single normal thought into my head when Alex was around. I couldn't even listen to the others properly when he was this close to me. I realised this and as I realised it and it landed in the centre of my mind like a big new idea, I found myself thinking, was it really possible that I'd never ever realised it before?

And then I felt confused.

I heard Sam laugh loudly in his show-off Sam way at something Diana was saying, but even if I tried to listen I couldn't quite pick up what the thing was. Alex was just too close – so close he made all the rest go unclear.

I heard Mouse say something to Dog and then I heard Sam say something to her. I looked at Dog and he slid in and out of focus. I blinked and he was back and I looked again and Mouse had her arms around his neck. Next time I looked, Mouse was asleep with her curly head in Sam's lap.

The baby started crying and then the baby stopped. Someone else said something. The baby hiccupped. Or maybe it was Mouse.

I felt Alex take a swig from the bottle and then he passed it to me. Even though his hand didn't touch mine, there was this feeling I got whenever any part of him came near. Even the bottle looked different and more special suddenly because he'd been touching it. I sipped a small sip of the wine stuff and waited for the burning-rocking feeling it gave me.

You're always doing that, Alex said from a long way away even though I knew he was still close.

Doing what?

Thinking secret things – things you won't tell anyone about.

That's not true, I said.

Yes it is.

No it isn't, I said rather stupidly. No I'm not.

Yes you are. Like when you smiled just then. I really wanted to know what was funny.

Yeah?

Yes and you wouldn't tell me.

Well, I said, struggling to think of an answer that might satisfy him, maybe it was just – that for a minute I felt a bit good.

Good?

I mean happy.

Hmm, Alex said as if he didn't believe it and I held my breath as his leg touched mine for a second. I pulled mine away, not because I didn't like the feeling but because I did.

That makes it sound like you don't feel happy very often, Alex pointed out.

I thought about this. I had slid down so my head was nearer the ground and now Alex moved himself down on the rug so he was down there level with me.

You don't have to pretend to be interested in what I think, I told him then, mainly because it was so nice that he was.

What a stupid thing to say, I thought. Maybe he thought so too because he looked at me as if I was a bit mad.

What makes you think I'm pretending? he said.

I shrugged. I tried to do the kind of careless shrug that Diana would have done but it didn't quite come out that way. It felt too lumpy and on purpose and anyway it was kind of hard to shrug while lying down.

Oh well. I waited. I was liking talking to him so much

that I wanted to be ready for when he stopped. So I wasn't too disappointed.

But Alex was looking at me.

It's like you're always having all these mysterious thoughts, he said. And no one is ever allowed to get anywhere near them.

No one, he said again. He said it as if it was partly a bad thing, but his voice was still gentle and interested.

I was lost. I didn't know what to say back. I'd never thought of myself as mysterious before. That was surely the last thing I was. Was this how it felt to be Diana? I knew that Sam would have laughed loudly at the idea of anyone finding me mysterious.

But doesn't everyone think things? I said slowly. I mean the kind of things they can't really say out loud?

Alex seemed to think about this for a minute. There was something lovely and sort of wobbly and unfixed about him when he was thinking.

No, he said after a moment. No I don't think they do.

I said nothing. I wanted the talking to go on but I just really didn't know what else to say. It was all so strange and vague. I didn't even know what we were talking about, not really.

Flynn? he said then in a voice so low it was nearly a whisper.

Yes? I said.

I'm really glad you came. With us I mean.

Straightaway I went all hot with pleasure.

Really?

When Sam didn't want you to, well I just didn't know what to say, you know?

Oh, I said.

I mean, Alex went on, you have a proper home and every-thing.

Suddenly I thought of that day on the lawn when Alex had picked Anna up and handed her back to me. Then I'd given him food from our fridge.

Yes, I said, I do.

But I really wanted you here, said Alex.

Did you?

Yes.

Why? I said.

I don't know. I can't explain it. Because you're fun, I suppose. You're really nice to have around. You're easy to talk to as well.

So are you.

No, it's you. I think it's you, Flynn. You're so open and quick and — well, you're not always making judgements like some people.

I smiled. I thought how Alex was determined to only see the good side of me.

Thanks, I said.

You don't need to thank me. I wouldn't say it if it wasn't true.

I thought about this. It was true that Alex didn't say things he didn't mean. It was almost impossible to believe I'd only met him a couple of days ago. It seemed years and years, a century at least. I was a different person then. Suddenly I knew I'd never be that person again. Tears came into my eyes.

Alex looked at me.

What is it? he said.

I don't know, I said.

We were silent for a moment then. Just listening to the others talking and laughing. Well, just Sam and Diana actually. Smoking and talking and laughing. Even though they were near, they sounded very far away. Mouse and Joey and Dog were all asleep. I wondered if Sam liked Diana. I thought that I would definitely like her if I were a boy. How could you not like someone with long blonde hair and mauve eyelids who had slid a whole baby out of her just like that?

Don't drink any more of that, Flynn, I heard Sam say, trying to boss me. I ignored him but Alex took the bottle from me anyway.

Can I ask you something? he said then.

Yes, I said.

I lay back and I waited. I shut my eyes and my body tilted so I opened them again. I knew in that moment that he could ask me anything he wanted.

Yesterday when you and Sam were having that argument, remember?

Yes, I said gloomily, wishing he could have asked me something better. I remember.

Well why was he so desperate for you to go home?

I don't know, I said as all the magic of talking to Alex seemed to slip away. I just think he didn't want our mum to be worried that's all.

No, Alex said. When he said about you doing it before – what did he mean?

Nothing, I said. He meant nothing. It's not interesting.

It is to me, Alex said.

I tried to think. I felt Alex waiting. Suddenly he seemed like the one person in the world I couldn't tell and also the one person I couldn't lie to. I gulped.

Do I have to say it?

Yes, he said, you do. I'm your friend, he added.

Are you?

Of course I am. You know I am. I like you a lot.

Well if I tell you, you won't like me any more, I told him.

He laughed.

Oh really, he said. And how do you know that?

I just do, I told him. I just know.

Suddenly I hated myself. I hated the droopiness in my voice and the way I couldn't be normal when he was near me. His whole self was unbearably close to mine as well as unbearably far away. I was feeling miserable because I did not know how to cope when he was next to me, but at the same time I didn't think I could possibly survive the moment when the evening was over and he got up off the rug and moved away. Had any one person ever had so many confusing thoughts in one night?

I put my hand on my stomach. I tried to breathe.

There was this time, back in the winter, last winter, when I ran away. From home, I mean.

He stared at me.

That's all, I said.

You ran away? Really?

I just disappeared, I said. For about four days.

He said nothing. I couldn't tell if he was very shocked or not at all shocked.

But – why?

I don't know. I just did. I was sad. I just found myself doing it.

What were you sad about?

I don't know. Stuff.

Where did you go?

Go?

When you ran away. Where did you sleep?

I don't know, I told him. All over. Not very far. I don't remember.

A lot of dark places flicked through my head.

You must remember.

No, I said, I really don't. I can't think about it very much or I feel —

Feel what?

I tried to think.

Like — the same feelings. I get the same feelings all over again.

Of wanting to run away?

Kind of. Yes.

Alex was silent.

What are you thinking? I asked him because I decided that even if it was something bad, I would rather know than not know.

I don't know, he said. I don't know. I'm not thinking anything. I'm just trying to take it in, that's all.

I took a breath. I felt some tears coming on my cheeks and I wiped them away quickly before he could see. I didn't know why telling him was making me want to cry but it was.

I'm just a bit surprised, he said then.

What, because I don't seem like the kind of person who'd run away?

Maybe, he said, I don't know. I don't know you that well. And I'm not sure there is a type of person. There are just situations, aren't there?

I thought about this.

I was in a situation of confusion, I said.

Confusion about what?

I tried to think. I thought of the out-of-breath feeling. I saw Sam's bedroom light on in the middle of the night. I saw my mum putting the phone down and just crying and crying. I saw my dad sitting on the edge of the bed, all emptied out like there was nothing left inside him.

I don't really know, I said. If you know what the confusion's about then you're not really confused are you?

Alex smiled.

But – weren't you scared?

No, I said. I mean yes. I was a bit. I don't know. I don't remember what I felt. I don't remember a lot about it actually.

This was a lie. Alex looked at me.

Did they find you?

No, I came back. In the end. I had to. My mum went crazy.

We were silent for a minute. The others were all far away and blurry. It felt like there was no one else in the room.

Why did you do it? Alex said at last.

I don't know, I whispered.

Yes you do. Alex was whispering as well now.

I dared myself to look at him.

I told you. Because I was sad. Because I'd been having so many bad thoughts, I said.

What sort of bad thoughts?

All sorts of thoughts.

So – instead of thinking, you just ran away?

Not exactly, I said, because it sounded stupid when he put it like that.

Then what?

Alex waited. I felt like I was this tight hard shell that had been prised open. I'd never talked to anyone about this, ever. He didn't realise. I literally didn't know if I would be able to bear it afterwards, that I'd told him this.

It was more like disappearing, I told him. I wanted to see if I could. And I found that I could.

Did it make the thoughts better?

Not really. But it made me better.

I understand that, said Alex, and I felt him move a little closer.

Would you ever do it again? he asked me. I was worrying he'd ask me this.

I don't know, I told him. I hope not.

Why? What would make the difference?

I don't know. I've never told anyone any of this before, I added after a little pause.

I know, he said.

More tears started coming then. I pushed them away. I hoped Sam and Diana couldn't see. I felt Alex's leg up against mine.

It's like disappearing makes me feel, I don't know – the more I can disappear, the more it makes me –

I stopped and looked around for the word. Lots of other pictures came rushing at me then. My dad's hands, the dark hole at the bottom of the garden where the foxes went, Alex's feet scrambling up the wall, the smell of my mum's clean clothes, Anna's sticky morning face, Dog's careful brown ears.

Safe? Alex said.

The world went around once and everything slipped and I shut my eyes. I felt a bit sick, then I didn't.

Yes, I said, wondering how he could possibly know. Yes. Is that bad?

No, Alex said. No stupid, of course not, it's good.

And suddenly out of nowhere his hand came into mine. One minute it wasn't there and the next it just was.

I stared at it a moment because I didn't know how it had got there. Then I understood. He had put it there himself.

Night closed in deeper and the house settled around us, drew us in. Its pulse was slow and steady, calm and slow. I didn't know a house could have a heart but this one did.

We all slept. Even Joey. No noise seemed to come out of him all night. None of us moved an inch from where we were. Certainly no one wanted to go up the creaky old stairs and look for beds or blankets, even though we knew they must be up there somewhere.

You could have said it was strange that we all preferred to sleep on the floor of a room that contained a dead man, but now that we were here in the house it was like the normal rules of life were turned upside down. We should have been afraid but we weren't. None of us were. Again and again we should have been afraid and we just weren't.

My sleep was strong and startling and sweet, it took me down to a good place I hadn't dared go before. I was down at the bottom of the pool, so deep down that the waterfall sounded like it was pounding on my head but it was all right. I was safe. Alex was there.

Everyone's waiting for you, he said, and I lifted my head and sure enough, golden light was pouring down from above, a light so bright and strong that it meant the sun was shining loudly up there through the water and somewhere the people were waiting. My mum, my dad, Anna, the foxes, Sam, my dad, my mum, everyone. Yes even my dad.

I could hear the waterfall pouring, pouring.

Any minute now, I thought, he'll come.

Any – minute – now.

In the night I woke once, surfaced, and Alex's hand was still in mine or mine was in Alex's I don't know which. Then I woke again and it wasn't but his whole self was wrapped around me instead. I lay still and tried not to breathe, just examining the feeling of his heart shivering against mine, quick but steady. I knew it was a dream but I didn't want the dream to end, I wasn't going to let it. I knew I would do anything to stay in this lovely feeling. I would be as careful as I had to be, to stay in the dream.

I felt the big heart of the house gently beating. Water rushed through the pipes, a door banged softly, the chimneys remembered how it felt to have smoke in them, sending great soft puffs up into the sharp night air. And maybe outside the

166

dragonfly had found somewhere safe to go to sleep, wings balanced shut, head laid down on a pale flower petal. I hoped so. Somewhere down in the softest part of my own sleep, I smiled.

But next time I woke, Alex had rolled away from me and the windows had gone pale and cold and you could begin to make out the tangled shapes in the room. All of us all over the floor, legs and arms, cushions and rugs, the sound of so many breaths coming and going. Mouse with her thumb in her mouth, the sad stiff outline of the man still sitting dead in his chair.

We'll bury him tomorrow, Sam had said.

Dog was on the sofa curled up very tight, his chin on his tail, and one of his eyes was open, looking at me.

It was later, much later, it was day – an achingly bright blue day. We'd all slept late. The sun was high up in the sky and Mouse's legs were flying through the air. Every time you looked at the window you saw her two bare feet come up and then go down again. Out of her mouth came a mad cry of happiness so loud it scraped against your brain.

There's even a swing! she'd shouted, shoving her head round the door as she burst back in from exploring the garden at the back of the house. D'you hear that? A swing just the very right size for me!

A Mouse-sized swing, well fuck me, groaned Sam.

The house had everything. It was like we only had to think of something and the house provided it.

Come and watch me go on it! Her voice came bellowing in the open window even though we were all still half asleep. Now! Can one of you come out right now, I don't mind who – just come now!

Mouse was the only one of us who felt OK. All the rest

of us, our heads hurt, our bodies hurt. Just the idea of going on a swing made me feel sick. It hurt even to look at Mouse hurtling through the air. Mouse was the worst person to be with when you felt like this.

C'mon, she shouted, racing and tilting around the room, tripping over cushions and knocking into all the furniture. Get up, get up all you fucking lazy people, I want to go and swing!

Go and swing then, muttered Diana. She sat up. Her face was completely white.

Can you hold him a minute? she said to me and she passed me Joey.

I need to breathe, she said. She stood up and walked around which was a mistake because Mouse grabbed her hand.

Not swing on my own. With you watching!

When Mouse was being demanding she talked like a baby.

Shush, Sam said, and he pulled a cushion over his head. Mouse, I mean it, we really can't do this. Just be quiet, OK?

Joey started to cry. Diana took him back from me and started to undo her shirt.

I'm not gonna be quiet! Mouse was yelling in Sam's ear now, until you help me find Dog.

She did one more quick circle round the room but then she seemed to forget about Dog because she ran straight back out to the swing and soon there were her two feet again, flying up and down, up and down.

Are you watching? she shouted as the swing flew past.

Yeah, Sam grunted.

No I mean ALL of you! Are you all watching?

I sat up. It felt like my head sat up slower than the rest of me.

We are, I yelled. We're all watching you do your stupid swinging, OK?

Wheee! went Mouse.

I threw myself back down on the sofa and my jagged head followed me. Then I realised what was wrong with the room: Alex wasn't in it.

I think I might throw up, Diana said, and she put Joey back into my arms and ran outside.

Minutes went by and she didn't come back. Sam was probably asleep again. His eyes were still closed and his arm was over his face. His feet were on the sofa and his body was on the floor and his mouth was wide open and I saw that he needed to shave but only in one or two places, the rest was smooth.

Mouse's feet were coming and going backwards and forwards through the air. There was no sign of Dog anywhere.

The empty bottle of wine stuff was on the floor next to a flowery china plate which Sam and Diana had taken from the kitchen to use as an ashtray. There were too many stubs in it to count. That's how much they'd smoked and that was why the room felt like all the air had been sucked out of it. That was why I could taste cigarettes in my mouth and in my hair and on the edges of my eyes.

I hoped they'd managed to smoke up all the cigarettes in one go and that the house wouldn't give them any more.

Diana still didn't come back so Joey and me walked out into the garden. Not the part at the back where Mouse was madly shouting and swinging, but the front bit where the path and the chickens were.

And I stood for a moment by the blue front door with the letterbox falling off and the yellow hollyhock and the pink one and I realised something. The door was a little way open. The chickens were scratching. The sun was shining in a blue sky. This was exactly the picture that Alex and me had seen yesterday morning from the other side of the pool except that now one detail was different. Now Joey and me were in the picture too.

I wondered how it would look to someone standing on the other side right now. I was too young to be the mother of the baby, but would they think the house was mine or that I belonged to the house?

For some reason this idea – maybe the idea that I might belong to the house, or maybe just the idea that there could be someone on the other side looking – made me shiver.

A big long shiver went down my back. Joey felt it too.

We won't go round the back, I whispered into his squished-up ear, because I think Mouse is there. And she's just too annoying, isn't she?

Because he couldn't reply, I did it for him.

But it's only because she's little, he said kindly.

And she doesn't have a mum, I reminded him.

Not in the way that counts, he agreed.

You have a mum, I told him.

Yes, he said. She's beautiful and lovely and she has a tattoo.

She's cool, I agreed. But I'm not sure she likes me.

I waited for him to tell me that she did, but he didn't. He just said nothing and blew a whitish milk bubble and I felt silly for wanting to know something as stupid as what Diana thought about me.

It doesn't matter, I said.

He said nothing. The bubble just got bigger and then it burst.

Pop! I said. He was too little to laugh but if he had been bigger he definitely would have.

The conversation was going nowhere so I did some big

loud kisses on his head to make it sound as if I was eating
him up. Actually I could've eaten him up.

You're delicious, I told him. I could gobble you whole.
Put salt and pepper on you and gobble you whole.

It didn't matter that he didn't reply.

We looked around the garden together. We went slowly,
looking at everything, one thing after another. We weren't
looking for Alex particularly. We were just looking.

It was boiling hot, hotter than ever. Chunks of warm air
hit me in the face. Every time I showed Joey a new thing,
I kissed him. One thing, one kiss. For example a big bee was
crawling into a flower. We watched him squeeze his fat furry
body right into the secret centre of the purple bell, then
come out again.

If you smelled that flower and didn't know the bee had
gone in, I told Joey, you might get stung right on your nose
and you wouldn't want that, so don't do it, OK?

I kissed him for listening even though his face was pointing
slightly the wrong way. Then we looked at the pool together.
The top of it glittered and sparkled in the sunshine but you
could see deep shadows moving underneath. Two little ducks
were on it. Or more like hen things. Their beaks were red
and you could see their thin black legs moving under the
water.

I always thought it was quite brave to be a duck, paddling
your legs along and not knowing if a fish was going to come
up and take a bite out of your foot. It was one of those
thoughts that wasn't really scary in the daytime but which I
had to force myself not to think about at night.

Joey gazed at the pool as if he knew stuff I didn't.

After that we turned and watched the waterfall come
tumbling down. I'd almost stopped noticing the sound of it.

Maybe if you sleep all night with the sound in your ears,

171

I told Joey, it gets so deep inside you that you forget to hear it any more.

We looked at the chickens scratching around and jerking their heads up at me and it occurred to me that they might be expecting someone to feed them. Maybe that was what the old man did at this time of day. I didn't know what chickens ate. Grain or oats I supposed. There might be some chicken food somewhere round the back door. We decided to go and look.

Joey was still wrapped in the pink towel and he'd only made a little bit of yellow mess in it. I stopped and wiped him and folded it over so it wouldn't get on my hands and I held him tight against me and rocked him. It bothered me that he still didn't have any nappies. I wondered if there might be any in the house and as I wondered it I straightaway knew the answer.

We'll get them later, I told him. First we need to feed the chickens.

I wished my head didn't hurt so much. I would never, never drink wine stuff again as long as I lived. And I would never speak to Alex again, that was certain. I had ruined everything now. I don't know if I really believed this but it was definitely the exact thought I was having as we went round the side of the house to look for the chicken food and there he was.

Oh, I jumped.

It was like me thinking about him so hard had made him appear. I went bright red.

He had a big spade in his hands and his face was smudged with dirt. He saw me then looked away shyly then looked back again.

He wiped his face on his sleeve and then he smiled.

I saw that what he was digging was a grave.

Hey, Flynn, he said, but his voice didn't sound quite right. And then I saw why. I saw that Diana was sitting on the ground right next to him.

Burying the man took half the day. I swear I would never have thought one hole for one poor normal-sized man would take so long to dig. You see people digging graves in films or whatever and you think it must be pretty easy but it's not. Really we could have done with a digger or some kind of proper machinery to help us.

There was only one spade so Sam and Alex took turns. Sometimes I had a go but I got nowhere. You needed more strength and the earth was so dry that the spade wouldn't go in very far. As you got down deeper, it turned blacker and softer and bigger and bigger bits came away but by then they were so heavy – way too heavy for me to shovel up and throw out.

Flynn, you're wasting time we just don't have, Sam said when I insisted on trying to help.

I threw the spade down and went and sat on the edge.

You can have another go in a few minutes, said Alex, but I knew he was just being kind.

It's OK, I said, because I didn't want to be treated like a baby. I don't want to. I've actually had enough, thanks, I added because I didn't want him to think I was sulking either.

Diana didn't even try helping.

All sorts of strange things were revealed as you went down in the earth. There were big jagged stones and lumps of wood with bent and rusty nails stuck in them. There was an old padlock with the key still in it but too stiff and jammed up with old soil to turn. And a silver spoon with the letter V on it.

V for Victory, Diana said, to no one in particular. I looked at her and I looked at Alex. I didn't know what I was looking for.

There were lots of bits of china, mostly blue-and-white, from dishes that had been used over the years. And the worms – there were bigger worms than you'd ever seen in your life down there, some of them the length and fatness of small snakes. I tried not to think of them eating their way through the man once he was under the earth. I knew it had to happen but still I didn't want to have to think about it too much.

Sometimes for maybe a few minutes at a time it was possible to forget all about the man and think we were just digging this great big hole. Just for the fun of it, like you do at the seaside. Then it would come back to me in a jolt that it was an actual grave and that it was for a real dead man, the last place he would end up in at the end of his whole life.

This was his grave. It was a shaky thought. I could only let it come into my head in short little snatches.

Somehow I worried that just by wanting to be in the house, we'd killed him. I knew we hadn't, but it was hard not to think it anyway.

What if it was us who killed him? I said before I could stop myself.

Sam stopped digging and looked at me and began to laugh. But Alex didn't laugh.

What do you mean? he said.

I don't know, I said. I don't know what I mean. But he died somehow, didn't he? Something made him die on the day we came here.

Not on the actual day, Diana said. The smell, remember?

Natural causes, said Sam, and he shrugged as if he needed to convince himself. He definitely died of natural causes.

We don't know that, I pointed out.

I do, said Sam.

What? I said. Suddenly you're a doctor or something?

Sam laughed again. Considering this was the death of a real person, I didn't think he was taking it seriously enough.

Alex said nothing. He was looking at Diana who had pointed her face into the sun and shut her eyes. Her mouth was a straight line.

I think somehow we might know if we'd killed him, she said softly.

Would we? I said.

Of course we would, said Sam and he started digging again.

I tried to separate out my thoughts. I couldn't help feeling we were ignoring a whole lot of questions about the house just so that we could go on being there.

Diana opened her eyes.

He was old, she said. People die when they're old.

He died in his chair, said Sam. It's not so strange. It's a good way to go.

I glared at him.

How do you know? I said.

The thing that got me about Sam was that he made all these pronouncements about life and stuff as if he'd really been there, but he was just a teenage boy who'd never done anything really. To him the old man was just the old man and that was all. He would never bother thinking that once he must have been someone's child for instance – a baby that was once as sweet and perfect as Joey.

I wonder if he has any family, I said.

I doubt it, Sam said, but you knew it was only because he didn't want him to have any.

How do you know? I asked him.

He shrugged.

I don't know. I just don't think he did that's all.

At first I thought the hole would never be more than about a foot deep, which is how it was when I found Alex starting it. But after an hour or two, the boys were actually standing inside it and only a little while later they'd disappeared right up to their waists. That felt like progress.

But how deep does it have to be? I asked them. I mean isn't that enough?

I've seen a grave, Diana said in a dreamy voice. A real one. And it was way deeper than that. It was about the height of a man or something.

Where did you see it? I asked her, not because I didn't believe her but because some of the things she said just seemed to drift around so vaguely that you really wanted to grab them and look at them a bit harder.

Was it your nan's? I asked her.

No not my nan's. She was cremated.

Whose then?

She stared at me for a moment in that way she had as if she'd just imagined me or something. Then she yawned.

I don't know, she said, and she picked up her whole hair and twisted it round her hand and pulled it round to her other shoulder. I don't know where I saw it. Just somewhere, OK?

OK, I said, and she looked at me.

What? she said.

Nothing, I said, though what I was really thinking was that somewhere wasn't much of an answer. At the same time I was thinking how nice she looked and how it suited her with her hair on one side like that.

She had laid Joey down on the ground and he seemed

happy just lying there gazing up through the wavy light of the trees and kicking. For a minute, without him in her arms, she just looked like a normal girl with long blonde hair pushed round to the side and long brown legs and this way of saying 'somewhere' and getting away with it.

Yeah, Sam said, and his T-shirt was soaked with sweat on the back and front as well as under the arms. That sounds about right. Six feet under, that's what they say, yeah?

Yeah, Diana said, and she smiled back at Sam.

I felt annoyed. Why was she starting to agree with just about every stupid thing he said? If Sam was going to show off all the time then a part of me wished she'd at least see through it.

I sighed.

Alex stopped a moment and looked at me. He looked serious and full-up, as if he had something he might have wanted to say. I looked back at him but then I took my eyes away because I knew that if I didn't, I'd just go red and then I'd feel flustered and then I'd feel stupid.

That was another thing about Diana. She never went red. Not even when Alex was looking at her. And he looked at her a lot. I pushed the thought away quickly.

Alex stuck his spade back in the soil.

The reason it has to be deep, he said, is we just don't want him to be found, OK?

I stared at him. For a moment I couldn't remember what we were talking about. Bad thoughts were sliding in and out of my head so fast I was having trouble keeping my balance.

I suddenly had this idea that we might bury the man and then Dog would come, missing his master, and dig and dig furiously not stopping till he unearthed him like a bone. Only he wouldn't be bones – not yet. He'd just be this cold grey piece of meat with worms slipping in and out of all his holes. And he'd get up and walk back into the house to find us all lying around and eating his food and drinking his wine stuff and then –

Are you OK, Flynn? Alex said.

I feel sick, I told him.

It's called a hangover, said Sam.

Suddenly there was a long and terrible scream from inside the house.

Where's Mouse? Alex said, and faster than I'd ever seen anyone jump, he jumped up out of that grave.

After all her swinging and shouting, Mouse had at last fallen fast asleep on the old brown sofa and we'd pulled a blanket up over her and then not given her another thought.

Actually we'd completely forgotten about her. There was so little peace from Mouse most of the time that when she was suddenly quiet you didn't waste time stopping to wonder why. You just got on with what you were doing and the time flew by.

We all ran into the house, even the boys with their feet full of mud and dirt.

Mouse's screams filled the house. She was screaming and screaming. One scream followed another with hardly any gaps in between for her to take breaths. She was sitting up on the sofa with her legs drawn tight up under her and her face and her skirt all wet from crying.

Diana put her arms around Mouse. She rocked Mouse against her so her hair fell like a blanket on her but Mouse struggled and tried to push her away.

The ma-an! The ma –

Mouse could hardly get the words out. She squeezed her eyes shut and stuck her hand in her mouth as if the words she had to say were almost too bad, as if they were a taste she had to get rid of.

The man.

We all turned at the same moment and looked at him. He was still there. He was still in the chair covered in the bedspread.

What about him? Sam said.

Instead of answering, Mouse just screamed again, even louder.

Hey, hey, look, Mousie, it's OK. Alex knelt down on the floor by the sofa and put his hand on Mouse's head, We're here now. Tell us what happened, what is it, what about the man?

The man, the ma-an —

Mouse covered her face and sobbed louder. I felt really sad for her that she didn't have a mother. I thought of my mum's cool hands on my face in the middle of the night. I thought of her holding my forehead when I was sick into a bowl. Suddenly I would not have wanted to be Mouse.

The man, sobbed Mouse. He came and he — he breathed on me!

We all looked at each other.

How do you mean breathed? I asked her and straightaway her eyes went dark with anger.

Just breathed, OK, with his mouth, get it?

She opened her mouth wide and showed me all her pointy baby teeth.

No need to be rude, Alex said. Flynn was only trying to find out what happened.

Mouse gave me a quick look and screamed again. It wasn't a real scream this time, it was just naughtiness. We all stood there and waited for it to be over.

He couldn't have done that, Mouse, Sam said at last.

The man's over there, said Diana. Look.

It's OK, Alex said. You had a dream.

He breathed on me! Mouse sobbed, but she wasn't shaking so much now. I smelled his smell.

What smell? said Sam.

That smell, cried Mouse. His bad smell!

Alex looked at Diana.

The smell's gone, Diana said. He doesn't smell any more.

In your dream, Alex said. In your dream he breathed on you.

It was a nightmare, I told her in the same voice my mum would use. Nightmares are horrid. But it's over now.

Mouse glared at me. Her eyes were furious and black.

I was scared, she said in a small voice. I was scared he was going to do things.

Of course you were, Alex said.

Mouse yanked up her dress to wipe her nose and as she did it, it was completely obvious that she hadn't any pants on. Everyone pretended not to see. She stuck her thumb in her mouth and sucked hard. The sucking sound was so loud it would have been funny if it hadn't been such an upset situation.

We looked at Mouse sucking and we looked at the man. Or at least we looked at the shape in the sheet.

We're going to bury him, Alex said quietly. Then he'll be gone. He won't be here any more.

Mouse said nothing.

All right, Mouse? Alex said.

Mouse looked at his face and nodded very slowly. She took her thumb out of her mouth and a string of spit came out with it.

All right, she said, and stuck her thumb back in.

We were all quiet for a moment as we thought about this.

You could hear everyone breathing and thinking in the room. Mouse sniffed.

I don't want to watch, she said then.

You don't have to, Alex told her.

Will you do it now?

Alex nodded.

Right now this minute?

Not yet. In a minute, he said. Very soon. As soon as we've finished digging. And do you know what we're all going to do afterwards?

Mouse put her thumb back in her mouth and, keeping her eyes fixed on Alex's face, she shook her head, a very exaggerated side to side shaking.

We're going to have a swim in the pool! Alex said, and he looked at me and Diana and Sam so we would back him up.

Yay! shouted Mouse and then she wiped her fingers on her dress and sighed a big sigh.

Where's Dog? she said. My dog. Where is he?

I don't know, Sam told her. He's gone again. But we'll find him. He's probably outside.

Suddenly I had a very uncomfortable feeling like a whole part of me had gone prickly with worry. I didn't know why. Then I realised why.

The baby! I said.

Diana's hand flew up to her mouth.

We all ran outside with Mouse zigzagging along behind. It felt like we were running from one new emergency to another, like there were just too many people to look after here.

But it was OK. There was baby Joey exactly where we'd left him, kicking happily and gazing up into the big dapply tree. And lying calmly on the ground beside him, chin on paws, as if we'd somehow magicked him up just by mentioning him, was Dog.

Even though he'd seemed quite thin, still the man was heavier than anyone could have thought. Alex and Sam brought him out of the front door, one of them holding each end of him, still wrapped up tightly in the bedspread. But Sam had said he would be stiff and light by now and he was wrong, it was the opposite. He was soft and heavy.

He weighs a ton, Sam said. And boy does he stink.

Funny, said Alex. I can't smell him. I would have said the smell's completely gone.

You must be joking, Sam said.

I thought about this and realised I agreed with Alex. I hadn't noticed the man's smell in ages. I turned to Diana.

Can you smell him? I asked her. And she thought about it for a second and then she blinked at me with her pale blue eyes.

He smells foul, she said. He's rotting. You must be getting a cold or something.

Even though she'd said she wouldn't, Mouse stood with us and watched. Her hands were deep in her pinafore pockets and her face was tight with worry.

Horrible man, she whispered to Diana. He breathed on me. He's a big bad monster.

It was a dream, Diana said. You had a dream.

No, said Mouse.

Yes, said Diana.

No, said Mouse again a bit louder.

She looked at me then but I said nothing. I'd run out of things to say about her dream.

The boys were dragging the man. Sam was much stronger than Alex. Alex seemed about to cave in under the weight.

Mouse pulled at the front of her dress and put her head down and sniffed.

I smell of wee, she said.

Diana gave me a look.

That's why we're having a swim, she said. When the man is buried, then we're all going to get clean together.

Mouse looked at Diana as if she was an idiot.

But I like it, she said.

No you don't.

Mouse smiled.

Yeah I do. It smells nice and hot. The monsters don't like it so it keeps them off. I like it. I like being dirty.

I thought the idea of Mouse fighting monsters off with the smell of her wee was quite funny. But Diana didn't seem to think so. She just sighed.

OK, she said. But you want to go swimming, don't you?

Mmm, well, the thing is, said Mouse in her exaggerated slow way which meant she was trying to sound grown-up, I don't probably think I can swim.

We already know that, I told her. And it doesn't matter. We'll teach you.

Sam can teach me, she said. Or Alex.

It was Sam this, Alex that. Mouse really was obsessed with boys.

You ought to put some pants on, I told her.

She sighed.

I don't know where they are.

But you used to have some?

She nodded.

Someone took them off me, she said.

Who took them off you?

Mouse looked solemn.

I think the man did.

183

Diana was standing and sucking her hair. She took the piece out of her mouth and let it drop but it stayed stuck together.

The man couldn't have, she said. The man's dead. Don't make things up, Mouse.

Not making it up, Mouse said. I set fire to his pants. The man took away my pants so I set fire to his ones, tat for tat.

You mean tit for tat, said Diana.

No I don't, said Mouse. I don't mean tit. Tit is a stupid word.

Diana looked at me.

Pants on fire, said Mouse in a steady voice, That's what happens if you don't shut up. You get hurt, ha, ha.

You're being stupid now, Diana said to Mouse and Mouse didn't seem to disagree.

She yawned and sat down for a minute and picked at the dirt between her toes.

I'm piggling my toes, she said to Diana.

Yeah, she said, you are.

Then Mouse laughed to herself and called out to Dog who sat a little way away under the trees.

Dog! she shouted in quite a loud rude voice. Dog come!

He didn't budge.

I said come! Come HERE!

I knew she was saying it rudely on purpose as if to show she didn't care about anything. But Dog just kept his eyes on her and didn't move one muscle. But if he was trying to make a point it was wasted on Mouse. She just kept on calling to him again and again until at last he gave in and his tail slowly thumped against the ground. He stood up and stretched his whole body backwards. Then he came over to her very slowly.

Mouse smiled.

He knows the man is dead, she said. He knows and he doesn't care not one bit, in fact he's very glad.

Oh really? said Diana. And how do you know that?

He told me. He said the bad man shouldn't have breathed on me.

He talks to you then does he? I said, and part of me was so sick of Mouse I wanted to wind her up.

Mouse nodded.

Yup. And he says he wants a biscuit now so I'm gonna fetch him one.

She trotted off to the house, followed by Dog. Diana and I watched them go.

Are there any biscuits? she asked me. I said I didn't know.

But I expect she'll find one, I added, because a part of me just knew she would. That reminded me about the nappies.

We must look in the house for nappies for Joey, I told Diana, I think there are some.

She didn't seem that interested.

Great, she said.

We watched Mouse tug open the side door with both hands and disappear with Dog into the house. After a few moments, Diana looked at me.

Did you smell anything, Flynn? In the room just now?

The man, you mean?

No. Not the man. Another smell. In the room when Mouse was screaming.

I tried to think what she meant and my heart turned over.

What, you mean –

Yeah. Just now. Did you?

I thought about it. The house seemed to have a million different smells. The first smell I'd smelled when I went in with Alex, the smell of flesh and deadness, had all gone now and been replaced by – what?

I shut my eyes. I saw waxy petals. I smelled pink.

Flowers? I said, I might've smelled flowers.

Diana took a breath.

Not –?

No, I said, just flowers. Why?

No reason, she said, I'm just – I'm really glad that stinking body is out of the house at last.

We both looked at the boys. They'd stopped to rest for a bit and now they were having to half lift, half drag the man. I was very glad the bedspread was on him and we couldn't see his face.

Half of what she says isn't true you know, Diana said. Mouse I mean. She makes it all up.

She sounded like she was going to say something else but then she stopped because suddenly Sam cried out. The part of the bedspread he was holding was suddenly wet – a pinkish-black stain spreading fast across it.

Oh, said Diana. Oh gross.

Just do it, Alex said. One two three –

They tipped him quickly into the hole. Then Alex sat down on the ground and put his head in his hands and Sam turned and was sick into the bushes.

WATER

5

A strange thing about the house: it had three staircases. We discovered this when we ran up and down them looking to see if there were any swimming costumes to borrow.

Diana, me and Mouse went looking. We let Mouse run ahead and we both followed. The main staircase that led up from the hall was wide and wooden and creaky but had a thin blueish carpet on it which was worn out in the middle from being trodden on so much and a banister rail that was just about wide enough for a person to slide down.

A person with a small bottom.

Whoooh! Shouted Mouse, half slithering, half hanging on.

Now she went tearing up this staircase, giggling crazily. She seemed to have forgotten all about her bad dream and she didn't seem scared of anything. After about half a minute she disappeared ahead, only to come running up the stairs behind us again.

Boo! she burst out on us, laughing.

Hey, said Diana, where'd you just come from?

It goes all the way round! yelled Mouse as if it was her own big private joke. You can go all the way round without even stopping! D'you want me to show you?

So we followed her up the first staircase and across a small dark landing with no windows, then along a narrow creaky corridor and then some quite steep stairs with no carpet led us back down again. At the bottom of these stairs was an old black wooden dresser thing that was thick with cobwebs. It was piled up with china – cups and plates, all with little flowers sprinkled on under the dust.

The scent of something was heavy in the air.

Why does everything in this house have to have flowers on? I said. I tried not to breathe in. The smell was making me feel sick.

Mmm, really pretty, Diana said in a boring voice as if she was a friend of my mum's or something.

I don't think it's pretty, I told her. I'm beginning to find it really creepy actually.

Creepy! shouted Mouse and went thundering off up the stairs again.

Really, Diana went as if she wasn't listening.

Can you smell that? I said.

What?

She wrinkled her nose at me. She seemed to have forgotten asking me about the smell before. Every time you talked to Diana it was like the last conversation hadn't happened. It made it quite hard to get to know her.

Why would flowers be creepy? she said.

I thought of the two hollyhocks standing guard outside and I shivered.

I don't know, I said.

She smiled to herself.

You're funny, she said.

Am I? What do you mean?

I don't know. Just some of the things you say. They're so weird.

I thought about this.

In what way weird? I asked her and she shrugged.

I've never heard anyone talk like you. Not a kid anyway. I don't always understand you, she said, and then she paused. But Alex does.

I said nothing.

Why're you going red? she said. I thought it was pretty mean of her to point it out.

I still said nothing, because what was the point? I just waited for the hotness in my cheeks to go down. She looked at me and laughed.

Don't worry, she said. It's OK. I won't tell anyone.

Won't tell anyone what?

You know what.

I made a point of ignoring her. She was trying to wind me up, I knew that. It was hard to tell from her face if she really meant it or she was just joking. I hoped she was just joking.

Upstairs you could hear Mouse's feet pitter-pattering about. She was all alone.

Do you think she's OK? I said. Diana shrugged.

We'll find out, won't we?

I thought it was funny that out of all of us Diana, the one with the baby, seemed to act the least like a parent.

Just then on the dusty dresser, I noticed something else. A stack of white folded towelling things. All crisp and hard like they'd just come out of the wash. Why hadn't I seen them before?

Nappies! I said.

Diana looked at them.

They're not nappies.

They are, I told her. They're the old fashioned kind. Look —

I showed her. Next to the nappies in a little china dish were some great big safety pins. The ends of them were pale blue.

Blue for a boy, I said, laughing because somehow I just wasn't all that surprised. They're nappies for Joey.

For you, look!

Diana held Joey up and showed him. Then she hesitated.

I don't know how to put them on, she said.

Neither do I, I said. But we'll work it out.

It was funny because the dresser that just a moment ago had been really thick with greyish dust suddenly seemed a whole lot cleaner. In fact it looked like it had just been polished till it shone. The perfect changing table.

I spread out a nappy and made it into a triangle and we rubbed Joey's bottom clean with the old towel and then we laid him on it. He seemed to like lying there staring into space and kicking and kicking.

I knew a bit about how to put a nappy on because I used to help my mum change Anna, but that was with disposables. Mum would lie her on the bed and I would rattle a toy in the air to keep her happy. I liked to watch as my mum cleaned her really carefully and put cream on. It made me feel all safe inside just watching her do that.

We need to do it up so it doesn't rub on his tummy button, I told Diana because Joey's stump still stuck out and I worried it might be sore.

But putting one of these nappies on was harder than I thought. There seemed to be too much material and not enough baby. In the end I had to just scrunch all the corners of the nappy together and then it was pretty impossible to get the safety pin through. I pushed and pushed. I didn't want to hurt him.

Here, said Diana, give it to me.

She grabbed the nappy and pushed much harder than I had.

Careful, I said, but I needn't have worried. Joey seemed to be really enjoying it. Finally Diana got it done up and picked him up. The nappy hung a bit loosely but it was better than the old bit of towel he'd had before.

Suddenly Mouse's head poked down the stairs. She looked fed up.

Are you coming or not? she said.

Coming where?

I found the secret stairs! she said as if we ought to know what she was talking about.

Mouse had discovered the third staircase quite by accident. After running around for a bit she'd leaned against what she thought was just a cupboard door and suddenly it had sprung right open. Inside was the tiniest twistiest little wooden staircase leading up again.

I'm not allowed to go up on my own, she said. So I camed to get you.

We peered up the stairs.

Now we were there and she wasn't scared any more, Mouse had to be the first. She pushed in front of us and went scrambling up and we followed her. The staircase had no carpet and it smelled dusty and old with a second smell that caught at your throat, a musky oily kind of smell I'd never smelled before. It was such a small tight twisty staircase that Diana had to actually bend her head to go up.

At the top was a door. Just a normal old door with a dull metal knob for a handle. Mouse tried to push it open but it wouldn't go, Diana had a go but she couldn't do it either. But when I tried, the handle turned smoothly and easily just as I knew it would.

At that moment I felt a strange tightness all over my skin and my hair went hot. Most moments have a texture of newness and surprise, but this one didn't. It was an old moment. It was grey and old and falling apart with oldness. It felt like the thing I was doing, I'd been doing for a hundred years or something, maybe more. It scared me. It felt like someone had scraped a knife down my heart.

Flynn? What's the matter? Diana said.

Nothing, I told her, but I had to swallow hard because a sick taste had come up into my mouth. Just the strange decayed rhythm of what I was thinking was making me feel sick.

Mouse was standing very still and pale with her arms by her sides as if she'd just heard or seen or felt something.

As if he felt it too, Joey started to cry.

Don't you start, said Diana, and she rocked him up and down and kissed him loudly on his face.

We found ourselves standing in a small bare room. There was no furniture in it, not a single object, nothing. It was airless and hot. One dead fly lay on its back with its legs in the air on the windowsill and one single light bulb hung from the ceiling and the wooden floorboards were dusty and the walls were painted a slightly shiny brown, like the brown paper old people wrap parcels in.

The musky smell was strong in here. I looked at Diana to see if she could smell it too.

What is it? she said, and I wished she would take her eyes off me for a second and let me breathe.

I don't know, I said.

But I did know. The room wanted me in it. It wanted me in it much, much more than I wanted to be there.

Mouse had been very still and quiet but suddenly it was as if she woke up again.

Hey, a secret room! she shouted and her bare feet went bumpety bump as she ran from corner to corner. My room!

OK, Diana said in a lazy voice. OK, if you like, it can be yours.

My own room! Mouse echoed in a stupid way.

I looked at Diana. She'd taken off her glasses and was wiping them on her T-shirt with one hand, while she held Joey against her with the other. I knew that she didn't mean what she said, that really she was just playing a game of saying yes to everything with Mouse.

There was one small window in the room. It was fairly high up, too high for someone as small as Mouse to see out. I walked over and put my eyes level with it but before I even looked I knew what I'd see: the pool with Alex standing beside it. He looked so sad and forlorn. He was looking into the water as if he'd lost something, as if he knew all the same sad stuff that I knew.

Somehow the beat of my heart was stopping me breathing.

But not to sleep in, Mouse was adding. Just my room just for playing in, yeah?

OK, Diana said, agreeing with Mouse for the millionth time, and that was the last thing I remembered before the floor and ceiling snapped together and the room tipped over and swallowed me.

A moment had gone by, or maybe more, maybe loads of little moments, I don't know how many. I was lying on the

dusty sunlit floor and I felt so wonderful. A pure delicious-
ness had crept into all my bones. I was so light. Nothing
mattered. I wondered if this was how it felt to die. Or be
born. Or both.

Diana was bending over me and Mouse was patting my
head. I knew that and then I didn't know it and then
somehow I knew it again.

Flynn?

Are you OK?

Flynn?

I went away and then I came back again. I wondered who
Flynn was. I wondered if she was someone particularly crazy
or special, a person I might meet in a later life. My limbs
were all melty, my tongue salty. I didn't mind where I went
or who I was. I wasn't scared.

Am I dead? I said.

I heard someone laugh.

It's all right, Flynn, someone said and then the sound
moved backwards again.

You fainted, Diana said from very far away and I saw how
incredibly blue her eyes were when her glasses were off, not
like eyes at all but bright crocks of see-through glass. Are
you OK? You almost hit your head but we caught you.

It's all right, Flynn, Mouse echoed and her breath smelled
empty as if she needed to eat. We caught you. You didn't
hit your head.

I pushed her hand away. I felt like I was drowning in
honey, like everything bad had gone away and so had I. Now
I remembered. I'd fainted before and it was always the same:
all my bones dissolving, sticky lightness in my brain.

Suddenly I remembered about Alex.

Is he still there? I said to Diana.

Who? she said. Is who still there?

Alex. Is he still by the pool?

How should I know?

I told her to go and look out of the window and she did but it was strange because even though she was taller than me, she had to stand on tiptoe to look out. She stared for a long time then she turned back to me.

No, she said. There's no one there. You can't really see the pool from here anyway. It must be round on the other side.

I shut my eyes and then I opened them again. Joey was looking straight at me. He looked like he was waiting to see what I thought about that.

The boys were lying in the tall pale grass by the edge of the water. You could see Alex's tattered brown trouser legs and next to them Sam's denim knees. Dog was with them. He was biting his tail, biting and biting furiously as if he was trying to comb something out of it with his teeth.

The pool shimmered and shimmered, its surface never seemed to stop glinting and shimmering. If water was a language you would have said it was trying to tell us something.

The boys looked asleep but they weren't. They were just knocked out by what they'd done. They'd covered the man up with the soil and Diana had whispered something like a prayer and made a sad little sign with her fingers that none of us understood and that was that, that was the end of him. He would rest in peace for ever, we hoped.

Does that mean it's our house now? Mouse asked me as we walked across the grass to where the boys were. She'd slipped her hand in mine. It was a bit sticky but I let her keep it there.

I don't know, I said, partly because I was sick of Mouse's questions and partly because I really didn't.

Well – shall we pretend that it does mean that? Mouse said in a whisper.

If you want, I said, because I didn't see what harm it would do.

Straightaway she took a big breath and looked all around her.

Oh what a fantastic place we all live in, she said, and stretched out her other hand in a fake way.

I tried not to smile. Mouse tugged at my hand.

Go on, she said.

Go on what?

Now you say something.

I don't know what to say, I told her.

Just say anything.

OK – anything.

Mouse wailed and I knew I was being mean. But she didn't give up. She tugged harder on my hand and looked at me.

No, no, not that! Just say – say you are happy to be living in this perfect house.

I'm very glad to be living here, I said.

Not like that! she said, pulling so hard on my hand that it hurt. You have to say it properly, say it like it's true!

I sighed and tried to take my hand away.

I just can't play games right now, I told her.

It's not a game, she said, and her eyes were all shiny and mad. It's for the house. The house wants us to do it.

I looked at her. And I was suddenly afraid that she was right about the house, that it did.

Alex's face was so white, or maybe it was just that his black hair made his skin look whiter. His face was full of shadows.

Sam had taken off his T-shirt. Even though he had no

hairs on it, his chest was getting to be muscly like a man's chest. Sam already looked like he was on the edge of growing up properly, but there was something slippery and sad about Alex that made you think he would never grow up but stay a boy for ever and ever. But I liked boys. I couldn't imagine ever liking men, with their bristly bossy gruffness.

Mouse got sick of me not playing the game and she let go of my hand and bounced over and threw her arms around Dog. Dog shuffled sideways a little so he could go back to biting his tail, but he didn't shake her off.

We're gonna live here for ever and ever! she told Alex.

Oh yeah? he said, but he kept his eyes closed and I was glad he did because it meant I could keep on looking at his face.

And Flynn got sick and fell over, she added then. She fell right over, bang!

Straightaway Alex twisted round and looked up at me, shading his eyes against the sun.

You did? Are you OK?

She fell right over on the floor, Mouse told him a bit too happily. Yeah, really. We thought she was dead.

No we didn't, said Diana who had followed us from the house. Don't be silly, we never thought that. She just fainted that's all.

But she didn't bang her head, Mouse added, because we catched her.

Caught her, Diana said.

She sat down in the long hot grass and undid her shirt and began feeding Joey. I watched his small hands open and close as he sucked. Diana didn't seem to notice. She had a look on her face like she was slightly bored with feeding him.

Alex was still looking at me.

Are you OK? he said. You look kind of funny.

So do you, I said, because he did, he looked really pale like someone who needed to lie down.

He looked at me.

I'm OK, he said. I'm just knackered, that's all.

It's the heat, Diana said. Everyone's so hot.

She's fainted before, Sam told them. One time she picked up this dead baby bird and just keeled straight over just like that.

Mouse looked at me with real interest.

Why?

Why what?

Why did you pick up a dead baby bird?

I don't know, I said, remembering the weirdness of that day and how much I'd hated Sam for laughing at me. I just did.

Did you want to see if it was OK?

I smiled.

No, I knew it was dead. I think its neck was broken.

And did it – did it come back to life? Mouse asked me with a serious face.

Of course it didn't, Diana said.

Well I would have made it alive again, Mouse said.

Yeah right of course you would, Sam said, and Mouse could tell he was laughing at her.

But I fucking would have! she cried and punched the ground hard with her fist.

And maybe Flynn would have, Alex pointed out, if she could. But she couldn't. People can't. It's not how it works, Mousie.

Otherwise we'd bring the man back to life, I said.

Mouse looked completely horrified.

I don't want that man to get back alive, I want him to stay being dead.

You shouldn't say that, Diana said. Poor man.

And she flicked a glance at Sam. But Mouse ignored her and looked at me.

But why did you?

Why did I what?

Pick it up?

The baby bird? – I thought about it for a moment – I think, I think perhaps I just wanted to see what it felt like.

Did it feel nice?

No, it just felt – cold, I said, remembering the chill bluish skin with just a few dark scratchy feathers. Not nice at all. Just the feel of it on my fingers made me go all dizzy.

Yuk, Diana said.

Can we please not talk any more about dead things? Sam said, but you could tell he only said it because Diana had said yuk.

We all looked over at the old man's grave. The soil on it was dark and fresh.

I thought I was going to shiver but I didn't.

You brought it up, I told him.

I noticed that Alex was smiling to himself. He didn't know I could see him, lying there in the grass with his eyes closed, smiling. I wondered what was so funny.

Now you're doing it, I told him as quietly as I could.

He opened one eye.

Doing what?

The exact same thing. Having secret mysterious thoughts. Smiling to yourself.

I realised I was getting braver with Alex. I was getting braver about everything. Was it just the house making me brave? I thought about what Diana said about him under-standing me and I wondered if it was true. I wanted it to be true. Because if I didn't then why had I gone red when she said it?

He shut his eyes and smiled again, though I wasn't sure this time if it was to himself or not.

They're not mysterious and they're not secret, he whispered, but he said it in a nice slow stretched-out voice as if he really quite liked that I'd accused him of it.

OK, I said. So tell me then.

I'll tell you later, Alex said.

Why not now?

No, not now.

Why?

He still didn't open his eyes.

You'll understand when I tell you, he said.

Later when? I said.

Just later.

It was already later. The sun was already not as high in the sky as it had been. The light was growing deeper and shadows were stretching themselves around us. It was still burstingly hot but time had slowed down.

It's later now, I told Alex. His face stayed dead still.

Yeah, he said, but not quite later enough.

I sighed. I watched an insect land on a leaf then take off again. I watched another do the same. The sound of the waterfall still pounded in our ears but we were used to it now. It had begun to feel like the normal background noise of our lives.

So did you find anything up there in the house? Sam said.

Only stairs, Diana replied. Loads and loads of stairs.

And a little secret room, Mouse added. By the way, it's mine.

Oh yeah? said Sam looking at her. How come it was secret?

It wasn't, I said quickly. It was nothing special. It was just an empty little room with nothing in it.

I bit my lip. I knew this was a lie. Why was I lying? The room was alive. But how could anyone else possibly understand that?

Everyone was silent for a minute.

Is that where you fainted? Alex asked me.

Yes, I said, wondering how he knew.

Oh, said Diana. We found nappies. For Joey.

For baby Joey! echoed Mouse, but the boys didn't seem too interested in this.

But we didn't find any swimming things, Mouse said. So we'll just have to go swimming in our pants.

You don't have any pants, Diana reminded her.

Oh, said Mouse in a disappointed voice. Oh I forgot.

And she rubbed her eyes and sat down on the ground next to Sam. She looked at her thumb for a moment then put it in her mouth.

You could always wear a nappy, said Sam. This was mean. Mouse stared at him.

You're horrible, she said.

I didn't mean it, he said.

Go away, she said.

The light in the sky had turned strange. Violet and yellow. Creamy spikes of sun poking through the fat dark clouds.

Feels like it's going to thunder, Diana said, and she put Joey down in the grass and stretched and yawned.

That's just what we could do with right now, said Sam, keeping his eyes on her. A great big electric storm.

Yeah, it would cool things down a bit, Diana said, and she looked at him as if what he'd just said was so unbelievably fascinating.

Clear the air, Sam agreed.

I didn't say anything and neither did Alex. I just kept my eyes on the clean safe curves of Joey's face as he lay staring up through the tall grass. I felt suddenly fed-up with the fake way Sam and Diana talked. Why were they talking about the weather just like grown-ups? Was it a way of showing they liked each other, to keep on saying really boring things all the time?

Mouse glanced at them and carried on sucking her thumb, but stared up at the sky, keeping her head still but moving her eyes around the way Dog did.

When're we going to swi-im? she asked with a little bit of a moan in her voice.

Soon, Alex said, but he didn't move either.

Diana glanced down at Joey then flicked a ladybird off her arm and yawned.

I feel like I can't be bothered to do anything, she said.

But the pool had other ideas. The pool wanted us to swim in it. It wanted us in it so badly it was quite hard to ignore. You could see it glinting at us, hoping and hoping. You could almost hear the words falling out of the waterfall, hitting the bright water hard before they came bubbling back up again: come on, come on, come in, come in!

We kept on trying to ignore it, to pretend it wasn't true. But it was holding its breath, waiting for us.

And although there wasn't a puff of wind, still even the tall grass around the edge seemed to be bending towards us, beckoning, trying to push us, pull us, suck us in.

In a minute, we said, because it was yesterday and we had other stuff to do first. Like eat, like sleep, like bury the man.

Come on, said the pool.

We will, we said, but not yet.

But whe-en? went Mouse who couldn't even swim.

In a minute, we said.

Soon, said Alex, because suddenly time had speeded up and it was today.

Now, said Sam.

By the time we went in, it must have been late in the afternoon. The air was still so hot it crackled.

The sky had turned a dark scrubby violety colour like someone had filled it in with a felt-tip. Thunder was grumbling far away. Now and then the horizon lit up with blue flashes. On the second flash, Dog ran back into the house. He ran so fast that no one saw him go.

On the third flash, Mouse started squealing.

I don't like it, I don't like it! she said.

She stood on the edge of the pool in the shallow bit and she hugged herself. She had no clothes on. She'd pulled off her dress and didn't seem to mind that she was completely bare, standing there in front of all of us with everything showing. But maybe I wouldn't have minded either when I was just six like her. Apart from her little sticky-out belly, she was so thin you could see all her bones, like someone's drawing of a small stick girl with no clothes on.

Don't like what? said Sam, who was already in, swimming up and down with long lazy strokes. What don't you like, Mouse?

That − that − thing over there. The nasty flashing thing.

She gazed miserably at the thin blue light which kept appearing in the gaps between the trees.

It's just a bit of lightning, said Sam, and Mouse gave him an evil look. Maybe she was remembering the remark about the nappy.

Make it go, she said, still hugging herself and tramping her feet up and down in the water to make as much splashing as possible. Just do it! Make them stop it right now!

Sam laughed and kicked back in the water.

We can't stop it, he said to Mouse. It's not a person doing it, it's the weather.

Mouse stared at him and scratched between the cheeks of her bottom then she sniffed at her fingers.

Don't do that, said Diana who was sitting on the bank behind her, it's dirty.

But Mouse wasn't listening and she carried on doing it.

Alex swam over to where Mouse was. His skin was white in the dark water.

Look, Mouse, he said. There's nothing to be scared of. The storm isn't here yet, it's still miles away. And anyway you're not scared of thunderstorms are you, Mousie?

Mouse shook her head and her teeth chattered and then she changed her mind and started nodding.

I am, she said, I – am – scared.

Well you never used to be.

I was little then, Mouse told him. I had my mum then. I was two. It was before I was six.

Sam stretched out his hands to her. Come on, he said. I'll take you swimming.

Mouse just looked at him.

Come on, he said again.

She kept on looking at him and tramping her feet up and down like she half wanted to and half didn't.

You said you wanted to swim, he reminded her.

She licked her lips.

I can't swim, she wailed.

It doesn't matter, said Sam. I can teach you.

He's a good swimmer, I told her because it was true and anyway I thought Sam was being very nice and patient with her. He's got badges.

Oh, said Mouse politely, although she probably didn't

know what swimming badges were. She looked down at her feet as if she was looking for a way out. Then she looked as if she'd found it.

If I wiggle my toes, mud comes up, she said. Look.

The boys had taken off everything but their pants and dived straight in off a fat grey rock that jutted out by the waterfall. The rock was the perfect shape and size. It looked like it had been put there specially for them.

First Sam went in, quickly followed by Alex. They had to make sure to jump far enough out so they wouldn't hit their heads on the rock.

At first as they went in, they seemed to stay down there for ever in that dark water. For a few seconds I felt panic. I looked at Diana but she seemed perfectly calm, as if she couldn't care less whether the pool swallowed them or not. I was very relieved when their heads and shoulders came bursting back up, first Sam's big man's ones then Alex's thinner ones. Bright sparkling drops exploded everywhere as Sam shook the water out of his hair. The thunder was still rumbling.

Even though I could dive, I couldn't do it in a pool like this one. I had to creep in slowly. Not because of the cold but because of what might be down there. The pool had pebbles and mud in the shallow bits but after that you pushed off into something deeper – thick sloopy water that stopped being see-through and turned black. There was so much I couldn't let myself think about. Cold faces waiting for me in the black tangle of weeds.

It was important not to show Mouse that I was afraid.

Diana didn't swim.

Why not? I said, and she made a face.

I just had a baby, didn't I. How can I?

I felt really bad for forgetting about the blood. So much had been going on that I'd almost forgotten how new Joey still was.

I took off my trainers and shorts but I kept my T-shirt on over my bra and pants.

Diana said that was silly.

It will take for ever to dry, she said. You'll be sopping wet. You'll get cold and then you'll have nothing to put on.

I said I didn't care. It was all right for her. She had a proper bra with lace on it. No way was I going to have Alex see me in the stupid childish underwear Mum had got me.

It can dry on me, I said. It'll be nice. It'll cool me down.

Don't be an idiot, Diana said. Take it off. No one's even looking. You've hardly got anything to hide.

I looked at her with her long blonde hair and her long brown legs and thought how easy it was for her. It didn't matter what you did or didn't have, how many clothes you took off or put on, when you were as gorgeous as she was. It didn't even matter whether anyone was looking or not. Diana's beauty was a definite, reliable thing. She carried on being beautiful even when no one else was there.

Who're you worried about anyway? she said. Are you worried about Alex, is that it?

I tried to smile.

Don't be stupid, I said, and quickly, before she could see me go red, I turned my back on her and waded into the water.

My feet wobbled on the stones. I felt the suck of the mud. I took a big breath and pushed off and floated. It was lovely.

Come on, said the water.

OK, I said.

I felt really sorry for Mouse, not being able to swim. It was so easy. Once you were in you just gave up and let the pool do the rest. Once I was in I wondered why we'd all waited so long. Why hadn't we just dived straight in on that first morning, Alex and me, why hadn't we just jumped right off that grey rock into the pool the very first time we saw it? In one way being in the water seemed to solve everything. It was the waiting to do it that had been difficult.

I told you so, the pool was saying.

Yeah, I replied, I know. You did.

I kicked out and swam towards the waterfall where the boys were splashing and shouting.

Even though I'd never been a brilliant swimmer, not like Sam, still my arms and legs went easily and smoothly through that cool water. It felt like the pool was holding me. Even though my T-shirt ballooned out and then drifted around me, even though something I didn't want to think about brushed against my legs. Weeds, I thought, just little ordinary weeds. I was quite pleased with myself for not shuddering.

Once you were in it, the pool seemed bigger than it had looked from the bank. Because three of us were in there swimming, the surface had changed, going from smooth and green and calm to this shivery jumpy thing which kept on breaking up. Rings broke into smaller rings, little waves bounced and slapped at the shore. Diana and Joey and Mouse suddenly seemed a very long way away.

I turned onto my back for a moment and looked at the house. Our house. Or whoever's. Like a lot of other things, it didn't seem to matter any more.

I could see the two hollyhocks, one pink, one yellow, by the door and the two brown chickens scratching. I knew that Dog was probably somewhere in there, curled on a sofa, paws sticking out. I knew that further round to the side was the rectangle of darker fresh earth where the poor old dead man lay, but I wasn't going to think about that. Another thing I wasn't going to think about was the idea that up a small twisty staircase in the house, a room was waiting.

Instead I looked at the bank where Mouse was. She had got a pile of small pebbles and was playing a game of throwing them in, plop plop.

The pool's hungry! she shouted. Watch me feed it!

I didn't watch. I turned away. The reason Mouse was tiring was she always needed someone to watch her.

Sam had swum back over to where Mouse was, maybe hoping he could get her to go in. But Alex was still by the waterfall. He called out to me but I could hardly hear him. His words kept going under, lost in the sound of the water.

He was trying to tell me that you could swim right round behind the waterfall. I saw that he'd gone behind it now and suddenly there was this loud sheet of brightness falling down between us. It was like looking at him through a window of water. Him just this dark blurry shape on the other side.

He called to me to come round. I wanted to but it was scary to swim too close to where it was crashing. I was worried I'd get pulled under or something.

No! I said as I got up close and he reached out and tried to pull me round.

What?

I don't like it, I told him as I gasped and tried to breathe as I treaded water.

But still he tried to pull me.

I'm scared, I admitted at last as I pulled away.

Scared of what?

Of that – that I might get sucked down.

I tried to laugh but I wasn't joking and you could tell from Alex's face that he knew it too.

Hey, it's OK, it's safe, he said. He held out a hand and even though I still wasn't sure if I believed him, I took it and this time I shut my eyes and let him pull me.

For a moment the weight of the water pressed on me and I felt a million bubbles fizzing up under my legs. Then suddenly we were both behind the sheet of water. He let go of my hand. I laughed. It felt like the water was alive and glad about what we'd just done.

Behind us was a low grey shelf of rock exactly like a little seat made for two people. You could sit there hidden from the world, your very own private waterfall tumbling down in front of your eyes.

Alex got himself up there and then he pulled me up after him. Our bodies dripped all over the stone which was warm even though it wasn't in the sun.

We sat there on the ledge with our legs dangling in the water. The light was eerie, half gloomy and half bright, wiggling around us. Alex didn't say anything. Because his hair was so short it looked completely dry. For a moment we just sat there, both of us, taking it in.

Even though it's so loud, I said, it's funny how peaceful it is.

He smiled and still he said nothing. I'd never been so alone with him. Just us and a crashing waterfall. I dared to look at him for a few seconds then and I noticed he had some little dark bruises on his chest and legs.

What are those? I asked him.

What?

Those marks.

I pointed and he glanced down.

Oh those. I don't know. Nothing.

Do they hurt?

He hesitated and I saw him looking down at them with surprise as if they were on someone else's body.

No, he said, I hardly feel them.

Still maybe you should see the doctor, I said, realising before I could stop the words how stupid they sounded. I was talking about a world we didn't live in any more.

Alex shut his eyes for a small second.

Maybe I will, he said. Thanks, Flynn. Thanks for the advice.

Straightaway I wished I'd never said anything. I hated it when he spoke to me all politely like that.

I felt suddenly miserable. It annoyed me that Alex could make me feel like that so easily. I wondered if he was thinking about Diana. Or if he wanted to be left alone. I wondered if I dared slip off the rock and into the black water without him helping me. But then I realised I dreaded drowning in that blackness even more than I dreaded being in Alex's way.

I looked at my harsh bony knees with the shiny scars where scabs had been and I wished for the hundredth time that I had knees like Diana's — smooth and pale golden. Until quite recently I hadn't cared the smallest bit what my knees looked like and it annoyed me that I might be turning into one of those girls who used a hairdryer and worried about stuff like that. All a knee was for was to join the two parts of your leg together.

I bit down on my tongue as hard as I could bear, to shake myself out of this stupid feeling and get back to being the person I normally was.

I was thinking so hard about all of this that I almost jumped when Alex spoke.

Flynn? he said.

Mmm.

Can I ask you a question?

If you want, I said.

Well I won't if you don't want me to.

I don't know, I said, because it was the truth.

Why don't you know?

What?

Why don't you know whether you want me to ask you a question or not?

We-ell, I said, I suppose because I don't know what it's going to be.

Do you really always worry so much about everything? he asked me.

Is that the question? I said, relieved.

No, he said, that's not it actually. But you do, don't you?

I thought about this and felt a sudden complicated wave of sadness.

Doesn't everyone? I said.

He thought about this.

No, he said, everyone doesn't. Or at least not half as much as you do.

Oh.

Diana for instance. She doesn't let herself think about everything all the time. She just gets on with it.

Yes, I agreed, thinking of the way she shoved the safety pin so hard into Joey's nappy without seeming to worry about hurting him. Yes, I suppose she does.

And I thought yes, the things that Diana was really good at were exactly the things that I couldn't do: keeping still and not thinking, getting on with things and being beautiful. And she didn't hurt Joey either, I reminded myself, he was fine. She got the nappy on.

Is Diana your girlfriend? I heard myself say then.

Alex turned and stared at me. Really stared. His mouth was open. He seemed as amazed by the question as I was amazed I'd dared ask it. Then he laughed.

No! he said. No, I mean she isn't my girlfriend. Of course she isn't. Why would she be?

He laughed again as if he was trying a bit too hard to make the point.

I told you. I've known her since I was a kid, he said, as if that somehow proved it.

Oh, I said, because I didn't see what difference that made.

I hope you believe me? he said suddenly and I looked at him.

I mean, seriously, Flynn, what a weird thing to ask me. I mean why would you even think that?

I don't know, I said, and I shook my head in a slow and baffled way but inside my heart was jumping with happiness.

We were quiet for a bit then. We could hear Sam and Mouse shouting and splashing over on the other side of the pool but we couldn't quite hear what they were saying. Mouse's laugh was very loud and high and Sam's was quite low and though the thunder was still rumbling, the flashes of lightning seemed to have gone.

Now is the kind of time when I really wish I had a cigarette, Alex said.

I looked at him in surprise.

I thought you didn't smoke?

He shrugged.

Not really. I don't, not any more. I didn't really like it. Except just occasionally I still want to. When I'm nervous.

You're nervous?

Now? A bit, yes.

He hesitated and opened his mouth as if he was about to say something, then didn't.

Anyway, he said, I only stopped because – well for a lot of reasons, but mainly because that child kept taking my matches.

Which child?

Which d'you think? Mouse of course.

Somewhere on the other side of the waterfall, we could still hear Mouse yelling at Sam.

Does she really set fire to things? I said, because I still couldn't quite imagine it.

He nodded and swung his legs in the water.

That's why she could never be fostered for long. All sorts of people tried but they kept on bringing her back. She's really dangerous. She couldn't be left alone in a room, couldn't keep herself away from flames. Still can't.

I was silent while I thought about this. I remembered Mouse going back into the house all alone to get a biscuit for Dog and wondered if we should have let her.

But she's been alone in a room here several times, I pointed out.

Alex shrugged.

It's different here.

Why? I asked him though I thought a part of me knew the answer.

He looked at me.

Why is it different? I don't know. It just is.

He was silent for a minute.

But that's why no one can love her, he said. I mean parent-type people.

But *you* love her, I told him, because suddenly somehow on Mouse's behalf I needed to know it was true.

He breathed in and flicked his fingers in the water.

I've known her since she was a baby, he said. But I don't know. She scares people. She scares me sometimes.

I tried to think about this.

But – you mean, she's really started fires?

Yes, he said slowly, she really has.

Where?

Kitchens, houses, all over, anywhere she gets a chance. At playgroup they gave her a surprise birthday cake and she crept in when everyone was playing and set it on fire.

I gasped.

Did anyone get hurt? I asked him.

No, he said. But she nearly killed herself once when she set light to someone's car.

She didn't!

It was horrible, Alex said. It wasn't that long ago. She used the lighter, learned how to work it and everything. She stayed in the car and when they pulled her out, she tried to get back in.

I stared at him.

What, back in the car while it was on fire?

Seriously. She ran back across to it and kept on trying to get back in there.

I thought of Mouse struggling to get back into a burning car and I suddenly wished I didn't have to have that picture in my head. I worried that I would never be able to think of her in the same way again.

I used to think, said Alex slowly, that she didn't understand about danger, that she thought it was a game or something. But lately I don't know, she's got so scared.

Scared of what?

Well, of everything.

Like the lightning?

Yes, he said. And all those dreams about the man and stuff.

All sorts of things. She drives me nuts sometimes, she's so jumpy.

I said nothing. I remembered how interested she'd been about the dead baby bird. And how keen she was that the old man should stay dead.

Does she think things can come alive again?

I don't know what she thinks, Alex said, and he bent and cupped some water in his hands and opened his fingers so it fell out. He did it again.

She has the strangest mind, he said. I don't get that mind of hers at all.

I said nothing. I didn't know what to say. I thought of Mouse running towards the flames, making her own cake catch fire.

She makes me laugh, he added gloomily, and he stared hard at the water for a moment as if Mouse might actually be down there somewhere.

My feet were starting to feel cold in the water so I pulled them out and hugged my knees to my chest. I was very glad I'd kept my T-shirt on so he couldn't see my awful bra.

I care about them both, Alex said, as if it was the answer to a question I'd asked. Her and Diana, both of them. They're my family. We've been through stuff together, that's all.

Like running away?

Alex looked at me.

You know, I never thought we'd do that. I know you've done it but, well, it was like all our lives we'd been stuck or trapped or something. Other people always in charge of us. I really wasn't sure we would ever get free.

But you did, I told him. You did get free.

Yeah we did.

★　　★　　★

There was some more silence between us then. It was Alex who broke it.

Flynn? he said.

Mmm.

Have you ever kissed anyone?

Straightaway I felt my face go hot. I couldn't believe he could ask me such an embarrassing thing.

A boy, you mean? The words came out in a croaky little whisper.

Of course a boy, stupid.

I don't know, I said. Why?

You don't know?

I couldn't look at him. His question was bumping around inside me so hard I could barely breathe.

Why? I said again.

It's just — it's something I'd quite like to know, that's all.

Why?

Alex laughed.

Why, why, why? Don't you ever stop asking why?

Don't you ever stop asking difficult questions?

He laughed again.

I'm sorry, he said, I couldn't help asking. Do you mind?

I don't know, I told him because I really didn't. But why?

Why what?

Why do you want to know?

He paused for a moment and even though I couldn't look at him, I knew from the feel of the air between us that he was looking at me.

I'm just interested, he said.

Interested?

Yeah, why not? I'm interested in everything about you.

Oh, I said, and I tried to take this in.

You're funny, he said after a second or two.

Diana said that too, I told him.

Did she? When did she say that?

I tried to think when it was. The day had gone all baggy and loose and the morning suddenly seemed years ago.

Earlier, I said vaguely. When we were upstairs. She said I say funny things.

Alex thought about this.

Well you do. But nice funny things. You make me laugh.

Oh, I said. Like Mouse?

No, he said, not at all like Mouse actually. You're funny in your own unique Flynn way.

I stayed quiet. I was glad the water kept on pouring down because it stopped me having some thoughts I didn't want to be having at that particular moment.

Are you OK? he said. I've upset you, haven't I?

Don't be silly, of course you haven't.

Are you OK though?

I tried to nod but my teeth were knocking together and I was suddenly quite cold.

You're cold.

No, I said, I'm OK.

That was the question by the way, he added.

That was it?

Yeah. Why? Did you think it was going to be something better?

You are cold aren't you? Alex said again after a few moments.

No, I said, even though I was. I was freezing. But I was worried if I admitted it we'd have to swim back to the others. I tried not to tremble.

You're not going to answer the question are you?

I said nothing. I was still trying to make my thoughts stay still so I could look at them.

Alex sighed and lay right back on the rocky ledge so all I could see were his knees and his feet. I let myself look at his feet. They were white and bony and strong-looking but they didn't have hairs on them like Sam's did.

If I tell you something, he said, will you promise not to think any differently about me? Will you promise to stay funny and not start being all soft and kind and sorry?

I looked at him and felt worried. I wondered what he could possibly tell me that would make me be sorry.

Why would I do that? I said.

He coughed.

Well – when you hear what it is. You might want to. But you've got to swear you won't.

I won't, I said.

You swear?

I swear.

Well, Alex sat back up again and took a breath. He looked quickly at me then he looked back at the water.

Do you ever think about dying?

I stared at him. In my head without meaning to, I saw the room, the small high window, the brown shiny walls. My heart turned over as something tried to grab at it. Out of nowhere I got the out-of-breath feeling.

Yes, I said as the answer rushed out of me before I could think straight about it.

You do?

He seemed surprised.

Yes all the time, I said, though like a lot of things I found myself saying to Alex, I hadn't known it was true till the moment I said it.

He stared at me for a moment and then he looked like he'd decided something.

What? I said.

Nothing. Just – I think you will live to be very old, he said, and he leaned towards me and screwed up his eyes. I can see you, Flynn, as this very wrinkled-up old lady walking along with a stick and looking out for dead baby birds to pick up.

This made me laugh.

But I don't ever want to be old, I told him then.

I thought of Granny Jane and the way she couldn't even open a jam jar without using a rubber grip and how she had to have a safety mat in the bath just like Anna. When you got old your whole life seemed to be rubber this, safety that, just like a baby. What was the point?

Alex kicked the water hard and it splashed onto our ledge, onto my knees.

You say that now, he said. But you will. When you are old you won't mind the slightest bit, you'll feel no different from how you are now. You'll just be glad about all the life you've lived, that's all.

Maybe, I said, though I felt far too impatient to even think about something so boring right now. But what about you?

What about me?

Do you want to live to be old?

Alex looked strange.

Well that's the point, he said.

What is?

I haven't been well.

I stared at him.

What do you mean?

I've been ill, Flynn. Really ill. I mean, technically I'm ill right now.

Technically?

According to some people.

What people?

Well, doctors.

I looked at his face and suddenly everything rushed closer. I felt my hair grow hot the way it had in the room.

When you said that thing about going to the doctor, he told me. Well it was quite funny because you see I have already been. I've been seen by so many doctors, I can't think how many, I'm losing track . . .

I stared at him.

Where? I said. It was the only thing I could think of to ask.

In hospital.

In hospital? I repeated like an idiot.

In and out. Months of it. Scans and tests and drips and people prodding me. Then treatment.

He showed me the back of his hand. His beautiful hand. The skin was mottled. A fading bruise the size of a plum. I wondered why I'd never noticed it before.

Until ten days ago there was a tube in there, he said. I pulled it out.

But – should you have done that? I said, still staring at him like a stupid person.

He grinned.

No, he said, of course I shouldn't have. It was a really stupid thing to do. But I couldn't do it any more. I'd had enough.

And, I said, because the thoughts in my head were all grabbing at each other now, and – so are you OK?

Somehow I already knew the answer to this.

Suddenly Alex looked tired. He looked the same as he always did but now I saw it clearly as if his skin was a window I could look into.

You're not OK, are you? I said.

He sighed. It was more of a bored sigh than an upset sigh.

Who knows? No one knows. I feel fine mostly. But they wanted me to go in again and I wasn't going to. I couldn't do it, Flynn.

I stared at him. He was so pale. His eyes were so bright. He was lit up from inside. I suddenly hated myself for being so thick and selfish as to – well – how could I not have known this?

So – you're not OK, I said again.

I'm OK. I'm very OK. Look at me. It's just – no one knows for how long.

What do you mean, how long? I said and my voice was suddenly so far away it made me dizzy.

I saw him look away. I heard Sam and Mouse on the other side of the pool shouting and laughing. Maybe Sam was teaching Mouse to swim, maybe not. What did it matter now? Alex shut his eyes and opened them again and looked towards the sound.

It was pointless to go into hospital all over again and have more of the bad stuff, he said. If you'd seen me a few months ago, Flynn, you'd have laughed. I had no hair.

I looked at his head with its thin layer of fur. I thought of my pretend pet fox cub.

I wouldn't have laughed, I said.

Alex made an impatient noise.

I'd like you without hair, I told him and I knew I meant it, but he just shrugged.

But if you went to the hospital, I began, I mean they must know –

But I stopped because I didn't know what I was going to say next. I suddenly didn't know anything.

What's the point? he said.

The point?

Of more treatment when I feel like this.

Do you feel OK?

I feel great. I feel very good when I'm with you.

With me?

He looked at me.

Flynn, he said.

What?

He smiled and then his eyes went suddenly from full to empty. I saw the brown shiny room again and I shut my eyes to it quickly.

Are you going to die? I asked him.

I looked at him and I'd never seen his eyes so empty and sad.

I don't know, he said. To be honest I really don't. What do you think?

I didn't know. I had no idea any more what I thought. I felt he was wanting me to say something but I didn't know what to say. Just when I needed to be strong and clever, I was feeling more stupid and hopeless than I'd ever felt in my life before.

Moments passed. The waterfall still rushed in our ears but I'd stopped hearing it. I'd stopped hearing anything except my own blood banging in my head.

Don't feel sorry for me, Alex said then. Please. Flynn, don't act differently with me. I mean it. I can't tell you how important that is to me. I'll never forgive you if you do.

I don't feel sorry for you, I began to say, it's just, I feel –

What? he was looking at me so sharply. What do you feel?

That – you've got to be OK.

He sighed and I saw now how pale he was, how pale

he'd always been. I felt cold then, very cold, really freezing in fact and I realised I was crying. The only reason I knew it was I felt the hot tears falling on my two cold bare legs.

There's no got to about it, he said.

He turned to me and his eyes were dark. I tasted salt in my nose and my mouth.

People can't always help what happens to them, he said quietly as if that wasn't obvious.

I know that, I told him and as I said it I felt so miserable.

No, he said. No I don't think you do know it. I don't think you know anything, Flynn. You haven't worked it out, have you? Do you know why I'm telling you this? Do you?

I stared at him. How could I possibly know?

He took a breath.

I'm telling you because I like you so much that it's making me feel —

Suddenly I couldn't look at him. Whatever it was he was going to say, I just knew I didn't want him to say it.

Don't, I said, but I must have whispered it too quietly because he didn't seem to hear me.

Please, Flynn, he said. Please don't look away. I've got to tell you this. I've started to feel — I don't know — for a while now. I feel like I love you —

Love? I whispered.

So much, he said, and now he wasn't looking at me either. I love you so much, I do.

I couldn't take it in. The word, it sounded like a joke, so unlikely. Love was something that happened in books, to other people, to grown-ups.

Don't hate me, he muttered. Seriously. You can't imagine how long it's taken me to say that.

I blinked. Was he completely stupid? How could I ever

hate him? It's just – this was so surprising to me. It was a shock, the whole difficult word love. I'd have been overjoyed just to have him say he liked me.

But Alex's voice was so unhappy now.

Don't laugh at me, he said.

I'm not laughing, I said quietly.

I didn't know it would be like this, he went on. It's almost the same as being ill, how helpless and stupid it makes me feel. I like you so much that I just – I can't think straight and I can't seem to do anything –

Me? I said, because I still couldn't believe it. Tears were standing in my eyes.

Yes you, he said, and his voice was all shaky. You – you're such a strange and funny person. I can't stop thinking about you.

I shut my eyes.

What are you thinking? he asked me. Please tell me.

Me too, I whispered. I'm thinking, me too.

Really? You feel it?

Yes, I said, because now it was coming clear to me. All the time. Even when I'm not thinking about you, you're still there in my head like a colour or a smell or something.

A smell?

Even though he was still half crying, Alex started to laugh.

Yes, I said. A lovely smell. Cake or flowers or holidays. Or – or a colour that's so bright it leaks onto everything else.

Alex thought about that.

I understand that, he said.

You do?

Yes, except for me you're a feeling. Not an emotion exactly, but a sensation – of hope, sort of, and excitement. If I think of your face I get this great big burst of excitement in here – or here –

He touched his chest and then his stomach.

And it's like whatever I do, whatever's happening, the feeling of you is always there, it's been there just about since I first saw you that time in the garden and it doesn't feel like it will ever go away.

I bit my lip.

You really felt it then?

Alex nodded.

And when you said that thing about wanting to disappear, he said then, I couldn't bear it. I wanted to pick you up and put you, I don't know, in my pocket or something –

In your pocket? I said, laughing, but I saw that his face was deadly serious.

So you couldn't go anywhere, he said.

I won't, I said, and for once I dared to look straight in his lovely face. I won't go anywhere.

Alex was silent for a moment.

Flynn?

Yes.

You can see why I needed to tell you the truth. But I meant it about not feeling sorry for me. I'm serious. I won't be able to bear that, OK?

OK, I said.

It would kill me.

OK! I said louder.

So promise you won't?

I've said, I told him. Are you deaf? I promise.

So that's it. We don't mention it again. Me being ill, I mean.

OK, I said again.

If you do, you'll regret it. Do you know what I'll do?

I stared at him and shook my head.

I'll do this.

And he scooped up a handful of water and threw it in my face so I couldn't see.

Hey! I shouted, but I didn't care. Suddenly I didn't want to see anything. I kept my eyes closed and I splashed him back and for about a minute we splashed each other so much that when I felt him take my face in his hands and hold it, I still couldn't open my eyes for how much water was in them.

Hey, he said as I tried to look at him. No, stay like you were. Shut your eyes. Hey, your face is all wet.

I smiled and kept my eyes shut.

You look like a –

Like a what? I said, worrying about what he might say. But instead he hesitated.

Like yourself, he said. You look lovely. You look like yourself.

And he held my face and looked at me and then I opened my eyes and I looked back at him as long as I dared and then because neither of us knew what to do next and it was the longest we'd ever looked at each other ever, he let go again.

The thunder was still rumbling far away as we swam back to the others. The storm hadn't come close yet, but the tick tick tick of insects was everywhere and the purpleness of the light meant that rain would come. Over by the edge of the water, two dragonflies were lifting and falling, zigging and zagging through the air.

Joey and Sam were lying fast asleep in the shade but Diana was sitting on the bank with Mouse held tight between her legs. Mouse was trying to watch the dragonflies but Diana kept on jerking her head back. She had her glasses on and she was looking through Mouse's wet hair, parting it and picking at it with her fingers. Mouse kept on twisting her head and complaining.

She has nits, Diana said as Alex and I walked up to them. Loads of them. Everywhere. Ugh, look you can see them easily now her hair is wet.

Get off me, said Mouse loudly. Fucking get off! I do not have any nits. I do not!

Keep still, Diana said. If you don't believe me, I'll show you one right now.

Don't want to see one, said Mouse, and she shut her eyes.

If you don't let me do this, said Diana, you'll be itching and itching for the rest of your life. Do you want that?

Maybe Mouse didn't like the idea of itching for ever and ever because she went still for a second or two.

Ow, she whispered, frowning up at Alex as if he might do something. Ow, ow, ow!

Shush, Mousie, Alex said. It's got to be done. Let her do it.

If you keep still it will be over quicker, I said.

As I said it Diana gave me a strange look. It wasn't cross and it wasn't friendly. It was just full of question marks.

It's hard with fingers, she said, and she carried on looking straight in my face. Then her eyes travelled down over my body. Really what we need is a comb. Do you know where there's a comb, Flynn?

There won't be a nit comb, I said, although even as I said it I knew that if we really needed one the house would probably provide it.

No, said Diana. Just a normal one. Any kind of comb will do.

Get her off me! said Mouse, losing patience again and struggling.

Keep still, Alex said more sternly this time.

I'll go and see if there's one anywhere in the house, I said.

I'll come with you, Alex said quickly.

I didn't look back to see what Diana thought of that.

Even though we weren't exactly dripping wet any more, still our two pairs of feet were damp enough to make dark footprints all over the tiles in the hall.

You wouldn't have had to be a detective to see that two fairly wet people had just walked over that floor. There were little bits of grass and stuff on our feet too. My mum would have made us go outside and clean them off. My mum would have made us do a lot of things.

The house felt cool and dark and quiet after the thundery hotness of the air outside.

Did you mind? Alex whispered to me as we went in the kitchen. He picked a shirt up off a chair and put it on. It was soft and bright blue, the kind of shirt that had been washed a million times to a perfect crinkly softness. I didn't know if it was his or not. I'd never seen it before. It looked perfect on him. It made him look perfect.

I realised I'd left my jeans outside and I was getting cold in my damp T-shirt but at the very same moment that I realised it, I also knew the house would give me something to wear.

Mind what?

Me coming with you?

Don't be stupid, I told him softly.

I didn't know why we were whispering. No one was in the house. No one except Dog. He was lying in a chair next to the stove, his paws all bundled up under his nose. He was absolutely still but his eyes were open. He was watching us as if he didn't know what to expect.

That made three of us.

I'm starving, Alex said, and he tore off a chunk of the crusty bread that was sitting on the kitchen counter. He tore off another piece of the bread and wiped it straight through the dish of soft butter in the way you'd never be allowed to do at home and he handed it to me. I took it.

I took it and then I felt suddenly not at all hungry. I felt shy. I didn't know what to say to him any more. It was like now that we'd said what we felt, all our words had been taken away which was odd as you'd have thought it would be the other way round.

I stood for a moment holding the piece of bread and butter and then I put it back down. I thought I might eat it later but not now. I was too full up with all our talking, I was filled to the brim with excitement and happiness.

Alex went over to the sink and turned on the old juddery tap and filled a glass with water and drank it down. I listened to the sound of him swallowing. Every sound he made was beautiful, every action kind of perfect. Did everyone see this about him or was it just me?

Something strange, Alex said, turning back to look at me. Have you noticed – the bread here is always fresh? Like someone just made it, I don't know, like it was actually made this morning or something. But this is the bread from the other day, right?

I nodded because as far as I knew it was.

The water too – he held up the glass and we both looked at it – it tastes so good, better than any water I ever tasted anywhere.

But the whole house is like that, I said. Haven't you noticed?

229

Even though I was with Alex, I felt myself shiver.

Everything that's here, I said, it all feels like it's been put here specially for us.

He frowned at me.

Did you say that once before? he asked me. Or am I imagining it?

I don't know, I said, because I really didn't, I might have.

He smiled and ate another piece of bread.

Aren't you hungry? he said. You should be really starving after a swim.

I shrugged and for once my shrug felt exactly as casual and convincing as one of Diana's shrugs.

Not really, I said, I'm too –

Too what?

I yawned.

Just too everything.

Alex yawned too and then he sighed in a happy way. He didn't look like someone who might die.

That's such a good expression, he said. Too everything.

I laughed.

Is it?

Yes, that's what I meant about you being funny. The things you say, they make no sense but, well – I understand them so perfectly.

I smiled. Was there anything he didn't like about me?

And I like how you always know things, he said.

I don't know things, I said, I don't know anything.

Part of me really thought this but another part of me was saying it just so he'd say something else nice. And it worked, he did.

Oh yes, he said, you do. You just don't realise it. Like you don't realise you're pretty. But you are. You're beautiful and pretty and clever. And you're brave. And good. And kind.

You're a good, kind, beautiful, brave and clever person, Flynn!

I laughed.

No I'm not, I told him, even though now I just wanted him to tell me more and more.

Don't argue, he said. I mean it. Just don't.

OK, I said.

And then, just as I guessed he would, he moved across the kitchen till he was very close, till there was only this thin slice of air left between us.

My heart felt like it was going to explode up out of my chest. Dog was watching, doing that thing he did where he moved his eyes without moving a muscle of his body. He sighed loudly then – the sigh that dogs do, a sigh that's like someone punching air out of a bag – and we both laughed.

He thinks we're boring, I whispered, but I only said it because I was feeling embarrassed.

Well he's completely wrong, Alex whispered back and he put a finger on my bare arm and it felt so good that my blood jumped. I stopped being embarrassed then. Part of me was happy and part of me was scared.

Are you going to kiss me? I asked him.

His eyes were blackest black. Suddenly they looked like someone else's eyes. Or maybe it was just that I'd never seen them properly and so close-up before.

I don't know, he said, and for once his face was even shyer than mine. Do you want me to?

I don't know, I said.

You never know anything.

You just said I did!

I know.

We both laughed again and he took a step back as if he was thinking something.

Oh, I said, because suddenly all I knew was I wanted him to stay near me, oh don't go.

Alex folded his arms and looked down at the floor.

I'll only kiss you if you answer my question, he said.

What question?

You know what question, he said.

I took a breath. The space between us felt painful. It hurt. This time I didn't feel at all embarrassed.

No, I said.

You won't?

No, I mean that's the answer. No.

No?

No. Never.

OK, he said smiling. OK. Thanks.

And before I could say anything else, he put his face right up close to mine. I felt his lips against my lips, hard and soft at the same time. I couldn't believe it. I didn't know whether to open my mouth or not. I tried not to breathe. It was amazing. I could feel his whole warm face touching mine and I liked it so much.

I couldn't believe it. It was something I thought would never happen. I was being kissed.

He took his face away and then he put it back again. Then he touched both my lips with his tongue and then the space in between as well and my mouth opened a bit, it couldn't help it, and I went hot and zingy all over. His tongue was in, slipping around and tasting me and I was tasting him back. I felt the feeling everywhere, in my arms and legs and right to the edges of my fingers and toes and my whole body.

I couldn't believe that just his tongue could make me feel like that.

I liked it so much that part of me wanted to look at him as well to see if he felt the same, but I didn't. Instead I shut my eyes and tried hard to concentrate on the kiss. It tasted of cold water and liquorice and maybe some other things as well. I'd never tasted anything so hard to take apart, so impossible to describe.

I was being kissed. It had happened. I knew what the inside of a boy's mouth tasted like. It was incredible. Nothing would ever be the same again.

It only took about four seconds. Wasn't it supposed to take longer? I was worried I wasn't doing it well enough. I opened my eyes for a second and then quickly shut them again. When he moved his face away at last so he could look at me, I felt like I'd lost something.

Is that it? I said.

No, he said, and he smiled and kept his eyes on me and touched my cheek with the soft inside of his hand.

No? I turned my head so I could put my lips against his warm fingers. It was like now I'd felt it once, I couldn't get enough of the feel of his skin, the up-close warmth of him.

No, he said again.

I waited.

You're so alive, he said.

Of course I'm alive, stupid, I replied. But I didn't mean stupid. What I really meant was, of course I'm alive and I'm just so happy that someone else can see it too.

I kissed his warm fingers and then my tongue came out and touched them. I couldn't help it. My tongue wanted to lick him all over the way a puppy dog licks.

But that's not it, he said again.

It's not?

No, he said, and he was still smiling as I licked his fingers. That's not it. There can be more if you like.

★   ★   ★

233

I did like. And I was about to put my arms up and pull him closer when the kitchen door banged and Mouse came storming in. Her hair was all wiggly from swimming and she looked blazing and fed-up and furious. I didn't think she'd seen what we were doing. I didn't think she'd seen anything. I thought she was still just busy being very cross about Diana finding the nits in her hair.

She says have you got the comb yet?

Who says? Alex looked dazed.

She. That horrible girl Diana. The one that keeps on trying to hurt my fucking head.

Mouse stared at us and waited.

Oh, I said, and I felt so strange, like parts of me were drifting around the kitchen. Oh no. We didn't forget. We were just about to look.

Alex took a step away from me. I felt him go.

Tell her we'll bring it out in a minute, I said to Mouse.

She says you've got to get it now.

Well tell her we can't, Alex said, and I felt him step closer again. Tell her she'll have to wait.

Mouse put her fingers in her mouth and looked scared.

She'll smack me, she said.

Of course she won't smack you, Alex said. Don't be silly. She's never smacked you in her life.

Someone else might smack me, then, Mouse said.

Who? I said.

I don't know. Just someone.

Did she tell you to say that to us? Alex said suddenly.

Mouse stared at him.

I just don't want to get smacked, she said in a small voice.

We didn't know what she was talking about. Suddenly I realised what was different about her. She was wearing pants.

Just pants and nothing else. They were pink with a little white bow at the top.

Where'd you get those? I asked her and she screwed up her face in a happy way.

I don't know, she said. Diana found them. Aren't they good? I've got some blue ones too. And matching socks.

Mouse stared at us for another moment and blinked. Then she blinked again.

I don't have any shoes though, she said, and she sighed.

Then she looked at the table. She saw the bread and butter that I'd just put down and she snatched it and crammed it in her mouth. Then, still chewing, she picked up a small metal frying pan and whacked it hard against the table leg with both hands.

Alex and I looked at each other.

What did you do that for, Mousie? he asked her.

She gave him a rude look as if it was obvious.

Because, she said loudly through the mouthful of bread, I wanted to kick something but I haven't got any shoes to do it with, have I?

Are you feeling very cross?

Yep.

Why?

Because Diana's cross that's why.

Why's she cross?

I don't know, she just is very cross. All the time. Cross cross cross.

Something occurred to me.

Is she cross with us? I asked Mouse.

Mouse shrugged. Her cheek was shiny with butter that had come off the bread. She put both her hands in her hair and scratched at her head.

Ouch, she said, and she scratched some more. Then she looked around again and spotted Dog.

Hey! she ran over and threw her arms around his neck. There you are! Alex, she said looking up from Dog, can a dog catch nits from a person?

I doubt it, Alex said. OK now off you go and find Diana.

But Mouse wasn't going. She kept on looking at us.

Have you got a biscuit? she said.

What, for Dog?

No for me.

Say please, said Alex.

Please, said Mouse.

I went in the cool pantry and found a tin I'd never seen before and opened it. Inside were thick round golden biscuits with sprinkles of sugar on them. I gave one to Mouse and she bit straight into it.

Say thank you, I said.

Thank you.

Now run back outside and tell Diana not to be cross and that we're just coming, OK? Alex told her.

OK, she said, and she tried to tug Dog down from the chair by his ears but he wasn't having it. He growled softly.

Leave him, I said. We'll bring him out when we come.

OK, said Mouse, and her eyes slid over to the table.

Can I have some of that? she said.

Some of what?

That cake.

What cake?

I saw that on the table was a blue-flowered china dish with a white doily and on it was a perfect pink-iced cake with a cherry on top and bright red jam squidging out of the sides. It looked almost funny, like a cake in a book.

I looked at Alex who was staring at it too.

236

Where did that come from?

I was just thinking I wanted a piece of cake, said Mouse, keeping her eyes on it. Now can I have some?

Just give her some, Alex said. I want her to go and leave us in peace.

I pulled a knife out of the drawer and cut her a slice.

Can I have the cherry? said Mouse. Her eyes kept flicking backwards and forwards from Alex to me and back again.

The cake was so light and fresh that when the knife went in it just bounced down and then up and no crumbs came off it.

When it's my birthday, said Mouse, I mean not yet but when it is, that's the sort of cake I'm having. With a cherry on it and everything.

And she held out her two hands for the slice and I tipped it off the knife, making sure she got the cherry too. She sat down cross-legged on the floor.

You can eat it outside, Alex told her.

OK, she said, and she got up carefully and turned to run back outside, but at the door she stopped.

By the way, she said. Guess what?

What? I said.

I can swim!

Seriously? said Alex.

Yep! I learned. Sam teached me and I can do it now. I'm really good.

That's great, I said. Well done.

Yes, well done, said Alex.

She looked at us both for one more moment and then she glanced down at the cake in her hands and then she went. We waited till we heard the back door slam before we put our faces back close together again.

★   ★   ★

We needed to go where we wouldn't be found. We decided to go to the room. We didn't know what we were going to do when we got there. We didn't know anything. All we knew was we needed to be squashed right up together for a while with nothing and no one to come between us.

In my head this was the only idea, the only thing I could think of, the possibility of lying my whole body down next to Alex's. I didn't worry about what Sam might think or whether Diana and Mouse might find us. I didn't think of anything except the idea of putting myself as close to him as possible, so close I could melt against him and stop being me and become something different that was made of the two of us.

He held my hand and I followed him up the long creaky stairs which seemed to lead everywhere now, in all directions, all over the house. There seemed to be doors and staircases everywhere, even more than before, exits and entrances, knobs and hinges. There were so many choices it made you dizzy.

On the first landing we stopped and looked around us and I tried to remember where we'd found the tiny staircase, Diana and Mouse and me, that first time which seemed like days or even weeks ago but was actually only this morning. Time in this house was stretchy. It came out in all different sizes depending on what you were doing and how and where and why and who with and how you felt about it.

Where are we? said Alex when I'd tried two or three doors and still not managed to find the twisty stairs. Are we lost or what?

He didn't seem too unhappy about it.

We're not lost, I told him even though I knew we were. We can't be lost. This house can't lose us.

I stopped for a moment to look around properly. It was

like the house was a puzzle I'd drawn and I used to know the answer but now I'd forgotten.

I don't get it, Alex said. I mean where did we come from? Which way leads back to the kitchen?

A strange kind of confidence bubbled up in me.

I don't know, I said. Does it matter?

No, he said.

My T-shirt was feeling all damp and uncomfortable on me just like Diana had said it would. There on a hook right in front of me was a soft brown jacket about my size with old worn leather patches on the elbows. I reached out for it.

Don't look, I said to Alex, and I pulled off my damp T-shirt and put on the jacket. Straightaway I felt warm all over. I hoped it didn't belong to the old man. I sniffed it. It smelled of the crackle of bonfires and winter nights.

Alex put his head on one side and looked at me. I pulled the jacket closed so he couldn't see my bra.

Do I look like a man? I asked him.

No, he said. You look nice. You look just like yourself.

I smiled. What he didn't understand was how I didn't feel like myself at all, how much I liked the feeling he gave me of being someone else. I thought how amazing it felt when you knew someone liked you. I wondered if I even did perhaps look a little bit beautiful now that I'd been kissed?

As if the house knew what I was thinking, suddenly on the landing wall opposite I saw there was a mirror – a slightly cloudy old one, but all the same. Without letting Alex see, I glanced into it. The girl in the mirror had straggly brown hair and a brown jacket like me, but her eyes shone right out of her face in a way I'd never seen mine shine.

Isn't there a room where we can just lie down? said Alex, and the impatient and longing way he said it made my heart go hot.

On the landing in front of us there was a wooden chest made of pine with some clean sheets neatly folded on it. They looked so fresh, like they'd just been put there ready to make someone's bed with. I rested the back of my hand on them. They were still warm and smelled of hot ironing, as if someone had only just that second smoothed them over. Like everything else, it wasn't really possible but that was how it felt.

Alex was holding my hand. It felt wonderful.

I don't think I've been on this landing before, I told Alex. It's not where I was with Diana and Mouse. Do you think we're on the other side of the house?

I don't know where we are, he replied and he let go of my hand and stroked and ruffled my hair till I got goose pimples all over. I've lost all sense of direction. I've lost all sense of everything.

We must have gone wrong, I said with a sigh.

Alex and me were lost in the house. We'd gone wrong, that much was definite. We didn't know where we were going or what we were doing.

But part of me could feel it telling us where to go, squeezing us along its passages and corridors and up and down its stairs. In a way, I suppose I trusted the house. But I don't think Alex did because suddenly he stopped and put his arms around me. My nose touched his shoulder.

What? I said.

Flynn, he said, and his fingers were in my hair again. Seriously, where are we?

I don't know, I told him.

I looked up at his lovely face and he touched my head. The feeling made my stomach go soft.

Well please, he said, and there was something like pain in

his voice, just hurry. This is taking too long. I don't care if we go to the room or not. Any room will do. I just want to be somewhere with you.

Somewhere?

Oh, Flynn, just anywhere.

I looked at his face, the face I liked so much. He looked pale and exhausted now. I looked at his mouth.

I want to be somewhere or anywhere too, I said.

I said it even though I didn't know where somewhere was. So many different places had opened up inside me in the last half hour, I didn't know what to think. Was that what love was, just all these endless confusing possibilities coming at you so fast you couldn't get your breath?

On the second landing we came to, which looked even less familiar than the first, there was a bunch of mauve sweet peas in a jam jar and a book of drawings of dragonflies with little arrows showing you what all the different parts of the body and wings were called. How did the house know? This was something I'd been wondering about ever since we'd seen the first one darting around over the pool. Also – surprise surprise – a nit comb. An actual one with a rim and teeth just like the one we used to have at home.

Actually I wasn't surprised, not at all. I held it up to Alex and he laughed and so did I and I put it in the pocket of the jacket.

Then suddenly there it was, the door in the wall that looked more or less like a cupboard door but which I knew wasn't a cupboard at all. I knew it led to the twisty stairs.

This is it, I told Alex and I opened it and sure enough there they were waiting for us – steep and secret and dark. I tasted the musky oily smell in my nose and mouth.

241

I closed the door again quickly before he could smell it. Flynn?

Alex put a hand on me somewhere. I didn't know where.

Come on, he said, and he opened the door and looked in, what's the matter? It's just a staircase.

I tried hard not to be childish. Even though I was shaking and trembling all over. I took a step up the stairs and then another and another and with Alex behind me I began to climb. But halfway up it was no good, I stopped. I sat down. The room was somewhere above me, Alex was somewhere below. Everything was tipping and going slightly off balance and making me want to lie down or hold on or something.

What? said Alex. He sat down on the step below mine.

There's something bad about the room, I told him.

What? What sort of bad?

I waited. Traces of musk filtered down the stairs.

Can't you smell it? I said.

Smell what?

Can't you smell the weird smell?

He looked at me.

I can't smell anything. What smell?

I hesitated and suddenly as if he understood his eyes grew dark.

Is it patchouli? he whispered.

I looked up at the stairs.

I don't know, I said truthfully. I've never smelled patchouli. I don't know what it smells like.

He sniffed and then he bit his lip.

I can't smell anything, he decided.

I looked at him.

I can't go in there. I can't go into that room.

I said it in a whisper because I didn't want the house to

hear me even though that was stupid because of course the
house could hear everything because the house was me.

Having this thought made me jump out of my skin.

Please don't make me, I said.

Hey, said Alex, I'm not going to make you do anything.
But seriously though. What are you so scared of?

I said nothing. I couldn't speak.

Flynn?

He touched my bare leg with his fingers and then he put
his lips on my knee – my dirty scarred knee – and kissed it.

Don't, I said.

What now? Don't what?

Just – it's not nice.

What, you don't like having your knee kissed?

No, I said, thinking of Diana's long legs stretched out in
the sunny grass. My knee. My knee isn't nice.

He laughed and kissed it again.

It's horrible. It's like a boy's knee, I said.

He laughed again and kissed it once more.

I mean it, I said.

Nothing about you is like a boy, Flynn, he said. So will
you stop saying it?

And he looked at me in a serious way and stroked his two
hands over my bare legs till I forgot we were sitting on those
stairs and I got the same turning-over-and-over feeling I got
when he put his mouth on mine. Suddenly he looked sad.

I wish you were a bit older, he said.

Do you? I said, dismayed. Why?

Well, thirteen's just so young.

No it's not, I said so quickly that I sounded a bit like
Mouse, and anyway you're only fifteen.

Nearly sixteen and that's a big difference.

No it's not.

It is.

It's not.

When will you be fourteen? he asked me.

I thought about this. I'd forgotten all about things like birthdays.

November, I said. Suddenly I thought of home and I saw Anna's face, her two small bottom teeth, her wispy baby hair. My heart went tight.

Hmm, he said, quite soon.

It didn't seem soon to me. It seemed a hundred years away. Autumn, school, cold air, real life. It wasn't possible. November would never come, I was certain of that.

I'll get you a present, he said in a happier voice and his finger traced a pattern on my knee.

I stared at him.

Will you? I said.

I couldn't take this in. It wasn't so much the idea of him getting me a present as – how would we get out of here? Why would we?

Of course I will. Why wouldn't I?

I had no answer to this. It all sounded so easy when he said it.

Thank you, I said.

Don't thank me yet, he said. You can thank me when you've got it.

OK, I said and I hesitated.

What? he said.

I hope I still know you then, I told him and I meant it. I meant it so much the idea made me want to cry.

He smiled and put his lips back on my knee. Warmth raced through me. My nose stung with tears.

Oh Flynn, he said.

What?

Just that. Just you. I like you. I like how stupidly crazily doubtful you are about everything.

We sat there a few more minutes. With the door still shut above us, we were half in darkness. It was like we'd forgotten that we were even supposed to be going up the stairs.

The thing is, I said as carefully as I could, I've been in the room before.

You mean this morning?

No I mean before. Before today, before – all of this.

He thought about this. I was grateful that he didn't laugh at me.

Why? How?

I glanced up into the darkness and caught a glint of the metal door knob. How could I explain it?

You know how you just know things sometimes? I said.

He nodded.

Well I just know it.

Or you think you know it, Alex pointed out.

I know I know it, I said.

We were silent for a moment. I shivered, even though I had the jacket on. Alex put his hands on my arms. He pushed his fingers right up inside my sleeves.

The room wants me in it, I told him at last. And I don't know why.

Well – Alex's fingers stroked my bare arms – in that case we just won't do it. We won't go in there.

No, I said as I felt the house get ready to laugh because it was hardly that simple. No, Alex, you don't understand – it's more than that. It's the whole house. I've been in the house before.

I took his hands off me and held them tight, not for kissing this time but for safety in the shadows. Because it was only just now sitting here on the dark stairs with Alex that I was thinking clearly enough to say what I knew. What I'd always known.

I know this house, I said, I know it so well.

The facts were arranging themselves around me. And I didn't like what I was working out.

It's me, I said at last.

Alex was looking hard at my face.

What do you mean, Flynn? What do you mean it's you?

That thing you said earlier – I mean about everything being here for us and the bread being fresh and all that?

What about it?

Well – it's me. Don't you see? I do that.

Alex was staring at me now with a look on his face like he had no idea what I was saying, like he almost didn't want to know.

I can't explain it, I said, but it's coming from me. I know it is. Everything that happens here, it's me, I make it happen.

Alex tried to smile.

No, I said, listen. It sounds mad and I don't understand it either but – well, every single thing that happens here happens just a few seconds or minutes or hours after I think of it.

Oh Flynn, Alex said.

I'm not crazy, I said quickly.

I'm not saying you are crazy, it's just –

Just what?

Just – I don't know, he said.

He didn't know. He didn't know so I put my head down, I put my face on his hand and breathed in the safe smell. Dragonflies were zooming round and round in my head, not letting me think in a straight line. I tried to put my thoughts in single file but they wouldn't go. What could I do? How was I going to make him believe me?

When I ran away, I told him, well I always had this place in mind, to go to, you know?

Alex nodded. I knew he hadn't understood.

No, I said, I mean it was this place.

This place?

He stared at me.

I mean I made up a place in my head, I told him. I could see it so clearly. A safe and perfect ideal place where I could really really –

Disappear, said Alex, and his warm hand moved under mine. I squeezed the hand.

And do you know what it was like, the place I dreamed up?

I'm beginning to guess, Alex said.

It was a little tumbledown house with a grey roof and hollyhocks round the door. It had a pool and a waterfall and chickens. And inside there was everything you could possibly want – food in the pantry and nice clothes to wear and pretty things with flowers on them –

This house, Alex said, and it wasn't a question.

This house, I said. It swallows me up. It lets me go. It takes me away. It loses me.

Loses you?

I nodded.

It lets me disappear.

Alex looked at me. I wasn't sure if he believed me.

But you're not disappearing now.

I stared at his dark, dark eyes.

That's because it's different now.

Why?

Because you're here, I said.

And that's the only reason?

I don't know. I've never been here with – others. I think – I'm realising now – I've only ever been here alone.

247

I shivered.

It's all in my head, I told him – and just saying those words frightened me. What if it was?

Alex said nothing.

In real life, I said, because he still wasn't getting it, this house doesn't exist.

He was silent a moment, thinking. His voice came from far away.

So where are we now, Flynn?

I shut my eyes. I hoped he would touch me. I kept my eyes tight shut and I really hoped he would.

We're not anywhere, I said.

Or somewhere?

I don't know, I said as I gave in and reached out for him. Yes. I suppose we're somewhere else.

Minutes passed. We were still on the stairs. I was in Alex's arms or maybe I wasn't. I felt like another person, not Flynn at all. I didn't know if we'd been sleeping or what. I didn't know what we'd been doing or how much I'd told him or anything.

I'm so thirsty, Alex said. Kissing you makes me so thirsty.

On the stairs was a bottle of something fizzy. I took the top off and handed it to him. He took a swig and stared at me.

Where did this come from?

I can get us anything we need, I told him. Haven't you realised that yet?

What do you mean? Get what?

I looked at him. I couldn't believe he could be so slow.

This jacket for instance, I said. Because my T-shirt was still wet and I was cold. And your shirt, your lovely blue shirt –

It's a really good shirt, Alex said.

It suits you, I told him.

Yes, he said, I really like it, it's —

But his voice trailed off and his eyes changed. I smiled.
He was getting it now.

Mouse's pants, he said slowly. She needed pants.

Two pairs, I said. One pink, one blue. And matching socks.
And nappies for Joey.

Even the nit comb?

I nodded.

And the wine stuff, and all Sam's cigarettes, and a biscuit
when Dog wanted one.

And just now, he said, Mouse's perfect cake? With the
cherry on top?

I nodded.

The exact cake she wants for her —

Next birthday!

Alex breathed out a big sigh.

Even the book about dragonflies, I told him. Think
about it. I'd been wondering about dragonflies, you see. I
don't think I even said it out loud. All I did was have the
thought. I just had to wonder and — do you believe me
now, Alex?

He said nothing. You could see he was thinking. He
knelt up there on the step and looked at me and his eyes
were dark with thinking. Suddenly he thought of something else.

But, Flynn, he said, the old man —

Quickly I shut my eyes.

Please, Alex, I said, I don't know anything about that. I
don't know who he was or what happened to him, seriously I don't.

You said what if it was us who'd killed him.

249

I stared at him. The words made my bones feel numb and cold.

Did I say that? I didn't say that.

It wasn't us?

I looked at him and said nothing.

Please, Flynn, he said. Please just tell me it wasn't us.

I don't know, I said, and all of a sudden a wave of pure misery went over me. I really don't know.

It was the truth. I had no idea about the man.

Suddenly there was pain on Alex's face. A different pain. He seemed to go away from me, back into himself.

What is it? I said.

It's nothing.

You don't feel well, do you?

I'm OK.

He steadied himself against the stair. I took the bottle from him and had some of the drink. It tasted brown like cola, and a bit flat.

You're not going to die, I told him. You're not. I'm not letting you.

He took the bottle back off me and swigged and put it back down on the step.

It might not be up to you, he whispered as he put his mouth back on mine. It tasted of cola.

But don't you see? I tried to say between the kisses. It is. It is. Everything's up to me.

What? Don't tell me. Am I real? Or did you dream me up too?

I tried to answer but he wasn't letting me. He was doing something to the inside of me now, something that made me feel I was going up higher and higher like on a swing. Suddenly I was scared.

Don't touch me there, I said, and I gasped.

OK, he said. Sorry.

Oh but please don't take your hand away, I whispered.

Two or three or maybe five seconds later, he seemed to think of something.

But Flynn?

Mmm? I breathed because it was hard to talk when he was doing what he was doing.

But I've just thought – don't you remember? Something important. It was me, not you.

Mmm?

I sighed and pulled him closer.

I mean I found this place, he whispered. Not you. It was me. I showed it to you, not the other way round, remember?

I did remember. Of course I did. I remembered the sheer pouring golden brightness of that first amazing morning, such a shock after the dark of the night before. I remembered it all and somewhere in the liquid middle of my new body I smiled.

You did, I said softly. Mmm, you did.

I woke you up and –

I touched his lips with mine to shut him up.

Yeah, I whispered, you woke me up and it was lovely. The most lovely surprise.

The memory of that morning uncoiled like a rope. Faster and faster. I saw Alex and me standing looking at the waterfall for the first time. Hot pleasure on my face.

I was so glad it was me, I told him now.

That what was you?

That it was me you woke.

Of course it was you. Who else would it be?

Well – I was waiting to see if you'd choose Diana.

Alex looked confused. He stopped what he was doing and looked at me.

You were awake already?

I wondered about this. I wasn't sure of the answer.

No, I told him, I was asleep. In my sleep I was waiting to see.

Alex frowned.

But I chose you. It was easy to choose you. I would never have chosen anyone else.

Inside my body I smiled again.

Exactly, I said. Easy.

But – so who actually found this house? he said. You or me?

I don't know. Maybe whoever woke first. Does it matter?

I don't know.

He paused.

I still don't get it, he said after a moment or two.

What don't you get?

I don't get anything about this.

There's nothing really to get, I told him and as I said it, I realised it was almost true.

The house folded itself around us. Slowly, carefully. It told us what it wanted us to do. Even though we tried not to listen, still it told us.

There were the weirdest noises going on around us. Far above us, I don't know where, there was a little sighing, cracking sound, like glass. It might have been an old window-pane which had finally decided to break. Why not? Everything has to go sometime. Or a roof tile might have been loose for ages and then had finally let go, slipped and fallen. Water might have rushed through the pipes, there might have been a leak somewhere, drip drip, undiscovered in the darkness. The stairs might have creaked a warning, but that was all. No other sound broke the silence.

I wondered if what we were doing was love. Making love. What does love sound like when you make it? And can you make it out of nowhere, can you just magic it up? And if you can then does that mean it must have existed somewhere inside you already before?

Alex didn't get it, I didn't get it, but did it matter? It wasn't that we didn't have the answers, it was more we didn't even know what the questions were.

Outside, even though the sky was warm and thundery, soon it would be autumn. When you're hot you can't imagine cold, you think that summer will go on for ever but we knew that very soon there would be a band of mist around the trees in the morning and the tall grass would be threaded with cuckoo spit and spiders' webs.

Everything was on the edge, smoky and sad, blue and hazy one moment, black the next. In some ways it seemed so simple and easy. When you're with someone you like or maybe even love, you can't imagine not being with them. You can't imagine anything else ever being worthwhile. You can't imagine the rest of life without that person.

I love you, I think I heard him say, and I love you too, I think I said back to him.

We hadn't known it was happening, we hadn't even bothered to know, but all the time that I'd been busy talking, trying to explain stuff, Alex had wrapped himself harder and harder around me till we were close up and tight together on those stairs like one single person, right inside each other's skin, our hearts slowed to the exact same beat, our bodies only moving for each other, with each other, when the other one moved.

I couldn't breathe. I didn't want to breathe. Why would

I want to? I didn't want it to stop. I couldn't stop. Everything had come undone but at least I knew something at last about the world. The taste of the room upstairs was in my mouth and nose but it didn't matter any more. It probably wasn't patchouli after all, it probably wasn't anything. I was safe. We were safe. We were somewhere else entirely.

Is this what love is? I might have heard myself ask the person who was Alex and very very far away on almost another horizon I might have felt that person explode.

But, I said, fifteen minutes or maybe eight hours later, do you know the real reason I don't want to go into that room?

I felt Alex shake his head. I held onto him tightly now, I wasn't letting go. There were tears on my face or maybe they were off his. I didn't care. I wiped them away on my sleeve.

Mmm? he said.

It's because of what I know I'll see. Out of the window.

He pulled his face back to look at me and I saw that they were his tears, not mine. He smoothed his hand over my hair. He said nothing.

I saw you there down by the pool, I told him. Before. This morning. Whenever it was. I saw you. Just before I fainted.

He kept on looking at me. I licked my lips, tasted salt.

Are you sure it was me?

Very sure.

Why? What was I doing?

You were just staring and staring at the water. It was terrible.

Why would that be terrible?

I don't know. You knew something no one else knew. An unbearable awful terrible thing.

He said nothing. He didn't ask what he knew. He knew what it was. He'd known all along, hadn't he, and then he'd told me and now I knew too.

But you don't understand, I told him. It's about the room. What I'm saying is I didn't even need to look. I knew I was going to see you and I did. And then Diana looked out of the window and she saw nothing. She didn't even see the pool down there.

But –

Alex stared at me then because a thought had come onto my face, a bad thought, one I could not stop. Now, even though I was in his arms, I was also in the room. Without meaning to, I'd gone there anyway. And now here I was –

Really? I drew a quick breath. Because how had I got here? How come I hadn't even needed to walk up the stairs and go right in to see it all – the brown shiny walls like old parcels, the bare dusty boards, the air that smelled of a musky oily substance, an odour that made my flesh take notice. And the little high-up window that looked down onto the pool when I was watching and didn't when I wasn't.

I wasn't even there but already I knew. If I looked out of the window now, what would I see?

Oh!

I knew the answer and I sucked in my breath.

The room was alive. It was shaking and banging like it wanted us to fall right out of it. Even though we weren't in it, it was shaking and shaking and we were falling right down into its single dark eye.

Mouse! I shouted because I didn't even need to see to know.

I gasped.

Mouse is in the water – !

And I let go of Alex and I jumped up and belted up the

rest of the stairs. I put my hand on the metal knob and yanked it so hard that it could not refuse me and in two quick steps there I was at the window in that shaky room with him behind me. But I already knew. I already knew what I'd see.

Mouse was a pale shape floating in the water.

The pale shape of Mouse. She was floating, her face was under, her legs were sticking out. Dog was standing on the bank watching like he didn't know what else to do.

Diana was screaming. Screaming and screaming.

After she'd had her cake and let her hair be looked at Mouse had crept back out of the house alone in her pants and gone in the water to show Dog that she could really swim.

She'd shown everyone else but she hadn't shown Dog. She was worried Dog wouldn't believe her. She'd said she was going to do this and Diana had told her not to, that she wasn't allowed. But she hadn't listened. She'd disobeyed and done it anyway. Diana had just turned her back for about three seconds, that was all. Mouse had sneaked off, just to be naughty. She'd been naughty on and off all day. Dog had followed.

She wasn't gone for long, just long enough. Just long enough to step in, laughing to herself, and walk a little further and strike out the way Sam had showed her and then a little more and then to put out a foot that went down suddenly and – what? – didn't touch the bottom. She'd been alone just long enough to put the other foot down and find that it didn't touch either and then breathe in a shocked breath of water, nose stinging, getting out of her depth and going down and coming up again and struggling and kicking and breathing in just enough water to make her go still.

256

Diana was screaming the words out – screaming and screaming them as if she would never stop. Her face was red and she was gulping and gulping she was crying so much and there was wet coming out of her nose as well. Joey was lying on the ground on his back and all uncovered and screaming too.

Dog looked at all the noise around him and took a couple of steps back and began to bark. It was so low and deep it made the air shake. It was the first time we'd ever heard him bark. Once he'd started it sounded like he'd never stop.

Sam was quick. He reached the water just before Alex and Diana and me and he dived straight in and hauled the little body of Mouse out. Water was falling off him and off her. His mouth was open. The air crackled around us. The air was black.

He carried Mouse dripping in his arms and it looked like she'd been folded in two. She was so small, she was tiny. Stick arms and legs. Wiggly hair. Her bottom hung down. She still had her pink pants on, dripping wet now.

Sam knew what to do. He'd done a life-saving course at school. He'd passed and got a badge. Even though our mum thought he was good for nothing, she was wrong, he was good for something. For trying to save the life of Mouse for instance.

A zigzag of lightning went across the sky. Drops of rain were starting. Big fat ones, one or two, then nothing for a few seconds. Thunder rattled the air.

Dog ran indoors.

Sam put Mouse down flat on her back on the grass and started blowing in her mouth and pushing on her chest. Blow then push, blow then push. We all stood back. The pushes were so hard they looked like they might hurt her thin little chest. I was trembling. My whole body had gone

257

shaky and scared. I think that Alex was trembling too. Even though we knew it was stupid, we all stared at Mouse as if staring could actually do something.

Her eyes were half open half closed and her hair was like black snakes in the grass. Her mouth was a blueish colour. Every time Sam took his lips away you could see that the colour of hers wasn't at all normal.

Diana was crying now. Just great gusty sobs instead of actual screams. She'd slowed right down and she'd run out of words. She was kneeling on the ground and sobbing. What had happened had happened. Words weren't going to do anything any more, we all knew that.

I wasn't crying because what was the use? I just felt frozen all over. I stared at the body of Mouse on the ground. The rain was coming down hard now but no one noticed it. No one could have cared less about things like weather or how cold or uncomfortable they were.

Let her be OK, said a quiet steady voice in my head. Let her, oh let her, oh let her.

Please, please oh please, Diana said.

Please, Mouse, I said aloud, please. We love you.

I said it because it was the only thing to say and also because it was true. Wasn't Mouse the one who thought things could come back to life if you just cared enough?

Sam stopped blowing and pumping and sat back on his heels. There were tears on his face or was it rain and he wiped them with the cuff of his sleeve. I'd never seen him look so terrible, so hopeless, like everything good had been dragged out of him. He looked like someone else, not my brother any more, not the one I'd gone over the fields with, but someone else.

He put his hands back on Mouse's small tummy and he looked in her face and I thought for a moment he might give up. But then there was a spluttery coughing sound and we saw it was coming out of Mouse.

Diana gasped. I gasped.

Quickly, Sam turned her over so she was on her side. A whole lot of water spilled out of her. More water than you'd think could be in such a small person. And as the water spilled out, Mouse started coughing and choking and then struggling and moaning in her usual way and we were all half crying and half laughing because we were all just so glad to hear that annoying sound again.

Mouse was alive. It was a miracle. Sam had saved her. Sam was the hero. I kept having to realise all over again that he was my brother.

Mouse was white in the face and still moaning and crying and complaining that she hurt all over, but at least she wasn't dead. Diana took the blue blanket of Anna's that Joey had been lying on and we put it round her, wrapped her like a baby. Mouse stopped crying and let us do it. She just did nothing and kept on sitting there all hunched up and sucking her thumb like she might die if she stopped.

Did Dog save me? she whispered through a mouthful of thumb.

No, we said. No, it was Sam. Sam did.

She kept her thumb in her mouth and fixed her eyes on Sam.

Please don't go, she said to him but in a very quiet, polite, un-Mouse-like voice.

Sam touched her wet head.

I'm not going anywhere, he said. I thought how old and exhausted he looked, as old as a man really.

I feel sick, said Mouse.

It's just the water, said Diana.

You've got to keep very warm, Sam said to her and you could tell that he didn't mind at all being the one to look after her.

Mouse's eyes were wide and fixed on him.

OK, she said, what else?

Sam touched her head.

Nothing else. That's enough for now. Just keep warm, OK?

OK, she whispered.

It was strange to have her be so quiet and agreeing with everything we said. Diana kissed her, I kissed her and she let us do it. She said her stomach hurt, but she said it in a small timid voice and kept on listening and nodding and doing everything she was told.

We should drown her more often, Sam muttered, but everyone knew he was only joking.

The rain was really starting to pour down heavily now so we all hurried into the house. Sam carried Mouse who giggled as he ran with her. He said she must have got fatter because she weighed a ton. She said he was the fat one. He told her to shut up. She said she was hungry.

You can't be hungry so soon after drowning, Diana said as we all shook the rain off us in the hall, but Mouse insisted that she was and then we all agreed — we were all hungry. We needed food.

Supper, said Alex, and he looked at me. A proper sitting-down supper.

A dinner, agreed Diana.

Not supper, dinner! shouted Mouse who was beginning to get loud again.

And maybe some of the wine stuff, Sam said.

Yeah, I said. Wine stuff.

But is there any left? Diana said.

I'll find some, I said, because part of me felt like having the wine feeling again only maybe with Alex's arms around me this time.

Do you think my nits drowned? asked Mouse who was scratching at her head and looking at her fingers.

I doubt it, Diana said.

Because they can swim or because they can hold their breaths? said Mouse.

Probably both, said Sam, and I could see he was thinking what we were all thinking – that it was just so good to be back with all of Mouse's stupid old questions.

We went in the room with the brown velvet sofa, the room where we'd lain around and had the wine stuff before. The room which once long ago had contained the old man.

The house smelled dark as old velvet with an underlying scent of musk which we all either didn't notice or ignored. Thunder and lightning lit up the room. Sam tried turning on the lights, flick flick flick, but they wouldn't come on.

That's weird, said Diana. Why won't they come on?

He shrugged.

Maybe the power's down, he said.

Because of the storm, Alex said, and he lit a candle. We all agreed that candles were nicer anyway. There were at least five candles so that was OK. They made the walls of the room look like underwater and they made all our faces look mysterious and wild and beautiful. It reminded me of that first night in Alex's shed.

Diana didn't seem very cross any more. She hardly looked at Alex and me. She just seemed tired. It was like the thing of Mouse nearly dying had got things into proportion. What was there to be cross about? We were all alive, weren't we?

She yawned and lay back with Joey on the old sofa next to Mouse who was still pale and slow and sucking her thumb and thinking about whether nits could swim or not. Dog had somehow found his way to her feet where he was curled up and of course Mouse loved that. She used her other hand that wasn't in her mouth to tug quite hard on his big soft ear.

Are you sure he likes that? said Alex, and she looked at him and blinked and as her thumb came out of her mouth so did a glittery string of spit.

Yeah, she said, I'm sure.

And she coughed and put the thumb back in and Dog sighed. We all sighed. It had been the longest day ever. Burying the old man seemed a million years ago. We needed to get comfortable now and relax and eat and shake off some of the bad things.

The trouble started when Alex went into the kitchen to get a drink of milk for Mouse who couldn't stop coughing.

And some water for me, Diana called from her comfy lazy place on the sofa where she was getting ready to undo her shirt and feed Joey.

Maybe a chunk of bread too? said Sam, who was famous for never being able to wait for supper.

In that case some of the green jam, laughed Diana. The one that's made of plums.

Greengage? I said, because the first time I'd ever heard that word was in this house.

Yeah, greengage. And butter.

Me too! shouted Mouse, I want that too!

Hold on a sec, Alex said. Is supper going to be just bread and jam or something bigger?

I want some wine stuff, I told him.

I want cake, said Mouse.

Just see what's there, Diana told him. Whatever's there is what we'll have.

The mood was happy. Because Mouse was alive mainly. Everyone was having fun ordering Alex around and he didn't mind. But when he came back into the room a second later he looked pale and shocked.

It's all gone, he said.

What? said Sam, who was feeling down the back of the sofa in case there were cigarettes.

Everything. It's just gone, Alex said.

We all stared at him and as we stared there was a loud clap outside and a flash of lightning lit up the room. For a second or two we thought he was joking. But he wasn't. You could tell from his blank, upset face that he was serious. I got to my feet.

What do you mean gone?

Alex turned to me. There were deep shadows under his eyes as if he'd never slept in his whole life. I wondered how I'd managed not to notice how bad he was looking.

I'm serious. There's nothing. No bread, no food, nothing. Even the water. I turned on the tap just now and nothing came out.

I stared at him.

What about in the pantry? I said, but somewhere inside me I already knew the answer.

Diana looked scared.

It can't all have gone, she said. I mean, earlier – there was so much there.

No one could possibly have taken all that stuff, said Sam.

Mouse began to cry.

Shush, Diana told her.

But Alex was staring around him and looking panicky.

No, you don't understand, he said. It's worse than that. Come and see.

There was a moment's silence. All we could hear was the rain pouring on the roof.

What d'you mean? said Sam.

Just come and look. I tell you, there's nothing, not a single thing anywhere. It's like – something's happened to the room or something.

We all ran to the kitchen, even Mouse, even Dog.

Alex was right. It wasn't just that everything had gone, it was worse. There wasn't a hunk of bread or a pat of butter or a lump of cheese anywhere. All the brightly coloured jars of jam had gone, so had the tins crammed with sugar biscuits and fruit cake and the big brown jug that always seemed to contain the creamiest freshest milk.

All gone. But it was worse.

The kitchen was dusty and sad and tired. There were some dead flies. There were spiders who had made their webs between the shelves. Thick webs that had to have been there for weeks or months. There were a few old containers with nothing in them. Rice said one of them, Sago said another. But they were old, some of them were rusty. You could see they hadn't contained proper food for many years.

Even the smell was different – a smell of old coats and dirty cupboards. There was a patch of damp on the wall that went almost up to the ceiling and the sink had a rusty stain in it like water hadn't been run there in ages.

In the corner by the stove, water was drip-dripping from the ceiling. There must have been a leak somewhere in the roof.

We all stood and stared.

It looked like a kitchen from a very long time ago, an old place that had not seen a meal or a crumb of food in months or maybe even years.

It looked just like what it was – a kitchen where a very old man had lived all alone with his dog and existed on not very much of anything and then sat down and died in his chair one day with nobody around to care about him.

We were silent. No one said a thing, not even Mouse. Even she seemed to realise that this situation was too strange and serious for either tears or words.

Slowly we walked back into the other room and sat around staring at the candles and at each other's worried faces. What to do now? It wasn't how it was supposed to be, but here we all were in a house with no food and no electricity and a full-scale storm raging outside and that was that.

The rain was pouring down loudly now, slapping the roof and guttering, hitting the hard dry ground all around the house. Sharp rods of rain would be piercing the smooth surface of the pool, the waterfall sound would be almost drowned out by it. All the flowers and plants would be bashed and flattened, all the birds and animals hiding wherever it was they all hid when really hard rain came.

It was hard to believe the house had ever been full of sunshine and pretty things and tasty food.

Every few minutes the room lit up with a blue light and then the thunder crashed. Flash, crash. Dog didn't like it. He had made himself very flat so he could wedge his whole body under the sofa. Only his tail stuck out.

Mouse began to cry again.

Don't, Diana snapped rather harshly. Just don't.

Come here, said Sam and he held out his arms but Mouse didn't move, she just sat there with her lip wobbling.

Diana sucked in her breath and took off her glasses and began to feed Joey even though she didn't have a glass of water by her. She ignored Mouse. She just got on with feeding the baby as if it was the only thing in life that she needed to do. Her lips were pressed tight together as though she'd had enough of talking.

Come on, Sam said again and slowly Mouse got up and climbed onto his lap. She made a point of not looking at Diana.

Are we going to die? she said softly to Sam.

Don't be silly, said Alex.

No one's going to die, said Sam, and he pulled the blue blanket up around Mouse.

I already nearly died, said Mouse.

That's right, said Sam. And that's why you're not going to die now.

Mouse snuggled under the blanket and she shut her eyes and then she opened them again. But she seemed satisfied with the answer.

I pressed myself against Alex. I sat on the floor as near to him as I could. I didn't care if anyone noticed. If I could have got right inside him I would have. It would have been a whole new way of disappearing.

I wondered what he was thinking. Even though his body was close, it was like his head and his mind were as far away from me as they had ever been.

He clasped his knees with his arms and I looked down at his thin white wrists coming out of his blue shirt cuffs and thought how even his bones seemed beautiful to me. You could see the blueish veins through the skin on his hands. You could see everything. I thought how I'd never realised how fragile and different and daring boys were. You could look right into them and lose yourself. Girls were these blunt things next to them, blunt and dangerous and small.

Are you OK? he asked me.

I nodded. Are you?

He said nothing. He shut his eyes.

Mouse sat on Sam's lap and listened to the sound of Joey sucking and gulping and she rolled her eyes and glared at him. It was a bit pathetic. Only Mouse would be jealous of a tiny baby, I thought. She scratched at her hair again and I remembered something.

We found a comb! I told Diana, even though as I spoke the words aloud I realised they weren't all that important now. All the same, I put my hand in my pocket. I felt around in both pockets. There was nothing. The comb was gone.

Good, said Mouse. Good bloody good.

We all sat in silence. A big empty silence. For once there really was nothing to say.

Sam sighed.

I'm fucking starving, he said.

So am I fucking starving, said Mouse.

How many days since we had something to eat? Diana asked then and no one could remember. Alex and I thought we'd all eaten something earlier that day, we just couldn't remember what.

We had bread, Alex reminded me. In the kitchen.

It was true. I remembered Alex eating bread and butter. I remembered Mouse taking my piece.

You had a biscuit, I told her, from the tin, remember? And then you had a piece of cake. With the cherry on top?

She looked at me like she didn't know what I was talking about.

No I didn't, she said. What tin? What cake? What cherry?

But you must remember? I told her. The lovely cake with the jam squishing out? Like you want for your next birthday?

She gave me a horrified look and put her hands over her ears.

Don't, she said. Don't make up stupid things. Stop it, you're scaring me!

Sam and Diana and Mouse insisted we'd been in the house for days without food. They sounded like they believed it too.

But we only got here yesterday, I pointed out.

Sam gave me a strange look.

Flynn. We've been here almost a week.

My stomach clenched. For once he didn't look like he was making it up.

No, we haven't, Alex said, and then he too suddenly looked confused.

We've had more than one night, said Diana slowly. There've been loads of nights.

I don't like the nights, said Mouse. That's when the man might come.

What night did we have the wine stuff? I said. Wasn't it last night?

I thought of me feeding Mouse like a zoo animal in the kitchen and suddenly it did seem a very long time ago. Just the memory of all that milk and cheese and cake made my stomach growl.

What does it matter? said Diana. If we don't get some food soon I'll have no milk left. Look at him. He's sucking and sucking and he's hardly getting anything.

We hadn't noticed but now she said it, it was obvious. Joey kept on squirming and crying.

Will he die? asked Mouse almost hopefully. Like I nearly died?

This time no one answered. No one really knew what to say. Just as I was thinking this, I felt Alex staring at me in a horrified way.

What? I said and my face went hot.

Flynn, your jacket – what's happened to it?

I looked down and everyone else turned to look as well. The whole of my jacket, all the brown stuff of it, the leather elbows, all of it, was in rags and tatters. Not only that but it looked grimy and sad, as though someone had gone and chewed it up and spat it out.

It was disgusting. I realised it smelled disgusting too. I pulled it off me. I yanked it off. I couldn't get it off fast enough.

But at that same moment my eyes fell on Alex's shirt. I'd just been gazing at his lovely wrists so why hadn't I seen? I wondered how long it would have taken me to notice that instead of the blueness and softness, there was nothing there now but wetness and grease? It was like an old rag you'd use to clean the floor with.

Alex was pulling his shirt off as I flung my jacket on the floor. The others were staring at us. Suddenly I thought of something.

Mouse, I said, your pants –

She blinked at me from Sam's lap.

I pulled the blanket off her to see but underneath it, just as I thought, she was completely bare, she had nothing on. She kept her thumb in her mouth and looked down at herself but she didn't look very surprised.

Oops, she said, I haven't got any on.

She grabbed hold of the blanket.

The blanket's OK, said Sam, looking at it.

The blanket's from home, I told him.

The room was getting darker. Alex had no shirt on, just his trousers. I was back to my T-shirt and even though it was dry now, still I felt colder and colder. Joey's nappy had of course gone too. Diana had to wrap him in Sam's jumper.

A long time ago Sam would have been horrified about this. He would never have lent his jumper to a baby to use as a nappy. But that was a long time ago, another Sam.

We stayed close together. We huddled together as close as we could.

Even though we had the candles, the light was running out. You couldn't even see properly into the corners of the room they were so black. There was the feeling of something ending. It was like the magic was over. I wasn't scared, I just so didn't want it to be over. I wanted to be back at the beginning with it all just waiting about to happen, with me just about to find Alex in the garden and −

Oh, oh, said Mouse, my tummy, my tummy hurts, and she started to cry again. She got off Sam's lap and she lay on the floor all wrapped up in the blanket with no clothes on and crying. Her bottom stuck out of the blanket and was so skinny it made you feel sad.

No one said anything because they didn't know what to say. Kids need to eat, everyone knows that. Normal flesh-and-blood children can't go very long without something to eat and drink.

My tummy, moaned Mouse.

Her crying got louder. You felt the house had just turned away and wasn't listening any more.

It hurts, she cried, it hurts.

No one did anything. It was like we'd given up, like no one had the energy to look after her and sort out her problems for her any more.

Suddenly I felt Alex stiffen.

Can you smell that? he said in a low voice.

What?

That.

I tried to breathe in the air.

What did you smell? Diana said and then before she'd even finished saying it she froze.

What is it? said Sam.

Her two hands were holding Joey but her face looked like she was listening for something. Joey's black eyes were open like he was joining in and listening too. It looked like the thing they were listening for was the single most frightening possibility in the whole world.

Christ, said Diana.

What?

It's like he's here in the room, she said.

Mouse turned and clung to Sam.

He can't be, said Sam, patting Mouse on the back. Forget it. It's OK. He isn't.

Alex looked at him and then he glanced over at the window, the glass which was so black with darkness you didn't know what was outside.

Pull the curtains, someone, he said.

But even as he said it he realised it was a pointless thing to be saying because there weren't any curtains there any more. Just the endless thick black darkness out there pressing against the house.

That was it. Mouse began to scream.

Moments passed. Nothing happened. Mouse's screams carried on. No one could stop her. Even Sam didn't try to stop her. What was the point? Letting her scream or not scream wasn't going to change anything. Diana sat cross-legged on the sofa and leaned forward to pick up her glasses. She looked very calm and gritty, like she'd decided something.

Shut up, she said, just shut up and I'll tell you a story.

Don't want a story! screamed Mouse.

If you just shut up a moment, Diana said, I'll tell you something really good.

Don't want good, wailed Mouse.

OK, Diana said. Something bad. I'll tell you something really bad if you like.

Shadows were marching round the room.

Something bad? Mouse sat up.

Yeah, said Diana with a look on her face as if she realised she'd accomplished something. Well, a bit bad and a bit good. Would you like that?

She'd given up on trying to feed Joey and she was holding him on her shoulder and bouncing him up and down quite hard to make him forget about crying. Joey kept remembering then forgetting then remembering. Then he burped loudly. Milk spilled down Diana's shoulder. Diana wiped it. Mouse looked at her.

I'd like bad please, she said, and she gave her a hungry look. She put her thumb in her mouth as if she was waiting.

All right, said Diana, and she took a breath but Mouse took her thumb out and interrupted.

You don't know any fucking stories, she said.

Oh, Diana said, I do. I know a real live story actually. It's about real life.

Mouse seemed to think about this.

And it's bad?

Diana nodded in an exaggerated way as if she was trying to keep her interested.

OK then, Mouse said. Tell me it. What is it? Is it about how you had baby Joey?

Diana looked at her for a moment and her whole body went stiff.

How did you know that?

Mouse blinked.

Because having baby Joey was good but a bad man did it. Jez did it.

Jez? I took a breath and looked at Alex. Jez? It was the first time anyone had said an actual name.

Alex's face was white. He looked like he was waiting to see what would happen next.

Diana shut her eyes and opened them again.

Did what? she said, and Mouse stared at her.

Put baby Joey inside you.

Diana looked at Alex and Alex looked at Diana. Sam looked at me. Nobody said anything.

Jez did it, said Mouse again and she waited. She looked half pleased with herself and half shocked. She seemed to have almost stopped breathing.

Everyone stared at her, Then, very gently, Alex spoke.

How do you know that, Mousie? Who told you that?

No one told me, said Mouse. I knowed it because he did it to me too.

Everyone looked at Mouse. No one breathed.

He did it to you? said Diana quietly.

Yep, said Mouse, and she patted her stomach. Except my baby hasn't started to come out yet.

I felt Alex go tense. His cold hand squeezed mine.

No one said anything for a minute or two. Alex and Diana were staring at each other.

Is it possible? he said to her.

Her face looked like I'd never seen it look before, like a piece of glass had come down over it. She shivered and looked at Mouse. Mouse's face was quivering as if there were tears inside it all getting ready to spill.

I don't know, Diana whispered, I've no idea if it's possible. How do I know?

It's OK, Mouse said with a gulp. He's gone now. He's all dead now under the earth.

It's not OK, said Sam, and Mouse looked at him with worry on her face as if he was going to tell her off. She blinked her eyes and then she started to cry.

Stop it, said Diana, and her voice was hard and tight. She's getting mixed up. The man who's dead is a different man, Mouse. That's not Jez.

Mouse looked at her.

You've got them mixed up, said Sam.

Mouse looked at him.

I told you, said Diana, and she sounded upset and almost angry, the old man who lived here was a good person and it wasn't his fault that he died. Jez was the one who followed us in the woods and –

Your brother, said Mouse.

Yes, said Diana.

Mouse looked scared of what Diana was saying.

Well it was him, your brother, the one that – that – Mouse was getting her words all twisted up now. It was Jez that always doed it to me.

What? Alex asked Mouse in a gentle voice. You have to tell us. What did Jez always do?

Mouse looked at him. She was sobbing now.

Do I have to tell you?

Yes, said Alex. Yes you do.

OK, OK, he – he showed me the thing that he put in Diana. The thing that if you touch it babies come out.

And did you touch it?

Mouse pushed some tears off her cheek and didn't say anything.

Not really, she said.

But did you? A few times?

She nodded.

Lots of times?

She nodded again.

Alex's face was very still.

When did he do it?

When I was round at Diana's, Mouse said. If I cried he said shut up, shut up, shut up Mouse or I'm going to have to hit you! I'm going to break you in two like one of your fucking sticks!

We all stared at Mouse in silence.

Did he – ever hit you? said Alex.

Mouse suddenly started hiccupping.

Not much. Only once I think, she said. Or maybe a lot more.

And she got up off the floor and keeping her thumb half in her mouth, held the blanket round her like a cloak. She looked all proud like a little queen. She hiccupped and then she laughed.

I hit him back, she said. I punched him and then he punched me and –

No one said anything.

Anyway sometimes I hit myself, she said as if that explained it. And then she looked around at all our faces and she laughed again as if she wanted us to join in with her.

We didn't. No one knew what to say.

I'm still hungry, she said then, because everyone was staring at her.

Still no one knew what to say.

I know, Alex said after a moment. We'll get you some-thing.

Are you cross with me? she said. Are you going to smack me?

No, of course we're not angry with you, he said. And

what's all this about smacking? We've never smacked you in our lives.

Mouse thought about this.

I want to go on Sam's lap, she said.

Come on then, said Sam, and he pulled her up and he held her tight and he rested his chin on her hair. Mouse closed her eyes and opened them again.

I'm scared, she said. I'm scared the man will come alive again.

That's a different man, said Sam patiently. And he won't. He can't come alive. It's impossible.

Mouse ignored him.

I don't like it, she said. I don't like the stinky smell. It's like him.

Diana shut her eyes.

I know, she whispered. It's him.

There were a few seconds of silence and Mouse looked around the room.

Is it the end of the story yet? she said. Is it the end of the bad story?

I looked at Diana then and saw she was crying. It was the first time I'd seen her cry and she looked like a completely different person, she looked all young and funny and not like anyone's mother.

Her face was down in her hands and even her hair was shaking. Sam reached out a hand and touched her shoulder. Mouse snuggled against him. I looked at my brother. I hardly recognised him.

Yeah, said Alex and he slid an arm around me and I could feel his heart bumping against me. It's the end of the bad story.

Is Jez gonna come here? asked Mouse. Might he come here?

No way, said Alex and he glanced at the window. You're safe. We're all safe.

Have we runned away yet? said Mouse.

Yes, said Sam, right now that's what we're doing. We're all running away.

Is it good? Are we good at running? said Mouse, and her voice had gone quite still and sleepy now.

Yes, said Alex, we're great at it. You are especially. We're getting there. We're all doing really well.

We were all running away but the house was standing still. It was starting to come apart around us. Once it had given us everything we needed – plus other stuff we didn't even know we needed. Now, almost as if it was enjoying it, almost as if it was finding it a thrill, it began to take things away.

It was getting darker and darker. We lit more candles but it didn't help. It was like the more candles we lit, the more the light was sucked away.

The walls which had once had all these elegant paintings of flowers and birds and fruit on them were just old and peeling and plain. There were no Indian rugs on the floor any more, just bare boards, dusty and scuffed and uncared for. The stripy and the flowery cushions had all disappeared. We'd never noticed before that the sofa had all this hard wiry hair and springs coming out of it.

I can't sit on this, Sam said finally, and he and Mouse and Diana and Joey moved down onto the floor. It was a good job they still had the blue blanket from home. It was the only thing they still had.

All around the house things were collapsing and going wrong, getting derelict and sad. Doors were falling off their hinges, windowpanes cracking, the dirt creeping in. It was like the normal kind of decay had speeded up. Even the screws in the old man's chair had started to come loose as if it might collapse at any minute.

That wasn't all.

At one point Sam went upstairs to see if there were any blankets or pillows left up there for us to sleep on. He came back down quickly and his face was collapsed with fear.

What? I whispered.

There's nothing up there, he said slowly. Everything's gone.

Everything? What do you mean everything?

I mean — it's total fucking darkness. I mean I got to the top of the stairs and I took a step and I almost fell. I put my hand out and there was nothing. I'm serious, Flynn. It's like — it's not possible but, well, there's no upstairs.

By the way it wasn't true, Flynn, Diana whispered to me out of the darkness. About me not knowing. I did know. Right from the start I knew.

That you were having a baby?

Mmm.

She held Joey up wrapped in Sam's jumper and she looked at him and opened her eyes and shut them again and he stared back at her. It was too early for him to smile but sometimes his mouth creased up at the edges as if he wanted to.

Did you feel sick?

Yeah. At first just the actual idea of eating made me want to throw up. And even though I was losing all this weight, they guessed. So they made an appointment for me.

Who? Who did?

My parents. Well, not my real parents. His parents.

But did they know?

About him? Jez? Yeah, they knew.

But — I didn't know what to ask next — I mean, what did they say?

She pushed her glasses up on her nose and rubbed her face.

They would never have said anything. It wasn't like that.

But, I said, feeling stupid, what was the appointment?

Diana took a breath.

To get rid of him, Flynn. Keep up.

I was silent. The idea of baby Joey not being alive made me go sweaty.

I was going to go. To the appointment. I didn't care. I didn't want a baby. I was scared. I preferred myself before, you know, the way I was before all of it started. But then — something happened.

She sniffed.

What?

I told them I'd lost it. Alex was the only person who knew I hadn't.

They believed you? I said in a whisper. But didn't you carry on getting, I mean, didn't you get fat?

I hardly put on any weight. In fact I lost some. By the end I'd only gone up barely one size. I could still get my jeans on. But I knew I had to get away from there before it was too late. If people knew about it they'd all be in the shit. So Alex said he'd help me — we knew we had to take Mouse but we had no idea that —

She looked at Mouse who was all rolled up in her blanket on Sam's lap, fast asleep, mouth open, thumb falling out.

I couldn't have done a thing without Alex, Diana said, and she wiped her eyes and looked at me.

I know, I said.

At one point, we thought he was — you know, that he might die.

I nodded.

I know that, I said again.

Diana was crying. She looked the type who wasn't used

to crying. She put her finger and thumb in the corners of her eyes to try and stop the tears but it didn't work, still they poured down.

He likes you, she said.

I said nothing.

He likes you a lot.

I put my hand on her arm and I rubbed it and she didn't stop me.

Oh God, she breathed, such a mess. Mouse used to be round at our place all the time, you know, Flynn. She was always there. She was so little – I didn't think about her being alone with him. It was all my fault. I encouraged her. I thought she liked coming.

Why did you? I asked her then because she still hadn't really said.

Why did I what?

Decide to keep him. Joey I mean.

Diana was very still now. I saw that Sam was holding her hand and I found I wasn't surprised at all. It made perfect sense. Part of him was touching Diana and part of him was touching Mouse. They looked like a safe little family, him, Mouse, Diana, Joey.

I don't know, she said softly, I don't know. Maybe I was just sick of being on my own all the time.

She looked at Joey.

It's not his fault, is it? she said. He's so small.

He is, I agreed.

She paused.

I don't know if I'll be a good mum though, she said. That's the only bit that worries me.

Why? I said, surprised. Whatever makes you think you wouldn't?

I couldn't imagine anyone finding it hard to be a good mother to someone as darling as Joey.

Diana looked at me.

I worry I'll be too selfish, she said. That I'll – you know – forget things.

What sort of things?

Just, you know, stuff that mums have to do for kids.

I thought of how my own mum always seemed to forget everything – exact change for dinner money, signing things, swimming notes. I thought of how she was always rushing round the house, racing from room to room, trying to keep up with the various tasks, and a big warm wave of love for her went over me. I blinked back the tears.

You won't forget things, I told Diana. And even if you do, it won't be fatal. He won't mind. He'll still love you.

She was looking at me with serious eyes as if it really mattered to her.

Seriously? You think so? But you don't know that.

Yes I do, I said, because suddenly I did. I do know it. I wouldn't say it if I didn't. Trust me, I do.

She looked at me for one quick second as if she was about to say something else and then she didn't. She just smiled.

That night we all stayed close together. I slept on the floor beside Alex, my hand in his, my face against his face. In the middle of the night we moved even closer. We tried not to make a noise. I don't know if the others saw or if they cared. We all did what we had to. Mouse sucked on her blanket all night to keep her growling stomach happy and I noticed that Sam fell asleep with his hand on Diana's long blonde leg.

And in the deep middle of the night when everyone was

stillest and you couldn't hear any breathing and Alex's arms had got loose around me, I found myself in the room.

This time I wasn't surprised or scared. I was just walking and walking across those bare dusty boards to get to the window. It took the longest time. I kept on walking but I never got to the window.

Instead, Alex was there. I was glad to see him. He was behind me and then he was in front of me. He was in our garden, down at the bottom where the foxes are. He was holding Anna, awkwardly but carefully, trying to give her to me. He was eating food from our fridge at home and things were just beginning and he was laughing at me from behind the waterfall and then, later, showing me how amazing kissing was. And then we were somehow in November and it was my birthday and he was getting me a present.

I couldn't see what it was. I tried to see but I couldn't and it was frustrating the way it is in dreams, when you can't see around the corner or look right into things and all that stuff.

Things slowed down. They almost stopped. I waited.

Then suddenly he was down down at the bottom of the pool under the water. There was no expression on his face and his eyes had gone dead. I screamed as loud as I could.

But somehow then the pool became the window or the window became the pool and there he was standing and looking out of it.

Alex! I said, but he wouldn't turn around, he just kept on looking. Alex!

I didn't know what he could see but whatever it was it had frightened him.

I woke up crying. I woke up and I was on the floor next to him with my face all wet and my head hot. The taste of the dream was still in me. A shaky taste. I couldn't get rid of it. I didn't dare move. Sometimes when you dream a dream it changes everything for a while, it grabs hold of you and you just have to keep on breathing and put up with it and hold very still until it decides to slip off you.

I was trembling and trembling.

Shadows kept on appearing in the room but they probably weren't anything. They were probably just imaginary things, just in my head. At one point I looked up and thought I saw a shape at the window, thought I heard a scraping and scratching on the glass, but I think I was still dreaming. I don't think anyone could really have been there.

For several hours the room had been filled with the scent of patchouli, musky, oily, red like blood, like poppies. We were almost used to it by now.

And then sometimes for a few brief seconds it wasn't really there at all.

Alex. His breath went in and out, in and out. I listened to it. Alex. I could have touched his mouth with my mouth but I didn't dare. I didn't move or do anything. I just waited to feel a bit less terrified and after a while the warm undone feeling of him calmed me and I did.

I must have slept for a while then because next time I woke, something had changed. I looked at Alex and his face was different, like there were traces of sweat all over him and there was something wrong with the colour of his skin. Not enough pink, too much blue.

As if he felt me looking, he opened his eyes then he shut them again. Then they were properly open and he was looking at me.

Are you OK? I said, but he didn't answer.

Alex? Answer me.

It was still night, blackest night.

Alex? I said again a bit more loudly.

Mmm, he went.

Talk to me. Say something. Tell me what you feel.

He shuffled closer. He smelled so hot it scared me. He still didn't say anything.

I'm scared, I said.

Hey, Flynn, he said, and his voice came out like a sigh. I could still smell the heat of him. He was so hot you didn't have to touch him to feel it.

It's OK, he said from somewhere in the dark middle of his sleep.

You can't do this, I told him, though I wasn't sure which thing I meant that he couldn't do. Living or dying?

He looked at me without listening, as if his eyes were trying to be polite but the rest of him just wasn't there. His eyes drifted shut again.

Alex? I said, Listen to me. You need to go to the hospital, don't you?

Hospital. Just saying the word gave me a jolt. Like I was ending something, like suddenly I knew what it meant.

He opened his eyes then, but just like in the dream I couldn't see what he saw.

MORNING

6

Part of me thought the night might go on for ever, but in the morning the rain had stopped and light came spilling in. Through the square of the window you could see the sky outside was bright liquid pink.

All the asleep faces looked quite peaceful in that pink light. Sam and Diana were curled up against each other with Joey in the crook of Diana's arm. You could see the little white bubble on his lip that he got from sucking.

Mouse's blanket had slid half off her but she didn't look cold, she just looked still and safe and comfortable. Dog was sleeping on the floor stretched out on his side as if he was dead only you knew he wasn't.

Alex was breathing. There was a bit of dampness still on his face, as if he'd sweated some more in the night, but he was sleeping, he wasn't dead either, I was sure of that.

I was the only one awake. I was the only one who could do it. I knew what I had to do.

Very carefully I got myself out from under Alex and crept into the hall and pushed open the big heavy door. Morning spilled into the house. Straightaway I turned around because I heard the click-click of claws on the stone floor. Dog had followed me.

I looked at him. He looked at me.

D'you want to go out, boy? I asked him.

He looked at me for one more moment as if I should have known the answer and then he pushed gently past my legs and slunk out. I watched him walk quite quickly around the side of the house and disappear. He looked like he knew where he was going and maybe I knew too. Maybe I just couldn't get the idea to turn to words inside my head.

The air outside smelled cool, it smelled of the end of summer. The chickens had gone and so had the hollyhocks but you could just about still hear the waterfall. Or could you? There was a roar in my ears but I began to think it wasn't water, it was something else just as familiar but much less lovely.

Traffic.

Cars. On a road somewhere. A hard tarmac road. Was it possible? Could there really be a road so close to here?

Because it was almost September and the air didn't know whether to be warm or cold, a band of mist had formed itself around the house. Like a ghost scooping us all up and hugging us tight, wrapping us in its arms and holding us until – until what?

I walked into this mist and right through it, out the other side. While I was in it, it was like I was the thing that had disappeared and I breathed in the wet which clung to my T-shirt and my hair. Then I walked straight out the other side. Now if I looked back, I could hardly see the house. Was it still there? I hoped so.

I didn't look back.

Instead I walked barefoot over the wet grass, round the side of the house and past the old man's grave which suddenly looked like a grave that had been there years and years, all covered in a tangle of ivy and falling-over weeds and with a little beat-up wooden cross on it that had come from I didn't know where. Someone, I don't know who, had been along and put some sweet peas on it in a jam jar. But it must have been there some time because the sweet peas had gone black and brown and the jar was all fuzzy and pale green inside. I stopped and stared at it for a second and then I saw that Dog was a few feet away on the other side and he was walking away fast.

Dog! I shouted to him to come back but something about the busy quick way he was walking made me think he really meant it. He was going.

Dog!

I tried once more and he stopped for a second and sniffed the air but he didn't look round, he acted like he couldn't hear me, and then his walk turned into a trot and then a run.

'Bye Dog, I whispered to him under my breath and I felt sad for a moment. I wondered what I'd tell Mouse. Maybe I wouldn't tell her anything.

I pushed my way through cow-parsley and past dangly elder bushes and alongside hedges strung with dewy spiders' webs where blackberries were growing. Some of them were tiny and pinched and green, just beginning to be red, but others were already ripe and black for picking. They looked a bit dusty but at least they were real. That could be Mouse's breakfast, I thought. It might stop her crying too hard when she finds Dog gone. Though berries can give you a stomach-ache.

Still the roar was in my ears. It must have been a main road, to have that many cars. I was getting closer to it. I kept on walking, even though I knew that once I hit the road that would be it, the whole brilliant adventure would be over.

The first car I waved at didn't stop. I suppose I must have looked strange, a skinny barefoot girl with messy brown hair and wearing just a dirty old T-shirt and knickers. I don't know – maybe they thought I was a boy or a homeless person or something.

But the next car was going slower and as it got close to me it slowed down completely and then it stopped. I stood and stared at it. It had its lights on because of the mist and the indicator was still going. In a way I couldn't believe what I was seeing. It seemed like it was out of another time with its shining doors and wheels and glass and light pouring out of it. Could it really be so long since I'd seen a car?

Hey, are you OK?

A lady had wound down the window. She was looking at me in a worried way.

Are you all right, love?

I stared at her kind normal face.

Look, do you need a lift? she said.

I said nothing. I couldn't find my voice. Instead I just kept on staring. I must have seemed quite rude but I couldn't help it. It was like now I'd seen a real live grown-up at last, my voice had just been swallowed up.

The lady frowned and opened the door and got out. She was quite young but she walked in a slightly stiff way. She had short fair hair and pearly earrings. She had eyeshadow on. I saw there were carrier bags on the back seat. A newspaper. A box of tissues. A red coat, folded.

She came and stood near me and she looked quite worried. She bent down slightly. I could see she was trying to smile but it was like she'd pressed the wrong button and what kept coming on her face were frowns.

What's up? she said in a gentle voice. Where are you from? You look like you're in some kind of trouble.

I said nothing. She bent closer. She smelled of lilac soap.

Tell me, she said. Tell me what's happened.

Then my voice started to work.

There's a boy, I said.

She waited, listening carefully with her head slightly on one side as if she didn't want to scare me.

A boy. Yes?

There's a boy who – who needs to go to hospital, I said then. He's got something bad wrong with him. He's really sick. And there's a little girl who –

I must have been shaking because she bent and put her arm around me.

Please, I said then. Please, there's quite a few of us and we've got a very small baby and I think – I think we need some help.

And then, just as if I was as little and helpless and stupid as Mouse, I burst into tears.

Out of all my possible endings for this story, this was not the one I'd planned. But what I know now is you can't always plan. Sometimes things don't work out the way you think they're going to. Sometimes you just have to shut your eyes and take a breath and go where they take you. The best and worst thing about this life is you can never know whether there's going to be something lovely or something terrible just around the corner.

You think you'll never do anything interesting ever again

for instance or never meet anyone nice or else you'll maybe stay unkissed for ever, and then, wham, suddenly it's happened. Everything's changed. You have to stay open to every little thing, every idea and possibility. I'm not sure I believe there is a God, but I know I believe in everything else.

Alex was right, I do worry. I am a worrier.

I worried about a lot of things that never even happened. I look back and think of how much time I wasted worrying and part of me wishes I'd just enjoyed things more instead.

I worried that a man would come – Diana's brother, Jez, I suppose – and he'd be carrying an axe or a gun or a knife and we'd open the door and he'd be standing there and he'd lift up the gun and take aim and shoot us. Or stab us with the knife. And we'd all be dead or injured or in a wheel-chair for life or something.

But that didn't happen. What happened was that Diana gave evidence and they prosecuted him for what he did to her and Mouse. And he went to prison and they made it so that when he comes out he won't even be able to think about going anywhere near either of them or any other child ever again or else he'll go straight back in there. And then because of everything she'd gone through, they gave Diana a safe place to live with Joey with a TV and benefits, so she was pretty happy.

I worried that Mouse would set fire to the house. I worried that somehow she'd manage to get hold of matches and the whole place would go up in flames and it would be all our fault. I worried that we'd smell this burning smell and rush up and down those confusing staircases but we wouldn't be in time, it would be too late to save anyone, even Baby Joey. These things happen. Fires start. People can die just from breathing in the smoke. You read about it all the time.

But it didn't happen. Instead Mouse was adopted by a

really kind couple who understood about her problems and made her feel safe. This time they didn't send her back. And it turned out that once she'd been able to talk to someone about all the bad things that had happened and once they'd convinced her that she was definitely safe now, then she didn't really need to set fire to things any more. She was even allowed to use a taper to light her own candles on her seventh birthday cake, which she made a great big fuss about.

And she has a little brother now and she's really pleased about that because it means she's not the youngest any more. She's even learning to read so maybe next time she gets a letter from her mum she'll be able to read it all by herself. She's going to be a vet when she grows up or else maybe work for a circus as the person who tames the dogs and horses.

I worried that the police would come and arrest Sam, having finally tracked him down for stealing the tequila and then our mum would chuck him out of the house for ever. But it didn't happen. Instead he came home and tried to behave himself. After Granny Jane's funeral, he made Mum a solemn promise that he would go to college and get some GCSEs. He got Diana to enrol as well. He still goes out a lot more than Mum would like and they do have some fights about it, but so far he's doing well. He babysits for Mouse sometimes and gets paid for it too. And Joey goes to the same nursery as Anna. He can't walk yet but last week he pulled himself up holding onto the table and let go for about eight seconds and didn't fall over.

When Dog ran off that morning I worried that we'd never see him again and Mouse's heart would be broken. I worried that Dog was somehow a part of the house and that meant we'd never be able to find him. But a man found him later, all starving and exhausted and cowering in his greenhouse.

And he handed him in to the police who put a notice up with Dog's picture on it saying LOST. And Mouse just happened to be walking by with her new parents and when she saw the picture she screamed with happiness and her parents said they would take him straightaway. So Mouse and Dog were reunited and when Sam goes round to babysit he always takes a biscuit for Dog. Mouse still drags him around by his ears though. I'm not sure she'll ever grow out of that.

I worried that Alex would die. I worried that he would just get sicker instead of better and I would lose him for ever. It happens. Just because you love someone doesn't mean they won't die, no one's safe, not even kids. But in my heart I knew I hadn't got to like him so much and shared such a huge adventure with him all for nothing. I knew from the first time I saw him standing there in the garden that there had to be a bigger plan. I can't explain it but I just knew. Lovely or terrible, sometimes you just have to shut your eyes and hope.

Alex is a lot better now. He just goes to the hospital for check-ups. They can't say he's cured for ever because he might not be, but then any of us could die at any time, couldn't we? His cheeks are the right colour now and his hair is quite long, almost to his shoulders. No one would recognise him. He looks cool.

I don't know if we'll always love each other, but he says we will. He says that when we grow up we'll get married and live in a house with roses round the door if I want and chickens and a waterfall and everything. He says he'll stick by me, that nothing would make him want to be without me now. I like it when he says that but I don't always believe it. I don't need to. He's young, I'm young. In a way it's enough just to know that he believes that – that right now at this moment there is a person in this world who thinks enough of me to say those things.

Oh and by the way I never ran away again. That was the very last time. Maybe it's just that I don't get the out-of-breath feeling so much any more, or that I like myself a bit better and don't really need to run. Or maybe it's that Sam and me are back in touch with our dad and even though he's a bit flaky and lets us down sometimes, still it feels so good to have him in our lives again. Why would I want to disappear when there's so much to stick around for?

I was wrong, the adventure wasn't over when I reached the road that morning. Quite the opposite, we'd hardly got started.

So none of the things I'd worried about happened. Instead what happened was this.

The lady parked her car carefully on the side of the road and then she took my hand and even though she was a stranger and I wasn't a baby, I let her, in fact a part of me was quite glad of it. And together we walked back along the hedge, past the blackberries and the spiders' webs and the bunches of elderberries that hung like creepy witches' hands. And she asked me what my name was and my age and what school I went to and I told her.

The answers sounded so strange. They sounded like a foreign language.

When we got back through the band of mist and saw the house where everyone was still sleeping, the lady took a breath.

Goodness, she said. Is this where you've been living? Is it a squat?

Is it? Was it? Now I thought about it, now I looked properly, the house did look a mess. I was surprised. It was like

I'd never noticed how many tiles were falling off the roof or how many of the windows were completely smashed and how there were rough old boards nailed up in quite a few of them. Another thing – someone had done graffiti all over the front door, great black dripping letters you could hardly read.

DANGER: NO ENTRY, the lady read out. Well what's that supposed to mean? Is this house dangerous?

I don't know, I whispered because suddenly I didn't. Suddenly I didn't know anything.

And I looked around then for the delicious greeny-blue pool and the crashing waterfall and the lilies and bulrushes and dragonflies zigzagging around, but of course they were gone. Instead there was just a muddy little pond at the bottom of the garden with hardly any water that you just knew would be smelly. And someone who didn't care what they did to the planet had gone and chucked a whole lot of junk into it including a baby's pram, some chairs with the backs falling off and a rusty old fridge.

ACKNOWLEDGEMENTS

This novel is entirely a work of fiction but it was inspired by some special people. So, thank you to Ian for giving me the songs that made me think of deep pools and strange places; to Eden, who, when once asked to keep quiet for five whole minutes, stuck her fist in her mouth and kept it there; and to the Yellolys for telling me how their dog Fred was discovered starving and abandoned, hiding in a greenhouse. Thank you as always to my three children for being the maddening, inspiring, beautiful teenagers that they are – sometimes to the point where all I want to do is stop being their mother and be thirteen again, running away across some dark fields with them. And thank you to Jonathan for understanding that, and being the best friend a writer could have. Lastly, this book was one big adventure to write but I'd never have dared do it without the confidence and security that Gill Coleridge and Dan Franklin always give me. I can't thank them enough for that.